The Saint
of Lost
Causes

The Saint
of Lost
Causes

Carly Schorman

atmosphere press

For Isaac and Henry,
in the hope you come to know a more just world.

Part 1: February

Jonathan

1

Jonathan Lambert stared at the tiny ball of fisted fingers jutting out from the newborn in a desperate show of life. She was too small to be real, he decided. He remembered his own father recounting the story of seeing him for the first time at the hospital in his plastic casing, surrounded by other newborns. Jonathan had been a plump infant, more than nine pounds at birth, with a swatch of dark hair atop his head that would fall away in the coming weeks to be replaced with soft, golden curls. He squalled, turning red, and Wallace said he swelled with pride. Of course he came into existence with an abundance of noise, but this infant was as silent as sleep.

This baby was not quite two pounds. She was red, but not from the exertion of crying. The infant lay as if already dead though she had entered the world only a few hours earlier. Only the sudden thrust of her tiny fist alerted Jonathan to the spark of life that lay inside her. An unexpected pang of guilt rose up in him with the knowledge that this short life was soon to end. He knew lives would be lost, but he hoped when the casualties started, the first victims would not be so young. Guilt and fear roiled inside Jonathan until he couldn't tell which emotion was stronger, but when he was honest with himself, he knew it was the fear.

The mother had named her Cadence. An old family name, he was told, but not by the mother. The nurse in the

Neonatal Intensive Care Unit had told him when he inquired after the infant's expected prospects. Less than one percent of babies were born earlier than 28 weeks. And here she was, fifteen weeks early, nearly purple and covered with downy hair. Jonathan thought of the kittens he had seen born when he was in second grade. Mewling and blind, he knew even at that age that he could crush them in his hand were he so inclined. This human infant looked just as fragile. Premature birth wasn't Cadence's only health concern. The lead she'd been exposed to during gestation had attacked her developing body. His guilt quickly turned to fear again. This couldn't have come at a worse time.

He would spare no expense to keep this child alive, but he had to make sure the money moved through the proper channels to distance himself from the paper trail it would inevitably create. After all, eleven other people sat on the board with him. Any one of them could have an infant on the way that he didn't know about. This could come down on anyone. There was no guarantee it would be him. But, as Jonathan looked down at the purple, paper-thin eyelids of tiny Cadence McNeil, he knew he would be the one made to pay for this just as surely as he knew this infant would not live out the week. Machines kept her breathing, other machines cleaned her blood in place of her kidneys. She would live what days she was given in the dark, sterile confines of the NICU and, when she died, he would be forced to pay a price for her life. The soft slapping of Michael's Salvatore Ferragamo loafers against the speckled, hospital linoleum told Jonathan it was time to leave.

"Looks like the family's en route, boss," Michael

whispered so as not to disturb the entombed infant before them. "Everything's taken care of. It's time to go."

Michael had his uses, probably even more than Jonathan could name. He would have addressed the bills and found the attending physician. Threats would have been made if necessary. Certainly not through violence— that wasn't Michael's style. Years of litigation, the promise of financial instability and possible ruin, these were the weapons in Michael's arsenal. And, for all Jonathan knew, when all else failed Michael could call in people who dealt in violence. He wasn't the type to get his hands dirty. Hours at the gym were passed so he would look good in an Armani suit, not so he could batter some loudmouthed contractor or angry citizen. He was surprisingly effective and he could be counted on no matter the task. That was more than he could say for anyone else. Jonathan inherited Michael along with the company when his father was forced into early retirement. Now, if only he could somehow keep the press from the story… but that might prove more than a little tricky, even for someone as capable as Michael Maestri. He wondered if it would be worth it to have Michael extend some monetary offer, but dismissed the idea.

It didn't matter. Jude would find out. He was onto them already, so it was only a matter of time. Jonathan had heard enough rumors to determine that they weren't just rumors. Of course, there had been a total press blackout on any mention of Jude or his purported organization, but when he saw the letter sitting on the boardroom table, Jonathan knew the rumors were true. He was real and Jonathan's name had been pulled from the man's black bag. The board debated on whether or not to call in the

FBI, but Jonathan had discouraged any hasty action. After all, it could be a year before anyone in Harrison actually *died* from the contaminated water they'd been drinking. The residents had only started to face the effects of lead poisoning, but Jonathan was told that they didn't need to worry about any direct loss of life for some time. And then he knew he would finally incur Jude's wrath.

If only Nicole had waited a little longer to get pregnant. Jonathan knew that the minute they got married she wanted to start a family so she could quit her job and focus on raising children. It wasn't like Nicki worked full time anyway. All she did was help with the books a few days a week at her father's car lot, but apparently that was still too much for doe-eyed Nicole Mason-Lambert. Jonathan shook his head with annoyance as he walked beside Michael through the hospital. In his own way, Jonathan knew he loved his wife above all the other women he had taken to bed, but the two years of marriage they'd shared hadn't quite proven as joyous as he'd anticipated.

These days, the only thing Nicki longed for was a child. And, now that the birth of a baby hinged on the horizon, this fiasco had to start and, with it, the threat to his unborn child. When the Charter Chemical leak had killed that boy up near Anchorage, it was Calvin Babcock's seven-year-old son who settled the debt. When a dam broke at a Colorado mine and spilled waste water into a nearby lake, covering 11-year-old Amber Williams in chemical burns that killed her, it was James Wolfe's preteen daughter that was taken. Jonathan's father had known James from their years at Yale together. That's what made Jude very real to him, more real than that minute infant back there, that two pounds of red skin and white fuzz and tubes connected to underdeveloped organs.

"What's the next move, boss?" Michael asked as soon as the door closed on the black Mercedes.

"I think it's time we reach out to the FBI."

"What about," Michael paused as his eyes flicked up to the driver, who was settling back into the front seat and fastening his seat belt, "that other thing?"

"It doesn't matter anymore. It's all going to happen anyway."

2

"Why didn't you call us sooner? When the note first arrived?" The agent began tapping his pen against a notepad in his hand in the short silence that followed his question. Jonathan Lambert grated under the scrutinizing gaze of the two FBI agents who'd arrived at his office within an hour of Michael's phone call. He supposed Jude was a national concern now. The Behavioral Analysis Unit was already en route from Washington. Jonathan would have preferred to wait for their arrival, but these two local yokels from the Phoenix division had been sent over in the meantime. He knew he was going to repeat all his answers once the real team of investigators arrived. He fixed his hard eyes on the young agent, locking on his muddled gaze, trying to get him to recognize his own impertinence without Jonathan having to verbally remind him of his position.

Michael answered for him, "You can certainly understand, Agent Garber, that in a company our size, we deal with a number of sensitive matters which are bound to give rise to threats on occasion. We don't need to trouble the authorities with every little matter. Once the threat became a viable concern, we contacted your department."

"I see. And what recently changed?" the agent continued.

"Excuse me?" Michael asked.

"Well, what made you change your mind? What made the threat suddenly *viable*?"

Michael looked over to Jonathan for a moment for some indication of just how much he should reveal to this federal agent. Jonathan offered a small shrug. What did it matter? It would all be a matter of public record soon enough if Jude had his hand in it.

"It would seem as if an infant was born at St. Mary's earlier today. She was born premature and isn't expected to survive the week. Lead exposure is suspected." Michael handled the question well. No assumption of guilt, but anyone with half a brain could reason out the rest if they were concerned about Jude coming down on them.

"I see," Agent Garber said in a pinched tone that suggested his mind was furiously working to connect all the pieces. The rumors about the Salt River Compact were true. Southwest Resources was dealing in contaminated water, at least, in certain areas. The number of people exhibiting the effects of lead poisoning would begin to rise rapidly.

"Can we focus on what's at hand?" Jonathan interrupted, no longer able to contain his frustration. In this building, he was the authority, not these *agents* standing on his antique Spanish Art Deco rug nearly a century old that sat on the floor of his office. The rug was an inheritance, just like this company and its crimes. "Jude, a known criminal, has threatened our board members and their families. I want to know, what are you going to do to prevent another child from being kidnapped?"

The two agents exchanged glances in an obviously noticeable way that irritated Jonathan even further, but he let it go.

"Mr. Lambert, do you happen to know if any members of the board have infant children or if they are expecting new additions?" the other agent asked. His name was Marquez or Martinez or something of the like. Jonathan couldn't remember.

"I am. I mean, my wife and I are expecting."

"Do you and your wife reside in Harrison?" Agent Garber resumed the questioning.

"No, we have a home in Phoenix."

"We'll get additional agents over to the house right away," Garber said in a reassuring tone that didn't reassure Jonathan one little bit. Nicki was going to be furious. Better angry and safe, Jonathan decided. Whoever this Jude was, he wasn't going to get a chance to snatch away their child. He didn't care what this bastard's record was. Jude didn't know who he was up against. Jonathan would have every cop in the Southwest hunting this guy. He would fly with Nicki to some secret location in the Australian Outback for the year. Whatever it took. The dark shroud of fear began to lift as he remembered who he was: Jonathan Lambert, son of Wallace, The Old Bull, who rose from nothing to become one of the richest men in the country. Let's see if Jude could match his resources.

Patricia marched straight in through the doors to his

office. The only time his mother came by to see him at the company was after a shopping adventure in Scottsdale. Large bags emblazoned with various logos confirmed Jonathan's suspicions. She was probably procuring more items for her impending grandchild, spoiling it with treasures before it had even taken a single breath. It didn't matter. The family had more than enough money to indulge Patricia's excitement about her grandchild. Nevertheless, Jonathan always felt like it was bad luck to buy so much for the baby before it was born and seeing his mother with her shopping bags made him feel like his concerns were more than superstitions.

At the sight of the FBI agents in their two hundred dollar suits, Patricia put down her bags and moved toward them with her arms stiffly at her side. Her face, almost unlined, formed a mask devoid of expression. It was a cultivated look she wore when she wanted to keep her emotions to herself. Jonathan had seen it on more than one painful occasion. Today, he knew, would prove no different. Jonathan wished his office assistant had the presence of mind to stop his mother, today of all days, before he permitted her to barge into his office unannounced. Unlike Michael Maestri and the rug, Jonathan requested a new assistant when his father stepped down once the full scope of the situation in Harrison was realized. Of course, Michael hired Stephen in his stead when Jonathan forgot interviews were slated early on a Friday morning. Still, the arrangement was working out. Jonathan ultimately trusted Maestri to select the right candidate, but Stephen had some ground to cover yet before he was as competent as Wallace's office assistant had been.

"Patricia Burwell Lambert. And you are?" his mother asked as her slender arms crossed in front of her chest with a casual air. Today, Patricia was wearing a silk shirt in hunter green she'd paired with camel colored slacks and a thin, gold belt to match the bands around her wrist and the chain holding the pendant around her neck. Jonathan was more familiar with the sharp, strong features of his mother's face than he was with his own, but he only now realized she was a handsome woman. Michael rose to offer Patricia his seat even though there was an empty chair one of the agents had chosen not to occupy. She nodded her head to decline the offer, but Michael did not return to his seat. Instead, he remained standing beside her.

"I'm Agent Garber and this is my partner, Agent Marcado," one of the agents said as the other offered his mother a curt nod to acknowledge the introduction.

"Would someone mind explaining to me what is going on? Last time I checked, I was still a shareholder," Patricia continued in an accusatory tone. Jonathan didn't know if the barbs in her words were intended for him or the FBI agents.

Michael stepped closer to Patricia and put a hand on her arm. "Why don't you come with me and I'll fill you in while Mr. Lambert speaks with these gentlemen?"

That man deserves a raise, Jonathan thought to himself. He was probably already paying him a small fortune, but it was worth every cent. Michael Maestri had come to him along with the company. He had been the executive assistant to his father, Wallace Lambert, who ran Southwest Resources for nearly four decades until the water contamination issue in Harrison set the company up for a PR disaster. Jonathan had been asked to assume the reins early to demonstrate that Southwest Resources was making sweeping changes before the inevitable public scandal hit. That scandal was about to break wide open. It wouldn't matter if it was his father's bad decisions or his own. Jonathan would be made to pay all the same.

3

Jonathan shifted uncomfortably in the overstuffed chair while he waited for his wife's reaction. He should have remained standing, but he didn't want to draw any unnecessary attention by changing his position at this juncture.

"What do you mean we have to leave? This is our home. I'm about to give birth!" Nicki's voice rose in pitch as it increased in volume. It was one of her more annoying traits. Second only, perhaps, to her tendency toward moodiness when she didn't get her way. Jonathan imagined the months of distemper that would result from this ill-timed escape in the middle of the night.

"Listen, darling," Jonathan began, trying to avoid the placating voice he frequently adopted when he thought she was being irrational. Nicki said it was "condescending," but he could never manage to avoid it entirely during their disagreements. "The threat the company received must be taken seriously. We need to move to a safe location. Michael has arranged for a security team to be in place day and night."

"You have got to be kidding me," Nicki said. "I can't possibly leave."

"We can't take this threat lightly," Jonathan contended, trying to keep his tone calm and reassuring while impressing upon his wife the gravity of the situation. "Jude has succeeded in the past."

"And what does this Jude person want with our son?" Nicki asked, lifting her head. Her angry eyes locked sharply on Jonathan's own.

He drew in a deep breath. He hadn't been told that Nicole was carrying a boy. They'd decided to keep the gender a secret until the birth, but Nicki had apparently taken a peek at the results without telling him.

"Jude is a vigilante. When he feels a child died as a result of some corporate decision, he takes one of the children of the highest ranking officers in that company. Apparently, he thinks he's got us for something."

"But you just took over at Southwest Resources. You can hardly be held responsible for decisions made before you got there," Nicki argued, her voice dangerously approaching a whine. "I mean, you've been to what, like, eight meetings, ever?"

"It doesn't matter. My name has been listed amongst the board members for years and I'm the director now. More than all that, I'm Wallace Lambert's son. It would seem like we're the most likely targets for any planned attack," Jonathan explained.

Nicki sat in silence for a moment, the features on her face hardening as she stared off into space. Jonathan married Nicki for her silence. She was beautiful and fun to be around, at least at first, but in a family like his, it was important to choose a wife who could maintain her composure in public and private. That was one of the many lessons Patricia imparted to her only child over their tennis games and luncheons while his father was busy working. Nicki's rage was quiet, not loud and messy, but he could tell that she was enraged. Jonathan felt a seed of anger take hold inside of him. Nicki never tried to come from a place of understanding. She only thought about herself.

Finally, she chose to speak, "What evil thing did you do that put my child's life in danger?"

Jonathan let out an exasperated sound and waved his hand in the air. "I don't know where you get off. I didn't get to pick what family I was born into and you seem happy enough to spend the money that comes from that family. The drought made the cost of every drop of water go up. We draw from twelve water providers for the town of Harrison alone!"

He didn't mean to, but his voice rose as he spoke, almost to the point of yelling. He could see the light in Nicki's eyes dim ever so slightly as her rage went quiet. Jonathan shifted under the hateful stare of his wife.

"The thing is, one of those sources might have been compromised." Jonathan paused and looked up again at Nicki, who stared back mutely. "It happened before I took over. And, when they found out, I was brought in to replace The Old Bull. Thing is, we didn't know for certain. It was decided that more tests needed to be run and then something was added to the water to lessen its toxicity, but the additives proved too corrosive, which is what we think might have caused the lead poisoning."

"Lead poisoning? Like what happened in Michigan and Colorado?"

"And Ohio and Alaska. All disasters, all paid for by someone's child," Jonathan said.

"That's ridiculous. I haven't heard anything about that," Nicki replied in disbelief.

"There's been a total media blackout on anything related to Jude. He's considered a domestic terrorist, so the press hasn't been giving Homeland Security a lot of pushback on this one. At least, for now." Jonathan didn't really know more than that. Hopefully, the BAU would have more information on Jude, but, for the moment, he was almost as ignorant as Nicki on the topic.

"What's a media blackout mean? I didn't think that was legal."

"Uh, it isn't, or wasn't. After the disinformation campaigns, the state established controls over the media. One of them is a blacklist on stories when terrorists are involved, foreign or domestic, amongst other things. And, for now, there's a media hold from the government on covering anything about water in Harrison until we have an action plan in place so the town doesn't riot when they find out," Jonathan explained.

Anger washed over Nicki's face and her voice became indignant, "Are people going to die? From this decision over at Southwest Resources? Is it going to happen here like it happened in those other places?"

"Yes."

"And we're in some kind of danger because of that?" Nicki asked.

"Yes," Jonathan answered. "I need you to pack. My mother and Val will help you."

Nicki's eyes began to well with tears and Jonathan moved closer to her, but before he could wrap her in his arms, Michael Maestri burst through the doors.

"Cadence McNeil just died," he stammered out as

Jonathan and Nicki stared back with a mixture of alarm and confusion.

4

"This is Special Agent Maurice Witlock. I'm Special Agent Richard Renn."

The man was tall, nearly half a foot above Jonathan's head. He had salt and pepper hair clipped neatly atop his head and no signs of balding. His charcoal gray suit was properly tailored and his shoes were polished to a shine. Jonathan already trusted this man more than Garber and Marcado, who were probably still on the property here somewhere but had wisely decided to remain out of his sight.

"Perhaps you gentlemen can tell me a little bit more about this Jude?" Jonathan asked. What little knowledge he had, Jonathan had gleaned from rumors alone. Hopefully, these agents could provide some accurate details.

"We're still trying to gather information, but we do know that Jude tends to move quickly once he faults a company in a child's death. We spoke with a Michael Maestri and he said that there might be a link between the death of Cadence McNeil and Southwest Resources. He also mentioned that you received a note you believe is from this Jude, is that correct?" Renn asked. Apparently, each duo sent out from the FBI included one agent who spoke on behalf of the pair. Jonathan wondered briefly which one was actually in charge. Witlock had a no-

nonsense look to him that suggested authority in spite of his silence.

Jonathan nodded to the affirmative.

"Is this the note?" Renn removed a letter sheathed in plastic from a folder—a clean, white sheet of paper with words scrawled across it in a child's gangly writing.

Jonathan didn't need to read it again. He remembered its succinct wording perfectly. He had never been hit in the stomach, but when he saw that note sitting neatly atop a pile of papers on their boardroom table, he felt a sensation he was certain was remarkably similar.

"We wish you would have come to us sooner. Cadence McNeil's death changes our timeline considerably. In truth, we've never dealt with a situation wherein the potential kidnapping victim has yet to be born. Jude usually moves within the first seventy-two hours, but, in this scenario, we expect he'll wait until the birth," Renn explained in a matter-of-fact tone that Jonathan assumed was intended to soothe him, to let him know they still had time to act defensively before the assault.

"What we're going to need from you are the exact details of your involvement with Southwest Resources and its decision-making process. It has been brought to our attention that there may have been some misdealings with the changes in water sourcing that has led to a community outcry over contaminated water. This would fit the profile for how Jude chooses his victims," Agent Witlock finally spoke up in a deep, rich voice that matched the square cut of his jaw. Despite the absence of an accusatory tone, Jonathan knew the accusation was there.

"Are you here to investigate Southwest Resources or to find this kidnapper? My unborn son is at risk here! I asked *you* what you could tell *me* about Jude. He's taken, what, *four* children by my count? What has the FBI done to find this guy?" Jonathan's indignation rallied his spirit. He knew the red blotches would start to appear on his face if he kept this up much longer. Who the hell did these guys think they were anyway? Didn't they know who they were dealing with? He wanted answers, not more questions.

"Eleven children," Renn said as he scribbled something down on his notepad.

"Excuse me?"

"It's eleven children that Jude has claimed responsibility for. There could be more if other companies have failed to come forward to report an abduction. We have to assume that some would be willing to hide the crime of another in order to keep their own crimes hidden," Renn replied.

Jonathan tried to get his mind around this new information. How could this have happened to so many and he didn't know about it?

As if in answer to his question, Renn continued, "With the media blackout on Jude, it's impossible to keep current. When there isn't a blackout, it's impossible to keep facts straight. It's our country's great catch-22."

"How can you be so glib about this? Eleven children taken? And none found?" Jonathan asked, appalled.

"I do apologize, Mr. Lambert. We're doing everything we can to locate Jude and his associates. If you could just help us by answering our questions, we can move this whole thing along faster," Special Agent Whitlock chimed in, trying to sound like the good guy again. Jonathan was done with the whole lot of them. He could see why some companies had decided against calling in the FBI. Maybe some of them had even succeeded in escaping the clutches of Jude and his "associates." Jonathan should have just put his family on a plane and been done with the whole business back when Wallace explained that he would be retiring early and why. Since that day, Jonathan spent a lot of time daydreaming about just that: cashing out, leaving the desert and Southwest Resources behind for good, maybe moving to an island in the Caribbean or the South Pacific. Nicki loved to sunbathe.

"Mr. Lambert?" Special Agent Renn said his name to recapture his attention which had slipped beyond the room to the beaches of Barbados. Jonathan brought his eyes back into focus on the men before him and Renn continued, "Once again, I would like you to outline for us …"

He was cut short by a scream coming from down the hall followed by yelling. It was his mother's voice. Jonathan was on his feet immediately. He tore off out of the room with agents Renn and Witlock just behind him as they raced across the house toward the source of the scream. Patricia stood clutching an empty carry-on bag to her chest. Jonathan came running down the hall in a fit of panic to where his mother stood in abject horror.

"She was just here!" Patricia screamed. "She couldn't have gone anywhere! She was just here!"

"Who? Mom? Nicki? Where's Nicki?" Jonathan asked in a string of frightened words.

Jonathan looked from his mother to the agents who were busy rattling off into some communication device that sent police and FBI alike scurrying around the house.

"He couldn't have taken her far," Witlock growled into his device and Jonathan faintly heard the static-charged chatter that returned but he couldn't make out the words.

Jonathan felt the room spin and grow silent. Although he could see the people moving, their mouths moving, he couldn't hear anything. His head grew light and the room grew dark as fear ripped through his chest like a bullet.

Haley

5

"Holy shit, lady, are you alright?" As soon as she asked the question, Haley immediately felt like an idiot. Of course this woman wasn't okay; she was laying in the middle of the road, bleeding out from her abdomen. Haley scrambled to find her phone. *Left pocket. No, right pocket.* She pushed her thumb against the button but realized it probably couldn't read her print with its coating of blood. She wiped her other hand against her jacket and hit the emergency call button so she could punch in 911. Waves of panic started rising inside her, but she fought to stay calm. *Do not cry. Do not freak out.*

"Nine-one-one. What is the nature of your emergency?"

"I'm out on the 87 and there's this woman lying in the road. She looks hurt pretty bad. There's a lot of blood."

"Do you know your exact location?"

"No, I'm just north of Fountain Hills. Southbound side. My hazard lights are on. She doesn't seem to be conscious."

"What is your name?"

"Haley, Haley Roth."

"Haley, we have an ambulance on its way to you, but I want you to stay on the phone with me. Can you do that?"

"Yes," Haley answered. She looked at the face of the woman and noticed that they could be the same age. She was young. Maybe no more than twenty-five. She looked blue and pale in the moonlight, already lost to death, but Haley noted the shallow movements of her ribcage against the thin, wet fabric of her bloody shirt.

She wasn't permitted to ride in the ambulance so Haley followed, at a prudent distance, to a hospital in North Scottsdale. The woman turned out to be Nicole Mason-Lambert, wife of Jonathan Lambert who, until their marriage a couple years back, had been one of the "30 Most Eligible Bachelors Under 30", according to *Sonoran Life Magazine.* She called her producer from the lobby while she was waiting for an update on the status of Ms. Mason-Lambert and explained that she was on the scene and ready to cover the story.

"Haley," he began in a voice that suggested disappointment would soon follow, "you're the weather girl, an admirable profession if ever there was one. Let's just leave the news to Cherie."

Cherie Rodgers, Haley's mentor-turned-nemesis as she moved from intern to weather girl, had become the thorn in her side. So far, Cherie had led a successful stonewall against Haley breaking any real stories on the Channel 9 News.

"I found her. Out on the road, she was just lying there." Her voice fluttered like a bird, overexilerated on a mixture of pride and panic.

"Listen, Haley, I get it. You found her and somehow you think that entitles you to the story. What were you doing out there anyway?"

"I was trying to get some decent footage of the meteor shower. I made Dennis meet me up near the lake."

"Anything good?" he asked, trying to derail Haley from her original purpose, but she would not be put off.

"I want this story," she said with finality, her voice steady and firm. After a brief silence, she added, "I'm part of this story now."

"All the more reason it's going to Cherie." And, without another word, he disconnected the call. She seethed for a moment, tempted to call him back, but decided against it. No sense in putting her job at risk by throwing a tantrum over the phone. She could talk to her producer at the station later. Try to make him see reason.

Haley looked down at her blood-drenched shirt. How could anyone survive the loss of so much blood? According to the staff, Nicole might pull through yet. Her family and the police were on their way down. Haley walked over to a nurse and asked if they might have anything she could change into. The sight of blood was beginning to sicken her slightly. The nurse looked annoyed, but she agreed to see what she could do and tottered away on the thick, white, rubber soles of her shoes.

"Ms. Roth?" a voice behind her sounded. She turned around and saw it belonged to the broad, but handsome face of a man she mistakenly estimated to be in his mid-thirties. "I'm Special Agent Maurice Witlock. I heard you found Ms. Mason-Lambert, is that correct?"

"Um, yes," she answered tentatively, distracted by the angles and planes of his countenance. *Get it together, Haley.* "Why is the FBI investigating this? Was Nicole reported missing?"

Haley saw a short comma form between his eyebrows for a moment before Witlock relaxed his face into its previously placid expression. "You wouldn't happen to be with the press, Ms. Roth?"

"Channel 9 News at 6. That's me. Well, I report on the weather, but we're a team down there," she rambled off with a warm smile. Special Agent Witlock did not look impressed. Rather, a dark cloud settled over his eyes and he stared at Haley with something that resembled disgust. "I'd really like to go home and change my clothes. Can I do that and come back? It shouldn't take more than an hour and a nurse told me Nicole should be in surgery for at least that long."

"I'm afraid not. We're going to have to ask you some questions first. I'm sure you understand."

"I guess," Haley answered, not entirely sure what sort of questions they would have for her. She tried not to grimace as she looked down at her blood-stained shirt. She hoped Nicole would survive the ordeal. It comforted her to see the blood as part of the struggle for life rather than its remnants.

6

"So, you have never heard the name Jude nor are you familiar with his organization?" a woman, yet another agent to whom Haley was required to speak to, asked her once again.

"Unless you are talking about "Hey Jude" and The Beatles, then no. I told you that before. I have no idea what you're talking about," Haley answered sullenly. The night had dragged on and on. All she wanted was a warm bath and a change of clothes, but it looks like no good deed goes unpunished, so she was stuck at a police station answering questions about this woman she didn't know who she found in the middle of nowhere. Apparently, the authorities didn't have much to go on in this case.

"What were you doing driving on the 87 last night?"

"I already told you, I went out there to try and get some footage of the meteor shower. Dennis Cardon, one of the cameramen from the station, met me up near Saguaro Lake. I was driving home when I saw Nicole lying in the road. I stopped my car and called 911. That's all that happened."

"And, how did you know that it was Nicole Mason-Lambert on the road?"

"I didn't. I only found that out when I got to the hospital. One of the nurses said her name."

"Do you have any tattoos, Ms. Roth?"

"Tattoos?"

"Yes, any tattoos?"

"Yes, but I don't see how that has any relevance…."

"Where is your tattoo?"

"Not that it's any of your business, but I have a star tattooed on my hip. It's small… from college."

The agent tilted her head to suggest that "college" didn't seem all that distant from Haley's present tense.

"No other tattoos?"

"Not yet. Maybe I'll get a prison tatt before you people finally let me go home and change my clothes." Haley had been given an oversized sweatshirt of unknown origin in place of her bloody blouse and jacket, but she felt feverishly warm and unclean in it and she was irritable after hours of waiting around before several series of confusing questions were thrown at her. This whole night had proven traumatic and she didn't understand why these people were berating her with questions rather than treating her like the hero she was. She saved a woman who was bleeding to death on the side of the road. And her reward? Distrust, contempt, and hours of questions while she sat with blood under her fingernails in a stranger's cast-off sweatshirt. Haley burst into tears. It was simply too much.

"Ms. Roth, we're almost through here. If you'll just give me a minute," the woman said in a cold and distant voice as she rose up from her metal seat. No one had shown Haley the smallest kindness tonight and her tears continued unabated until there were none left. Haley lost count of the seconds as they turned into minutes, but the woman eventually returned and told her she was free to leave. They would contact her if they had any further questions.

"Hey wait," Haley called out as the woman turned to leave. A stern face looked back at her. "Did Nicole do okay in surgery?"

"We don't know yet," she answered before continuing out the door, leaving Haley to pick up her own belongings and follow after her. A police officer, and not Special Agent Witlock, gave her a lift back to her car at the hospital. The sun was beginning to offer its first glow of morning light in the east.

She clamored out of the squad car and into the driver's seat of her Prius. She took a deep breath and started the almost-silent engine as the police officer, the first to extend her any warm words, waved and drove off again. Haley bowed her head forward against the steering wheel and cried, more from exhaustion than fear or sorrow this time. She wiped the tears from her eyes with the back of her hand. At least they had let her scrub her hands clean at the station. They hadn't been so mean as to deny her that, but they had been mean. Short and demanding, untrusting of her answers, and she had done nothing wrong whatsoever. Haley sniffled one last time and began to pull out of her parking space. She'd had a rough night. She needed a stiff drink, a hot shower, and a lot of sleep.

7

"Open up, Haley, I know you're in there!"

A set of three loud bangs sounded out from the front door, the second in an ongoing series. Cherie wasn't going to give up. The noise had yanked Haley out of the black of sleep. She looked at the clock and realized that less than four hours had passed since she collapsed into bed following her ordeal the night before. Haley stared wide-eyed at the ceiling until she realized Cherie would not give up and leave her alone. Instead, Haley admitted defeat and pulled a robe on over her pajamas.

"Hey Cherie, unexpected visit," Haley said as she struggled to remember through the fog of sleep if she ever actually provided Cherie with her address. She tried to sound casual, unalarmed, but the ace news reporter of the Channel 9 News at 6 showing up on her doorstep at such an early hour was tipping her interior scales toward a full-blown anxiety attack.

"Jesus, you're practically cowering," Cherie said with a certain measure of contempt as she pushed her way past

Haley into the apartment.

"You would be too if you had the kind of night I did," Haley said in her own defense.

"Doubtful. I'm not a pussy," Cherie said as she walked over to the couch and took a seat. She patted the cushion next to her in a gesture of invitation. Haley felt hesitant, but Cherie was the head news reporter at her station and, more importantly, Haley had always looked up to her. She pushed away her apprehensions and sat down. Cherie surprised her again by taking the younger woman's hand in her own in a show of compassion.

"Listen, sweetie, I do understand that you've had a rough night, but I really need you to tell me about it. What did the police ask you? Were the FBI present? I need you to remember all these things and to tell them to me. Do you think you can do that?"

Cherie had never shown Haley the slightest indication that she cared for her young co-worker, no matter how many times Haley tried to explain what a character-shaping role Cherie had played in her life. From an early age, Haley had watched her on television. After all, Channel 9 was the preferred news provider of both her parents. Cherie was always chasing down local scoundrels and making them set things right. She frequently crossed the line between journalist and activist and Haley always admired her for it. When she first met Cherie Rodgers in person, Haley was shocked by how cold and, well, disinterested she was. Haley thought it might be jealousy. After all, she was a hot, new talent on the news team. Maybe Cherie saw in Haley her own numbered days, or so she had to tell herself on occasion, but now, with her own cold fingers encased in Cherie's soft, warm hand, she wondered if she might have been wrong all along. Maybe Cherie did care about her, but it just took this proximity to tragedy to bring out that concern.

Slowly and carefully, Haley began recounting all the details exactly as she remembered them, from the moment she first spotted Nicole on the road to the moment the police officer dropped her off at her car at sunrise. Cherie listened intently, careful not to interrupt except to draw out additional details and, occasionally, give Haley's hand a reassuring squeeze. Haley felt a few hot tears slip out the corners of her eyes. She didn't want to break down into open sobbing in front of Cherie Rodgers.

"Thank you," Cherie said with one final squeeze of her hand before she rose up and made her way back to the door.

"Get yourself together before you get down to the station. No one wants to see Little Miss Warm Front looking red and puffy on the news later," Cherie said as she breezed through the doorway. "I'm going to the hospital. From what I heard, someone cut a baby out of that woman and left her on the side of the road to die. Maybe if you hadn't been there, she would have."

Haley wondered if that made her a hero in some strange way. She had saved a woman's life by being in the right place at the right time. The faint flush of pride did little to ease her embarrassment at being treated like a whimpering child by a reporter from her own station. She wondered what Cherie had meant when she said they "cut a baby out" of Nicole. Had she been pregnant? A new wave of sorrow washed over her as she sat in her pajamas and, once again, began crying.

8

"You can't do this!" Cherie shrieked as she followed the producer out of his office into the narrow corridor where Haley was passing by on her way to make-up.

"It doesn't come from me. My hands are tied." As if to prove it to her, he held up his hands with their invisible shackles. "There appears to be a media blackout on this one. No one is going to run the story so you better just shelve it for now."

"I spent all day chasing down leads including, I might add, finding one scatterbrained weather girl sleeping soundly after an interrogation by the FBI."

Their producer stopped dead in his tracks and turned on his heel to face Cherie. "What part of blackout do you not understand? This isn't the 20th Century. Act like you know something for chrissakes."

That seemed to give Cherie a moment of pause, but as soon as he started back down the hallway, she was right behind him again.

"Listen, I have enough to go on without the FBI corroborating the facts. We have witnesses. Our own damn weather girl is one of them!" Cherie shouted. Haley stopped walking and listened.

"I told you already. Media blackout. No one is covering this Judas guy or whatever his name is," the producer explained, his irritation growing by the minute.

"Jude, his name is Jude and there is a rumor that he kidnaps children as some form of vigilante justice. Come on, now. How is that justice?"

"You don't have enough to go on and I don't own this station so it's not up to me anyway."

"That hasn't always stopped us before," Cherie contended.

"This isn't like the Buckeye Butcher. This is something else entirely. The orders come from the HSA. I'm sorry, but if you continue to pursue the matter, you'll have to do it with another news station." Without another word, he left Cherie stunned in the hallway. Haley did her best to look away as she started toward make-up again, but she wasn't fast enough. Cherie's eyes honed in on her like an eagle and in three quick strides of her patent-leather heels, the woman was beside her.

"Can you believe this shit?" Cherie asked, looping her arm through Haley's and continuing along the hallway, even though it was in the opposite direction of the make-up room. "I mean, we're *journalists*. We're supposed to tackle the difficult stories; the ones they tell you to stay away from. It just isn't right."

In the silence that followed, Haley tried to think of the right words to say, but all she heard was the hollow clicking of their shoes against the granite floors. *Don't be dumb*, she thought to herself, *think of something to say*.

"I completely agree with you," Haley finally decided upon. She worried that was the wrong thing to say, but it was too late to recant.

"Good, we can't just let this injustice go unreported."

"Right," she agreed again.

"I think we should go back to the hospital together. I mean, you practically saved this woman's life single-handedly. It's perfectly reasonable that you would want to see her and make sure she's all right. Maybe give her a chance to thank you personally for coming to her aid when so many other people would have driven right by."

Haley couldn't think of anyone who would drive right by a woman lying in the middle of the highway at night, but she didn't argue with Cherie. She let herself be led right back to the newsroom while she nodded her head in agreement that they should both return to the hospital the following morning to check on Nicole Mason-Lambert.

"Okay, wonderful, I'll pick you up at half past eight," Cherie said with a nod and smile. "Try to keep it under wraps and don't go blathering around the station."

Haley tried not to feel glum. Cherie was known for being painfully straight-forward. She probably didn't mean to be insulting, but Haley couldn't help feeling insulted all the same. She looked around and realized she was back in the newsroom. She had to turn back and began making her way to make-up once again. Wardrobe had selected a yellow mini dress for her forecast of sunshine today and sunshine tomorrow. She'd kill for a decent weather event. A hurricane or tornado or even a tsunami that rolls up from the Gulf of Mexico and obliterates the entire Southwest. Anything but more sunshine.

9

Haley was up and dressed well before Cherie's arrival. She also had to empty the litter box or Daisy would piss all over the hallway rugs while she was gone for the day. The cat had been a present from her parents when she started middle school in exchange for a promise that she wouldn't drink or use drugs for the duration of her preparatory education. At twelve, it seemed like a reasonable exchange. At seventeen, she chafed against her sworn commitments, but by then she already had her sights set on a career in broadcast journalism. An arrest for drugs or underage drinking would not look good on her resume. Daisy had been a wise parental move, she decided later on. Haley loved the cat dearly even though old age had made her surly and smelly. For the most part, they left each other alone as long as both continued to adhere to their long-established domestic patterns. A clean litter box was Article One of their treaty.

Her cell phone rang, jolting her out of her thoughts.

"Hello?" Haley said.

"I'm here," Cherie replied and disconnected the call.

Haley shook her head, already annoyed with herself for agreeing to accompany Cherie to the hospital this morning. The woman didn't care about her. Hell, Cherie didn't even seem to like her. She just saw Haley as a step in the story. With a sigh, she made her way out of her apartment, careful to re-lock the door behind her, and then trudged down the stairs to the parking lot. Cherie was sitting in her SUV with the engine running, her eyes affixed to something on her phone. Haley walked over to the passenger door, but as soon as she opened it, Cherie stopped her before she could sit down.

"I thought it would be wiser if you just followed me over to the hospital," Cherie said as she continued to scroll through some body of text on her phone. Her eyes flicked up ever so briefly to acknowledge Haley and then they returned to her screen.

"Right," Haley said as she shut the door once again and made her way to her own car, her skin already starting to bristle. Cherie could be such a bitch.

The receptionist at the information desk informed Cherie that Mrs. Lambert was not accepting visitors, but she wouldn't take no for an answer. Instead, Cherie led Haley toward the cafeteria and then began a careful and discrete operation to seek out Nicole. Haley had picked out an overpriced vase of flowers in the hospital gift shop while Cherie inspected the directory for possible starting points. Eventually, it was a police officer standing guard in the ICU that tipped Cherie off to Nicole's whereabouts.

When she caught sight of the uniformed officer, she pulled Haley out of sight into a doorway that was blocked by the angle of the corridor.

"They might recognize me," Cherie said, worried. Haley did her best to suppress an eye roll.

"I'm sure it'll be fine. We're just bringing her flowers," she offered in reassuring tones. What a time for the veteran news reporter to get cold feet.

"You should go ahead of me. They might let you in if you're alone. No one will recognize *you*."

"Fine," Haley said with finality. What did it matter? She certainly wasn't going to ask this poor woman if someone cut her unborn child out of her belly. She could just drop off the flowers and maybe introduce herself before leaving. That is, if Cherie wasn't there. Who knows what this woman would ask Nicole if she were granted access to her room? Without another word, Haley began making her way toward the guarded hospital door.

She considered just going for the door as if she had every right to enter. That was a trick she learned early in her journalism studies. Sometimes you can gain access to restricted areas just by acting like you were *supposed* to be there. At the last second, she changed her mind. The officer had shifted his mass so that he was obstructing the entryway.

"Excuse me," Haley said in her most sugary tones. "I'm just dropping off these flowers for Nicole."

"I can take it from here," the man replied, looking down at the arrangement: one dozen roses in an array of colors called a "Rainbow Bouquet," according to the tag Haley had ripped off in the gift shop.

"I'd like to take it into her if you don't mind. You know, I'm the one that found her. I just wanted to make sure she's all right," Haley blurted out as if she had been holding her excuse in her pocket and was just waiting for the opportunity to show it off. Rookie mistake, she thought to herself. Never volunteer too much information. That's the fastest way to blow your cover. Her story, she reminded herself, was not a cover. It was the truth. She did find Nicole and call for an ambulance. She saved her life.

"Not at this time. You can leave it with me or you can take the flowers with you and come back when Mrs. Lambert is accepting visitors." The officer's voice had become stern, reproving. She hated the idea of returning to Cherie without even setting eyes on Nicole, but she didn't know what else to do.

The door to the room suddenly opened as if in response to her wish. Haley looked in but couldn't see anything more than the edge of the hospital bed. Jonathan Lambert moved into the hallway. Haley recognized him from the picture in *Sonoran Life*. He looked haggard. His hair was tousled and his skin dark around his eyes. The same eyes shot toward Haley's face.

"Who the hell are you?" he asked, his voice accusatory.

"I'm-I'm Haley. I found your wife out on the 87," she managed to stutter out. In that instant, she watched his face soften.

"I'm sorry, we've had to chase off a few nosy reporters recently. I don't know why they can't just leave us the fuck alone right now. Nicki has enough to deal with."

"I totally get that," Haley said, hoping she wasn't blushing with shame. "I just wanted to make sure Nicole, I mean, Nicki, is doing okay?"

"Yeah, the doctors say she's going to pull through. She lost a lot of blood, but you got to her just in time. I can't thank you enough…." Jonathan's voice trailed off as Cherie made her way toward the door.

"Hello, Mr. Lambert… Officer," Cherie said with a friendly smile and a nod to both parties. "I see you've met my associate."

Haley felt her stomach plummet.

"You work with this woman?" Jonathan asked, not bothering to hide his contempt.

"Uh, yeah. I do the weather," Haley answered feeling increasingly foolish by the second. She flashed her most beaming smile and said, "Channel 9 News at 6."

"Just get the hell out of here," he said, his face reddening with rage. A second wave of shame hit. This man was suffering. She could see it in the way it twisted the lines of his face beneath the anger.

"I really did find her," Haley added in a hurry. "Honestly, I did."

"I don't give a rat's ass," Jonathan replied, his eyes hardening with hatred. He turned abruptly to the police officer and said, "Get them out of here, now."

Jonathan Lambert vanished into the confines of his wife's hospital room as the officer took both Cherie and Haley firmly by the arm and began leading them back to the elevator. He didn't say a single word nor did he acknowledge Cherie's demands that they be released immediately. Only when they were in the elevator corridor did he finally manage a curt, "Down," at Haley. She selected the appropriate arrow. At the chimes to signal the parting doors, the cop let go of their arms and said, "Get out and don't come back."

Haley made her way directly into the waiting elevator with Cherie reluctantly in tow. As soon as they were both inside, Haley selected the button for the lobby and watched the doors close. She felt nauseous and her face burned with embarrassment. Once the elevator started into motion, Cherie broke the heavy silence that settled over them.

"See?" she said. "I told you they would recognize me."

Cherie

10

Erick said he would see what he could dig up, but only if Cherie agreed to meet him for drinks at some downtown bar he described as *hip*. She was momentarily thankful he couldn't see her retch at the suggestion. Erick was always in search of the new hotspot in the Phoenix Metro Area to share with readers of the Lifestyles section of the local rag. The man was as lame as print media, Cherie had decided long ago. Did people still use the word *lame*? She shook her head and started texting Audra instructions to pick up her black Max Mara sheath dress at her condo to bring down to the studio along with a medium iced, quad-shot, skim-milk latte. Her phone automatically populated her coffee selection now which proved rather time-saving over the course of a week. Technology has its conveniences.

By the time she arrived at her office, her drink was collecting water droplets of condensation on her desk and her dress hung neatly in plastic on a hanger on the back of her office door. Audra might actually last longer than six months as her personal assistant. That would be a refreshing change. The last one, Kaya or Kira or something of the like, had only made it through a meager six weeks before she quit with a terse email. Another eager journalist chased out of the field, Cherie thought with a laugh. None of these young women had what it took to make it in broadcasting. She was saving them the trouble of several trying years before they came to that conclusion all on their own. Besides, what sort of person thought "assistant to Cherie Rodgers" was the best way to break into the business? Did they have fantasies that involved her locked in a bathroom with a vicious bout of food poisoning while the producer asks, "Can you go on for her?" It was ridiculous. She had attended the journalism school at Northwestern and been placed at the station by her university's residency program. She worked hard, made a strong impression, and secured a lasting job with the news provider.

Cherie continued to dream that a national news organization would take notice of her and steal her away from Phoenix, but no one came forward to stake their claim. Now that she had slipped past forty, she knew time was running out. If she didn't break a national story of actual worth, she would be blogging about cleaning products by the time she was fifty-five. She didn't care what she had to do to get her story. She would even meet Erick at his "hip" downtown bar. Or so she argued with herself later that evening as she slipped into her little black dress after her news segment. He promised Cherie that her name would be on the list so she could bypass the line in the alley, and a stiff drink, not too sweet, would be on the table waiting for her. Maybe Erick wasn't that bad after all.

By the time she found a parking spot and walked a block to the bar's alleyway entrance, Cherie had once again changed her mind about Erick. He sucked. If he didn't have some information for her, she would pour her drink on him and never call again. Assigning consequences in her head for future annoyances always made Cherie feel a little better about the irritation she anticipated. Erick had a table in a dark corner of the bar, far away from the skeeball machines. She shook her head. All the happening new spots catered to a younger, and seemingly classless, crowd. They had no sense of refinement, but held onto tokens from childhood as if the only quality shared by these burgeoning adults was an aversion to adulthood. At least this bar sought to appease both sectors.

"Isn't this place great?" Erick asked as he rose to greet Cherie. She opted for the vinyl booth style seating along the wall, displacing Erick so he had no choice but to occupy the metal chair opposite her. He pushed a drink toward her and Cherie eyed it with apprehension.

"It's called The Janet Napolotini. They name all their cocktails after famous Arizona politicians. Isn't that great?" Erick added with a smile. In their time apart, Cherie almost forgot his propensity for asking that same question over and over until it became infuriating. She took a deep breath to calm herself before downing a hearty gulp of whatever Erick had placed in front of her. She should have known the day wasn't going to get any better as she watched that weather girl storm away from her in the hospital parking lot earlier that morning. *What an idiot*, she thought as the girl drove off in her Prius in quite the huff. Cherie took another, more tentative sip from her drink and tried to let go of her annoyance from earlier.

After all, Haley Roth was little more than a child and a nitwit to boot. How she got so lucky as to stumble upon Nicole Lambert in the middle of the desert, Cherie would never know. She thought it might prove to be her own lucky day considering Haley's call to the show's executive producer in the middle of the night led him to alert Cherie to the possible story while every other news station sat around oblivious to the kidnapping. She had a jumpstart that no one else had. Only she was able to talk to Haley right after the FBI questioned her. Even if others heard about the kidnapping, she might be the only one who had a name to go on. She just needed a little more information but the research team at Channel 9 was off the table if the story was on the blacklist. That meant she had to put up with Erick.

He had a little gray starting at his temples. Cherie was surprised that he didn't dye his hair again, but then she remembered he was in print. What was the point? No one saw his face. Hell, most people probably glazed right over his byline. She ran her eyes over his face. Erick had a strong jaw and a shapely, well-defined mouth. Cherie's eyes paused at his lips, trying to remember what it was like to kiss him before she gave up and returned his gaze. His dark brown eyes looked black in the dim light of the bar.

"So, Erick, you said you might be able to find something for me?" she asked, cutting straight to the point.

"You're not even going to make with the nice talk for a minute before you dig in?" he asked, amused. "You were always too much business up front and not enough party in the back."

She supposed he intended it as an insult, but she didn't care. Men in this field could cut loose with hookers and cocaine and they'd be deemed as brash as Hemingway, but the minute a woman in her profession did the same, she was deemed a party girl, denied any serious assignment.

"I'm a woman, not a mullet. And, it's not that I don't appreciate the objectification, but I called you earlier for one reason. Can you help me with this story? I promise, you'll have first stab at the print edition. I'll give you my personal notes." It was a fair offer. As soon as she could break the story on the evening news, Erick could follow up with the ink the next morning.

"Then why don't you tell me what you know first, since we're in this together," Erick countered with a smile. Cherie stared at him trying to guess what sort of information he might be holding. This could all be a bluff. She decided to take her chances.

"It seems as if Nicole Mason-Lambert was abducted. She is currently in the ICU of the hospital on Shea. I heard the name "Jude" in connection. All I could find out from my sources was that this Jude might be tied to some sort of corporate crime vigilante group." Cherie didn't mention the part about the pregnancy or the possibility that the infant had been stolen at the moment of their birth. She gave Erick just enough to make him think she was putting her cards on the table. If he was smart enough, he would know that she was holding a couple back just in case he didn't come through on his end.

Erick slowly spun his glass in front of him. Bourbon on the rocks from the looks of it. He always had to order drinks that suited his masculine image of self, the rugged reporter, even if he wrote for the Lifestyles section more often than not. Cherie noticed, however, that he was always eager to sample the delicate concoctions he insisted on ordering for his female companions. Cherie watched the slight grimace, almost completely suppressed but not entirely, as he took a gulp and prepared to divulge his own findings. *He must have something good for all this build-up*, Cherie thought as she shifted forward in her seat.

"A guy over at the news desk heard something about this Jude. Vigilante is right. Apparently, the word is that he kidnaps children as punishment for corporate crimes. There's a total media blackout on coverage by order of the Homeland Security Association. Also heard that Southwest Resources is about to bring down some serious heat so maybe that's your connection to this Jude guy, but I haven't heard anything about his connection yet. We're just waiting for the go to run with what we've got," Erick said. Cherie could taste the smugness in his voice. He obviously knew a lot more about what was going on than she did. He gave a dramatic pause just so she could prompt him to continue.

"What's the story?" she asked without hesitation. Let Erick enjoy his victory. She would be the one to break the *real* story.

"Lead poisoning. Water contamination over in Harrison. Whole town is affected. Bad. We're just starting to hear about it so my guess is that it's been going on a while if people are starting to show the effects. Company shifted leadership four months back. We're guessing it was a defensive strike against the media fallout."

She heard stories about towns turned upside down by water issues and other environmental disasters. The Flint Water Crisis in Michigan which was drawn out into years of litigation and still wasn't resolved. The Denver Contamination which caused widespread rioting throughout the city and resulted in damages somewhere near a billion dollars. The Anchorage Disaster which turned almost a quarter of the city into a ghost town. What would happen here? This story was going to be even bigger than she had imagined. Her mind spun back to Nicole.

"So, you think this Jude person might have kidnapped Nicole over a decision made by Southwest Resources?" Cherie asked.

"I don't honestly know. My guy says there's nothing solid on Jude. Just rumors and faint ones at that. Something about a seven-year-old boy that went missing up in Alaska after that Anchorage thing and Vince heard something else about a girl in Texas disappearing after that oil refinery accident last year. Jude was a name that was tied to both events, but once the local media caught word of it, the big boys put the kibosh on the story."

Cherie leaned back in her seat and thought about what Erick had told her. The head honchos at the studio had already handed down the decision to cut the story, but she had stumbled into something bigger than herself, bigger than the station. A total media blackout on a group of high-profile kidnappings. She would get a Peabody for this. She also realized that she could lose her job. Cherie had to make a decision: go big or go home. Maybe another opportunity would come her way, one without so much risk attached, but she didn't think it was likely. Most people only got one chance to make it big. What if this was hers?

11

Cherie started the day early by canceling her session with the personal trainer. She couldn't trust her team to do the legwork on this one for her. She would need to see to the research quietly and personally. She even picked up her own coffee on the way to the station. Audra didn't start her official work shift until 9 a.m. and she usually put in close to twelve hours so Cherie decided to be generous and let her sleep. She, on the other hand, had a long day in front of her. Cherie ran through her list of tasks as she parked her BMW in the spot labeled "Cherie Rodgers". The SUV was almost two years old. She would need to start looking for a replacement soon enough. Just another task to add to the list, Cherie thought woefully. It felt like every completed assignment was replaced by two more.

She didn't have much to go on. Just a couple of names and incidents. She decided to start with the kidnapping in Anchorage. She could almost recall seeing something on CNN about the abduction of some kid with political ties a year and a half ago. There had been a lot of national news out of Anchorage at that time. The Charter Chemical Company caused an environmental catastrophe when one of the dams within their waste water containment system broke and a flood of toxic waste was released into the main water supply. Cherie poured through a bevy of articles on the event covering everything from the initial reports of effects to the widespread abandonment of certain parts of the city. Finally, she read stories of corruption in the wake of the disaster. Shady corporate restructuring to avoid the cost of clean-up, the early retirements and hefty bonuses for outgoing members of the executive board, the appalling inaction by the government, both state and federal, to see any retribution for the lives lost or irreparably damaged.

Calvin Babcock was at the center of the chaos. As the head of Charter Chemical, he was the general populace's choice for villain in this tragedy. It was Charter Chemical's executive board that failed to acknowledge warnings from safety engineers about due maintenance. They were the ones who didn't set up an effective wastewater treatment plan to reduce the hazardous levels of toxins in their water stores. And, once the dams broke, they were the ones who didn't warn the public immediately. They walked away from the whole fiasco with large payouts to second homes in the Florida Keys or Italian villas. During the disaster, it was reported that Calvin Babcock's seven-year-old son, Caleb, had vanished. No ransom note or body turned up, but the Babcock family had attached a staggering reward for information leading to the return of their son. And then nothing. No additional information surfaced in any search Cherie conducted.

She went back to her original queries on the Charter Chemical disaster in Anchorage and found a story about the children who died as a result of the incident. There she found the face of seven-year-old Malcolm MacDonald, one of a dozen children to perish. He had short hair and bright, friendly eyes in his first-grade photograph. He wore a mirthful expression that suddenly made the Charter Chemical event very real for Cherie. Malcolm stirred something maternal and long-suppressed. The image of her own mother pulling warm sheets out of the dryer on Saturday morning suddenly surfaced in her mind. Her mother worked as a secretary in a legal office during the week, so Saturday was her day to catch up on the domestic tasks, the ones Cherie's father never seemed to concern himself with doing.

Cherie moved away from her computer. She'd been trying to uncover additional leads for a little more than an hour and she already needed a break. She walked over to the window of her office. It was a smog-filled day for Phoenix. Her eyes moved to the east toward the town of Harrison out past Mesa. All those people unknowingly drinking poisoned water and the media is sitting on their hands waiting for the go-ahead from the higher-ups to warn the public. It seemed criminal.

Once upon a time, before the career and the accolades of modest success, she had decided to pursue journalism as a career because she thought she could make a difference. It sounded like such a tired cliché at this point in her life that she was almost embarrassed to have once been so young. A world-weariness had settled over her a long time ago. Now the only type of change she pursued with any tenacity had quantifiable results: money, exercise, a story with the potential to expand her audience beyond the urban, desert landscape outside her window. This thing with Southwest Resources could be the piece to launch her career to that next level. It might even be her last chance, but the lengths she would have to go to uncover the story, the whole story, overwhelmed her in that moment.

One step at a time, she reminded herself. Cherie heaved a heavy sigh and moved away from the window. She picked up the disposable cup from her desk and drained its remaining contents before tossing it in the small trash can. Someone always came by afterhours to empty her wastebasket and replace the liner, even if she had only tossed away a few crumpled pieces of paper. It bothered her to think that someone was in this space, her space, when she was away every night. She wondered why she didn't think of it before. Cherie gave her head a shake and returned to the questions at hand. She had one kidnapping to correlate to the Lambert abduction, but she needed more. Now, Erick had said something about a girl in Texas....

Cherie sat down at her desk and clicked her mouse to reactivate her computer screen. She compiled a list of search terms and set to work. Another hour ticked away and she had located her third kidnapping victim, Lacey Hardgrove, the fifteen-year-old daughter of a high-ranking Gulf Petroleum executive who had vanished a week after the GP Refinery Explosion. She found a couple stories about the kidnapping: one in the *Dallas Morning News*, the other in the *Houston Chronicle*. The news about the explosion overshadowed everything else that week. Twenty-seven people died and more than two hundred were injured in the blast. Cherie ran through everything she could find on the victims of the explosion. All were adults except for Isla Moreno, just three weeks shy of her fifteenth birthday. Cherie found a photograph that the girl's mother had provided to the *Chronicle* of the young girl holding up a puffy, pink dress she was planning on wearing for her quinceanera.

That was two high-profile kidnappings in the wake of a disaster. Nicole Mason-Lambert's child could be the third, if Cherie was drawing the right connections. She printed out a few articles and called out to Audra for another latte before she remembered it was not quite nine in the morning. Cherie decided coffee would have to wait as she began gathering her notes and printouts to show to the producers. The Lambert family might have a hold on the local press, but they couldn't stop the story from being told once the facts were in place. If the Channel 9 News team didn't break it, someone else would beat them to it. The people at the top had to see that. Cherie just had to convince them that she had more to go on than wild conspiracy theories. Three kidnappings seemed like enough evidence to draw a correlation. Cherie just hoped it was enough.

12

She made her way toward the executive producer's office to leave a message with his assistant requesting a quick sitdown when he got to work that day. "Sitdown" was the station's fresh and approachable way of saying "meeting" but it always carried a hint of irritation for Cherie, who took it as further proof that modern media was too much PR and too little hard-hitting news. To her surprise, Cherie found her producer had arrived early for work and he didn't look too happy to be here.

"I was just about to call you in for a sitdown," he said in a bland tone that didn't suggest trouble, but Cherie could tell from the tension in his face that her boss was not pleased with her today.

"What a coincidence," Cherie replied with a smile, "I was just on my way here to request the same thing."

The producer exchanged a brief look with his secretary and asked her to hold his calls before moving toward his office with the expectation that Cherie would follow.

"Cherie, I already told you to stay away from this one," he said, annoyance dripping in his voice before she had even finished closing the door behind herself. "I got a call from the higher-ups this morning telling me you hadn't listened."

"What does that mean?" she asked, trying to match the irritation in his voice. If someone called her producer before he even got to the station this morning, that explained his anger, but what Cherie didn't understand was how anyone knew she was looking into the matter.

"It means you've been looking into this Jude thing after I said there was a media blackout in place by order of the Homeland Security Association."

"I don't know what you're talking about. I was just looking into some unsolved, high-profile kidnappings that might have ties to the Lambert case." Cherie tried, unsuccessfully, to steer the conversation back to the reason she sought out a meeting this morning in the first place. How did he know she had been looking into this Jude person? She hadn't used any of the station's research staff to seek out information.

"The Lambert case is off-limits too," he said firmly before adding, in a softer tone, "for now, at least." Cherie didn't know if he was trying to assuage her or himself, but she could see him trying to relax his stance ever so slightly.

"And the contaminated water? That's off the table too?"

"Yes," he replied without hesitation. "Not until we get the go-ahead."

She had the answer she was really seeking. The station knew about the water already. They probably knew more than her about the kidnappings too. The higher-ups *knew* and they just sat on the information.

"I just don't get it. Aren't we supposed to chase down the stories that people in power don't want us to cover? Isn't that the way it works?" Cherie could feel her frustration mounting. A big story falls in her lap and she gets stonewalled. She wasn't so naïve as to think that the journalism of the present day had that same ethical core that propelled it in the past, but this seemed like a blatant disregard of the principles that ignited their profession. She stared at her producer as he paced behind his desk in his mint green button-down with its matching tie of aqua paisley. He certainly didn't look like a newsman. Too pretty, Cherie decided. He looked like he should be heading some division of a public relations firm. Maybe that's all the news was these days. Glorified PR.

"Jesus, Cherie, grow up. No one's changing the world today. We have you on that school shooting over in Gilbert. Doug and Renée are gathering witness accounts right now, but when they get back, I'd like you to help them select the right clips to use in the segment."

"That's it? I have to drop the story and I'm assigned busy work as punishment? This is bullshit," she protested. Cherie looked away from her producer in his spring-toned attire to the barren office he occupied. A sleek, modern desk of glass and metal, no bookcases or file cabinets for storing information. No books, no pictures of his family, no clusterfuck of files that Cherie had come to associate with journalists during her early days in the field. The office was cold and sterile. No, Cherie wouldn't be able to stir up enough passion to go against the HSA's blacklist here, but that didn't mean she was going to give up so easily.

Her producer picked up his cell phone from the edge of his desk and ran his thumb across the screen to check his messages. Cherie took this as a sign she was being dismissed. Apparently, that was it. She was expected to drop everything and move on. Well, they had another thing coming if the station execs thought she would lay down and die just like that. Cherie began her sullen march back to her office, but before she could reach the door, he added, "Stay away from it, Cherie. It could cost you your job and a whole lot more."

She paused in her step to listen to his warning, but she didn't turn around to look at him. She didn't want him to see the defiance burning in her eyes. Cherie continued out the door in full knowledge that her face was red with anger. She noted the smug look on his secretary's face as she exited. It was no secret to Cherie that she was not a staff favorite at the station, but she didn't care. She was focused on other matters. There was no way she was going to let another news team beat her to the punch, not when the story was practically handed to her by that idiot weather girl.

She noticed Audra was not seated at her desk yet. That was a problem for another day, Cherie decided as she stormed into her office. On the corner of her desk sat a chilled coffee drink, condensation slowly gathering. Cherie quickly dismissed her misgivings about her assistant as she sat down and activated her computer screen. How on earth had the studio execs known she was looking into the kidnappings? It had to have something to do with the search queries she put into her computer, but how could they know what she was researching? Everyone suspected that the government had access to all that information and probably Google did too, but how could *her boss* learn about her searches without someone looking at her personal computer?

A knock at the door jolted Cherie and she sat up straighter in her chair.

"Yes?" she asked, not bothering to mask her annoyance. Audra burst through the door with a clipboard in her hand. The young woman would best be described as "cute" and today was no exception. She had chosen a Pepto Bismol color sweater over a pea-soup green skirt. To this, she added an aged pair of clunky Mary Janes. Where did HR find this girl? The team over in Human Resources seemed to find no greater joy than locating these personal annoyances in the form of interns and assigning them to serve as Cherie's assistant. She took a deep breath and reminded herself that she didn't even need to text Audra this morning to remind her about her coffee order. That was worth one gold star, pink sweater or not.

"Don't mean to bother you but the D.A.'s office called and asked if they could move your interview with Chavez from tomorrow to Thursday?" Audra had a cheery voice that Cherie suspected hid a dour temperament.

"Yes, fine," she said dismissively and waved her hand to signal that Audra should be on her way. Cherie didn't even remember the scheduled interview. Her mind was preoccupied with other matters.

"And, I-uh, I hope you don't mind, but I told the

producers you already had a lunch scheduled when I saw the calendar update for an editing session later. I know you hate those."

"Do I have a lunch today?" She honestly couldn't remember what she was supposed to be doing with her day.

"Not really." Audra giggled nervously and tried to hold her mouth in a straight line.

"Why would you do that?" Cherie didn't know if she was angry or appalled. Everything about this young woman grated on her from the way she dressed to the way she spoke to the soft curves that spoke of dietary bread allowances, but Cherie was beginning to question her assessment. Either this girl was batshit crazy or she had something going on beneath the puerile wardrobe choices and upbeat attitude.

"I heard the boss was coming down on you hard so when I saw the calendar event in your inbox, I figured it was some form of punishment. Usually, I sit in on the editing and you're never there. So I just jotted off a reply letting him know you weren't available at that time," Audra rattled off her reasoning like she was giving directions to the library, punctuated by unnecessary inflection, without any concern or acknowledgement of her gross overstepping of boundaries.

"Don't you think that's a little presumptuous of you?" Cherie asked, more surprised than anything.

"Oh yeah, definitely," Audra said as her smile broke through again.

"Why would you do something like that?"

"Way I heard it, working as your assistant is sort of a rite of passage. If you last more than four months, you'll make it in news. No one's ever made it more than six. I've been here almost five months. As I see it, I'm already on my way out. So, you know, go big or go home. I figured you'd either be pleased or pissed," Audra explained.

Cherie leaned back in her chair, surprised for the first time in a long time.

"So, did it work?" Audra asked. "Are you pleased or am I fired?"

Cherie realized her assistant's brazen action had freed her from an afternoon locked away in an editing room with Doug and fucking Renée who masked the smell of cats with various scents sprayed from cans. She could keep working on her story and none would be the wiser. If only she could figure out how the higher-ups caught onto her in the first place....

"Audra, what do you know about computers?"

13

"All the computers at the station are connected through a Virtual Private Network so anyone with the right access can see what people are looking at all day online. I mean, if they really wanted to get creepy about it, they could set up keyword alerts that let them know any time someone types a word into a search engine. So, when you look up something you're not supposed to, it sends an alert to whomever set it up."

The computer on her desk became more menacing as Audra explained ways and means by which all her online time was likely monitored. Cherie didn't know how to pursue information without the machine.

"Are there ways around it?" Cherie asked after some deliberation.

"Well, sure," Audra said from the desk she had opted to sit upon instead of in one of the many seats available in Cherie's office. Audra's right foot swung back and forth from where she perched. "First thing I'd do is *not* run a questionable search from your office computer, especially if you work for some big corporate news conglomerate."

She gave Cherie a reproachful look that suggested any child should know as much. Cherie hated Millennials and every generation after, but even she had to admit that they had their uses. Audra's slumped posture leaned in towards the computer as if she were drawn to its invisible life force.

"Now," the younger woman continued, "I use a Tor browser at my own house and a Linux operating system to help protect my network."

"What are you doing from there? Running drugs?" Cherie could understand a little paranoia when it came to internet security, but Audra seemed to take this to a whole new level.

She laughed before replying, "Torrenting. What were you looking up anyway?"

"I think there might be some high-profile kidnappings happening as revenge for corporate crimes. I was just following-up on some names, but the story's been blacklisted."

"Well, you're sure as hell not going to find anything on Google. I'd start by making sure my system was secure, and well-hidden, but then I'd search message boards on the dark web using an onion service. Easy enough, really."

"You sure you don't want to go into Computer

Science? There's real money to be made there, unlike journalism," Cherie asked.

"I'm not in it for the money," Audra replied with a measure of pride. Cherie wondered if she was ever this young. Certainly not at twenty-two which, she was guessing, was roughly Audra's age now.

"Audra, it seems I am in need of a lunch companion today."

Cherie knew she had to get back to the station, but her time passed in Audra's two-bedroom bungalow downtown was well worth the hours she spent stewing in the mingled aroma of litter boxes and incense. Audra took a seat on the lumpy, flower-patterned couch and pulled out a battered laptop plastered in stickers until the original black plastic casing could no longer be seen. Cherie took a seat beside her assistant, hoping she wouldn't leave with cat hair stuck to every inch of her pressed skirt. She had thought to take her jacket off, but removing her skirt seemed impractical.

Together, they generated a list of search terms for Audra to investigate and then Cherie was sent to the kitchen to make some tea while her assistant fell into the black hole of the internet where she apparently felt most comfortable. The kitchen was small, smaller even than Cherie's bathroom, and instead of cupboards, shelves lined the walls which made it easier to locate the boxes of tea bags. A lime green kettle sat on the stove patiently waiting. Cherie filled it with water from a gallon container sitting on the counter and set the kettle on the burner while she began looking for mugs. By the time the tea kettle started its hissing whistle, Audra had uncovered a message board with an unusual number of hits for the word "Jude" but it seemed like it pertained more to requests for spiritual assistance than any sort of kidnapping operation.

Cherie was beginning to understand just how difficult it could be to access certain information with media controls in place. In response to the deluge of misinformation during the previous decade, the government instituted a media watchdog group as part of the Homeland Security Association after the Justice Department and Homeland Security merged in the name of streamlining communication on all matters of national safety while reducing the cost of red-tape bureaucracy. In addition to providing far-reaching oversight to many previously independent agencies, from the FBI to the CIA to even the NSA and regional law enforcement, the HSA also maintained a handle on the media blacklist and was able to prevent a lot of misinformation from proliferating amongst the American public. Or, so it was explained, but many had their doubts. Cherie herself was starting to have some serious doubts.

"Try cross-referencing with any names and locations we might have," Cherie suggested, setting down a cantaloupe-colored mug on the coffee table between Audra's laptop and a 1956 edition of *Better Homes & Gardens Decorating Book.*

"Looks like I've got something," Audra said as she leaned closer to her computer screen and began reading. "It says, 'Please pray for Isla Moreno,' and then a link to an article in the *Chronicle.*"

Cherie perked up and leaned in to look closer at the screen. There was the name. The message was signed by someone called ETW1, no email or contact information included.

"Well," she said, leaning back once again, "it's a start."

For the remainder of the hour, Cherie poured through the posts with her assistant until a ruckus at the front door startled her. She instinctively leaned forward to close the laptop as the door opened and a young man stepped inside. He was dressed from head to toe in dark colors: black slacks, a button-down grey shirt, and black tie. His clothes spoke of a profession even though his shoes were Vans' skate shoes, also black. He had a mop of dark, lank hair atop his head and piercing eyes that locked on Cherie with an accusatory glare.

"Marv!" Audra shouted as she jumped up from her nesting place on the couch and ran over to greet their new arrival. Marv, for his part, did not look away from Cherie as he wrapped his arms around Audra in a mutual embrace.

"Who's your friend?" Marv asked as he planted a kiss atop Audra's head, which only reached his shoulders.

"This is my boss, Cherie," Audra answered with a smile, turning back to her on the couch. "Cherie, this is my boyfriend, Marv. He's really great at research too. Maybe he could help us?"

Cherie shifted uncomfortably and noticed that Marv did as well.

"This is a very sensitive subject," Cherie began, unsure how to dissuade Audra from sharing the details of their query.

"Oh, I know, but Marv won't tell a soul. Will you, Marv?" Audra asked, turning back to her partner with a beaming smile. Standing side by side, they looked like quite the odd couple. Short, curvy, brightly-colored Audra with her pink sweater and pixie shock of white hair next to the drab, dark, beanpole of a man called Marv.

There seemed to be a heavy pause before Marv answered, "No, of course not." Cherie detected a hint of offense, as if she had suggested he was untrustworthy. She nearly rolled her eyes in irritation, but managed to control her face.

"See, there's this guy," Audra started explaining, "and we think he might kidnap kids from corporate bigwigs when their companies do something really bad, like poison a city's water supply or that refinery explosion in Texas."

"Uh huh," Marv said with a certain hint of suspicion in his voice. "And why aren't you over at the news station using your staff of reporters to look into this?"

Cherie realized the question was directed at her and not Audra.

"Well," she began, but Audra cut her off.

"The story is blacklisted!" she called out, practically shouting.

"What makes you think you can trust *her*?" Marv asked Audra, though his eyes remained fixed on Cherie.

"Well, she's here, isn't she? She wants to find out the truth," Audra answered.

"And, once you find out the truth, what are you planning on doing with it?" Marv asked, the question aimed back at Cherie this time.

"I'm going to release the story," Cherie answered firmly, annoyed, and not for the first time, at the evaluative gaze this Marv guy had locked on her. Who the hell was he? Some twenty-something kid was going to judge her level of commitment? If she didn't need Audra's help just then, Cherie would have taken him down a few pegs.

"I thought this story was blacklisted. Your station won't touch it."

"Then I'll take the story to another station or to the internet. I really don't care as long as we get it out there," Cherie answered. She wasn't sure she meant everything she was saying, but she hoped it was the answer Marv was looking for just so they could get back to work. And, now that she had time to think about it, maybe she would shop the story around if the station wouldn't budge. Afterall, this was her big story.

Marv smiled for the first time and Cherie could almost see what Audra might find attractive about this misanthropic young man. His entire face changed when he smiled, releasing its sullen hold.

"I guess I can help with that."

14

Cherie and Audra left the bungalow an hour later to return to the station while Marv continued digging into research. He'd already uncovered quite a few leads in the investigation including an unlisted, user-supported news site called XrX that reported on stories no traditional news publication would touch. Things that would also get them torched right off of a Google search bar. They published a lot of rumors and conspiracy theories, it would seem, but they did uncover a few stories about Jude. The writers didn't seem to know much more than Cherie herself, but they did provide a couple key pieces of information that could help her story, including a connection between Jude and the kidnapping of an Allied Motors CEO's grandson in New York. When the time came to return to the station to prepare for the evening news, Cherie didn't want to leave, but Marv promised to continue searching for information until they could return later that night.

Cherie offered to give Audra a ride home from work only to discover that the offer also had to be extended to her bicycle. She winced as she imagined her manicured hands cramming some bright pink, fat-wheeled cruiser into the back of her SUV, but reminded herself that Audra and that dreadful Marv were helping her chase down leads for her story. Not to mention, they were helping her keep her search *hidden*. Nothing else made her feel like she had drifted past her prime quite like these computer kids. They seemed to speak in an entirely foreign language. Audra tried to explain their secure network while Marv combed through entries on the message boards. Cherie finally cut her short by asking, "So we're safe, right?" She waited for the affirmative nod before saying, "Okay, great," with enough disinterest to convey to Audra that she didn't want any further explanations.

Cherie was preoccupied for the rest of the day, trying to connect the pieces of her story while also trying to avoid her producer at all costs. She showed up late to makeup so she would then have to rush to the studio before air time. She would only have time to offer a cursory nod to the boss before she took her seat for the start of the show. She had forgotten her coffee, but just at the moment she realized her error, Audra arrived with a fresh, ice-cold latte for her. A flush of relief and gratitude filled her unexpectedly.

Apparently, the most important quality in an assistant is the ability to predict her caffeine needs throughout the day.

Cherie only had a few minutes left on the clock and needed to review her notes before they went live but her mind was racing, filled with names and faces. Lacey Hardgrove, Isla Moreno, Caleb Babcock, Malcolm MacDonald, and, thanks to Marv, she now knew of Jeremy Sutter and Penelope Garland, one aged six and one eight and both connected to the Allied Motors incident a couple years back. Every time a child dies in some fatal corporate error, another child gets taken. Well, not *every time,* it would seem. Just when the first child dies, one child gets taken. Others may also fall victim, but it seems as if Jude just claims one child for the initial loss of life and then moves on to the next tragedy.

Just how many people died each year as a result of corporate corruption or mismanagement? She was beginning to wonder if she could even come up with an answer to such a question. Certainly, corporations would be reluctant to release figures of that nature to any research or media outlet. And, with the media blackouts in place, they might not even be able to find such statistics even if the information had been initially gathered. Cherie could feel a headache forming at her temples. She closed her eyes, careful not to scrunch them up and disrupt her carefully applied make-up. A voice startled her and she quickly opened them again.

"Two minutes, everyone!" the production assistant shouted. Her name was Ruth. Who names their child Ruth in this day and age? Then again, who was she to point fingers? Her real name had been Cherlene-Dean Roggers before she had it legally changed the year she turned eighteen. That was about as white trash as you could get. Cherie Rodgers had a much better ring to it. The all-American ace reporter, at least, that was what Cherie thought when she chose the name for herself. It was her homage to her past and future selves, although her mother hated that she had ditched the "Roggers" part along with Cherlene-Dean. Althea-Mae wore her hyphen proudly and could never understand why her daughter chose to exist in perpetual opposition to the men in her life, from her father to the pastor of her church. What Althea-Mae didn't realize then was that Cherie existed in perpetual opposition to everyone in her early life, especially her own mother. It just seemed like men were the only ones who chafed against her attitude. Perhaps women were more accustomed to dealing with general disregard from the people they encountered so they didn't think her behavior quite as offensive.

From her early days, she felt like she was born in the wrong place and looked forward to the promise of college in a distant zip code. Her parents were part of a disintegrating middle class that had gained hold in their chunk of South Carolina during the 1950s, only to begin losing their footing once again, slipping slowly back into poverty thirty years later. Her parents could afford trips to Disney World, but they still accused her of "putting on airs" when Cherie tried to speak like the newscasters on CNN. They belonged to a group that Cherie would later term, with only a minimal degree of guilt, the Proud-To-Be-Stupid people. They worked hard and earned a living wage, with benefits, but they didn't really have the expendable income or energy for enriching leisurely pursuits. Newspapers were depressing, art exhibitions boring, and the theatre overpriced. Television was a readily available escape in the evening. Cherie believed that sitcoms make us comfortable with our shortcomings and distract us from the harsher realities of our everyday. The misogyny of our fathers is passed off as a humorous quirk just as the intellectual or moral superiority of our mothers is downplayed to ensure comfort in the home. People laugh at how much it relates to their own lives without really taking the time to reflect on what that means. Cherie had enough of that during her first seventeen years of life that she didn't need it reiterated for her with weekly programming.

As she looked around the station, she began to realize that she was part of the programming. This news show, if it could even be called that anymore, had a blacklist. This was the second time she'd come across a story that she was told to stay away from, but this time, it seemed like they actually meant it. She noticed the flashing light that told her they were about to go live and looked down at her notes. Cherie usually used these last few minutes to review the evening's stories once again. It helped her avoid any misalignments of tone and content. The last thing she wanted was to end up on a John Oliver segment of embarrassing news moments. An abrupt hush fell over the studio as the red light went on, indicating the show was live. Cherie put on her biggest celebrity smile and faced the cameras.

Two hours later, she was helping Audra lift her bicycle into the back of her SUV. It was the color of orange sherbet with a lime green stripe, not pink. That was her one mistake when she predicted this moment earlier in the day. She also didn't imagine her producer would choose that exact moment to walk out of the building and over to his convertible, but he did.

"Flat tire?" he asked as Audra and Cherie finished loading the bike. Cherie closed her hatchback before answering.

"Just giving my assistant a ride home. It's a little late to be out riding a bike," Cherie said as she turned around to face him. She knew she should have gone with a different lie as soon as she saw the doubt worn clearly on his face. Audra rode her bicycle home every night, in all likelihood, and she'd never thought to offer a ride home in the past. She should have said it was a flat. At least that way, Audra might have *asked* Cherie for a ride home and it would have seemed less conspicuous. Cherie certainly wasn't the type to offer others anything that might be misconstrued as a friendly gesture, especially her personal assistants.

"I see. Well, maybe we can have a sitdown when you get in tomorrow," he added in an amicable tone. Cherie felt like she had been suddenly doused in cold water. "Just come by my office when you get here."

"Whatever you say, chief," Cherie replied dismissively, keeping her voice in check. She hoped her expression matched. "I'm heading out. Audra, are you coming?"

Audra looked startled to suddenly be included in the conversation.

"Yeah, thanks!" she chirped before rushing over to the passenger door and climbing into the vehicle.

"Stay out of trouble, Cherie," her producer said to her

as he started toward his own parking space.

"No worries, always do," she replied with a hearty dose of false cheer. She hoped she was telling him the truth. Audra nervously fiddled with the seatbelt.

"Do you think he's onto us?" she asked.

"Can he see what we're looking for at your house?" Cherie asked in return.

"No way," Audra replied confidently.

"Then he can't know. He's just trying to scare me a little to keep me in line," Cherie asserted as she started her ignition and put the vehicle in reverse. Something instinctual told her to trust Audra, but she couldn't stop herself from wondering if Audra could be certain about the security of her home computer system. After all, Cherie always thought her internet searches at the station were private until today. As if in answer to Cherie's unasked questions, Audra spoke up.

"The best hackers are the ones that are never identified."

Cherie maneuvered into the narrow driveway in front of the bungalow shared by Audra and Marv. She left Audra to yank the cruiser out of the back of her vehicle by herself and walked straight over to the front door. Without knocking, Cherie opened the door and found Marv exactly where she'd left him, seated on the floral sofa in front of Audra's laptop. Two mugs of tea from this afternoon maintained their earlier position as well. The only thing that seemingly changed was a pizza box left open on the floor beside the coffee table.

"Find anything?" Cherie asked as she heard Audra

walking up behind her. Marv looked up just as his girlfriend followed Cherie through the door.

"Ho-ly shit," he said smiling, drawing out the syllables as his eyes looked to Audra and Cherie.

Renn

15

He didn't trust this Michael Maestri within an inch of his life. The man seemed like a sleezeball the first time they met him over at the Lambert residence. He had an easy charm that led others to excuse his arrogance, but not Renn. He didn't like him and he didn't trust him. That's all there was to it. Jonathan Lambert was a spoiled rich kid and likely complicit in any number of criminal offenses on behalf of his family's corporation, but Renn didn't think he was bad at his core. It seemed like the guy almost convinced himself that he was trying to right the wrongs done by his father at Southwest Resources. Maestri, with his slick and ready smile, was the real double-dealer. After a week of him, Richard Renn had his initial suspicions confirmed. The man's official company title was "Executive Assistant to Mr. Lambert" and it would seem Maestri was up to his ears in misdeeds in the service of the Lambert family and the company.

Not that any of that mattered. The BAU had been called in to investigate Jude, not the criminal malignance of SWR or its board of directors and employees. Cadence McNeil would just be the first death. Others would follow. Renn had seen this all before. This was the fourth time he had been called in to investigate the phantom figure who steals children in the night, never to be seen or heard from again. He had sympathy for the parents, especially poor Nicki Lambert, who'd had an infant stolen straight from her body. The doctor told his partner, Maurice, that she wouldn't be able to have children again. The damage to her uterus during the birth had been substantial. A gruesome wound ran down her abdomen to remind her forever of the assault. Renn didn't know whether to be relieved or frustrated when Nicki explained that she had been unconscious throughout most of the ordeal. She had a hazy recollection of someone telling her to push, of pain, of a baby crying, and then nothing. The fog of a dream not quite lucid. Nothing solidified until the hospital. It was better for her that she not remember that horrible event, but as investigators, it gave them very little to go on.

Not that it mattered. They would be leaving soon anyway. After Jude made his abduction, he would stop all contact with the Lamberts and Southwest Resources. And the FBI would be left waiting for the vigilante to strike again. He had dared to hope, when that ditsy weather girl turned up with Nicole alive in the middle of the road, that she might be able to provide them with some sort of lead, anything they could use. After all, he had long suspected that Jude's organization had access to members of the media. He always seemed to know what stories were lying in wait, written yet unable to reach their audience because of the blacklist. Maybe Jude had been part of the media. That was one theory. They knew he had to hold a professional position, one with connections. At least, he did before he adopted the moniker "Jude" and went on a kidnapping spree. A professor or journalist or maybe even a high-level agent of law enforcement. He had money and he had somehow managed to infiltrate every sector of the public in order to accomplish his great heists.

He also seemed to know about corporate crimes before

they did. It was a puzzle with too many pieces that wouldn't fit together no matter how you arranged them. Either Jude was everywhere or they were dealing with an organization, the reach of which Renn felt he was only beginning to grasp. This most recent abduction had given them a considerable amount of information. Jude knew about the death of Cadence McNeil as soon as SWR was made aware. He extracted a pregnant woman from a house teaming with law enforcement—that suggested procedural understanding as well as advanced knowledge of the Lambert residence. The swiftness in which Jude delivered his brand of justice revealed that he was in proximity before Cadence McNeil died. There were signs of an attempted forceps delivery before the infant was extracted through caesarean section that suggested they wanted the infant born alive. The fact that none of the uterine arteries had been cut during the extraction and that Nicole had been stitched back together, however haphazardly, told them that either Jude or one of his associates had medical training, maybe even a doctor or surgeon. Nevertheless, Nicki could have easily died out there on the highway that night. And that, perhaps most importantly, showed Renn that Jude was not above violence or even murder in his quest for vengeance.

The garish stitching across Nicole Lambert's abdomen could have bled out if Haley Roth had not been on hand. There was no way of knowing that a car would pass by, or even stop, in time to save the mother. At first, it seemed like too much of a coincidence for the weather girl not to have a connection to Jude, but after questioning her extensively, he realized she was hardly capable of conspiring in a crime of this magnitude. The most arduous task of her day was predicting the color of her wardrobe so she could match her fingernail polish accordingly. She was the polar opposite of Cherie Rodgers. That woman had been calling him every day to ask about developments in the Lambert case. Every day, he would direct her to the press coordinator for their department, but that didn't deter her from calling again the following day.

Why did she call *him* anyway? Maurice was the senior agent. Most people thought Renn looked older. He supposed it was due to the effects of early graying at the temples. The stress of the job had caused some early lines to form on his forehead and at the corners of his eyes so, at thirty-four, he could pass for forty. Maurice, nine years his senior, still got asked for identification when he bought cigarettes. Usually, he'd just flash his badge and no one would give pushback. He'd do the same thing in a bar when ordering scotch. It always made Renn a little uncomfortable. If he was going to have a drink at the end of a long day, he didn't need that bartender knowing that he was with the FBI. He didn't want the questions that would usually follow, nor the automatic malignance some people adopt in the presence of law enforcement. Renn understood the aversion. He didn't much like cops either. Maurice, however, appeared to regenerate during conversations with strangers. His energy renewed and his mood elevated. Talking only wore Renn down further and the tired, repetitive conversations one has with strangers at a bar irritated him.

Nevertheless, when Maurice asked if he wanted to meet at the hotel bar, he said yes. He always did. It was important to socialize with those you work with in this field, to roll over the details of the cases outside of the office, to make sure everyone was handling the horrifying moments with a measure of reason. He knew that before he signed onto the team. His job was the type that eats away the rest of your life. Maybe that's the trade-off. Rich home life, dismal job. Meaningful work, miserable home life. Renn didn't believe in binaries and, even if he did, he knew that one didn't hold weight. Some people were happy with both aspects of their lives just as others were equally miserable at home and at work. He was just being self-indulgent. It didn't matter, he decided as Maurice walked through the open doorway that divided the bar from the lobby. He acknowledged Renn with a smile and a nod as the man started to make his way towards him. Renn held out two fingers as the bartender looked over. Just as Maurice took his seat, two fresh scotches were placed before them. Renn liked when the timing worked just right.

"Thanks for the drink. I need one today," Maurice said as he lifted his glass and took a swig, the size of which could best be described as "dainty". Maurice would sip a glass of scotch for an hour. Renn could take down three in that time, but he would curtail it back in the presence of his superior to two an hour and no more than four in total. By his count, he could manage six heavy pours without an effect on his external demeanor. "The hospital expects Nicki will be cleared tomorrow. You get a chance to set up time to talk to Wallace Lambert yet?"

"The Old Bull? Tomorrow, unless he has a heart attack when that story breaks," Renn said. "I'm guessing the lawyers will try to use it to buy him a few more days." After a pause he added, "I hate lawyers."

"Yeah, but you hate everyone so that's not saying

much. Now, I hate lawyers. That actually means something, Ricky," Maurice said with a laugh. No one other than Maurice ever called him Ricky. Everyone that knew him called him Renn. Even Sheila, his girlfriend back in DC, called him Renn. The only exception was his mother, who called him Richard. The nickname grated on him, but he figured that was Maurice's intention so he forced himself to ignore it. Thankfully, no one else at work picked up on using it, probably because they could read the irritation on his features when Maurice did. He hated it, but he hated it less than he hated lawyers.

Old man Lambert had hunkered down with his legal team at home for a week, claiming dire health and threatening to sue should he fall victim to a heart attack due to unnecessary duress. The Bull had become very timid indeed. They had gotten word from the local PD that the press was going to break the water contamination story tomorrow. It had probably been traded for the knowledge that Nicole Lambert was laid up in the hospital recovering from a miscarriage. Renn didn't like that the press was going to drum up sympathy for the family based on their misrepresentation of Nicki's situation, especially not when the real focus needed to be on the town of Harrison and its inhabitants.

Maurice was still wearing his suit from earlier in the day. Oftentimes, he dressed down when they met up outside of work, but not today. The bartender hadn't asked for ID, thankfully. Renn took it as a small sign this evening wouldn't progress as terribly as he'd initially thought. Maybe they could keep the chitchat to a minimum and just go over the case.

"How do you think the residents in Harrison will

respond?" he asked. Recent riots in Denver and Anchorage had begun to set a precedent for violence.

"No one can say. Some towns just don't have the energy to riot. I've driven through Harrison. They look tired and beaten. And they don't even know yet," Maurice said as he took another small sip from his glass.

"Sometimes it's the people that are worn down that yield the most destruction," Renn argued. He knew it was the quiet mix of anger and hopelessness that you really needed to watch out for.

"I guess we'll find out sooner rather than later. I suppose we should be glad that they're finally getting the word out to the residents. How long have they been drinking that water *after* Southwest Resources realized there was an issue? Months? A year? Maybe even longer than that." Maurice looked down as his phone began to buzz. He pulled it out of his pocket and read the screen.

"It's Nicole Lambert. She has something for us."

Looks like it would be a one-scotch night. Renn figured he should be glad he wasn't impaired if they needed to head down to the hospital immediately. Nicole had had a rough run of it. Aside from being kidnapped, cut open, having her child stolen at birth, and then left on the side of the road, she had also been subject to a raging infection following the surgery that removed her uterus. She was only now recovering from that event. They only had been permitted brief conversations with the woman. She couldn't remember the incidents leading up to her kidnapping nor most of what followed. She came to briefly in a haze of narcotics. She thought she dreamt she was in labor, but the doctors said there were signs that the kidnappers attempted to induce the child and extract it using forceps. Nicole remembered pain and screaming. She thought she heard a baby crying. And then nothing. Not until the ambulance sirens.

Nothing more. If only she could remember who had come for her in the house. It might have been someone already on the scene, someone Renn would have seen and never suspected was a threat, or it could have been a stranger who somehow gained access to the premises. There was no way of knowing unless Nicki was able to remember something about her abduction. Renn dared to hope as he climbed into the driver's seat of their rental car that Nicole Mason-Lambert had been able to recall something they could go on. As it stood, they were as helpless in this case as they had been in the previous ones.

16

The sterile scents of the hospital always evoked an uncomfortable level of anxiety for Renn. He learned to manage it well, as he had his other "quirks," as his mother often described them when he was growing up. Panic, as a teenager, was something Renn needed to learn to control. He'd trained himself to maintain a manageable distance from his fears so that he could function in his daily life without interruption, no matter what his level of internal discomfort. On occasion, however, he would be reminded of his adolescent life when those early associations went straight past his conscious mind to the confused inner workings of his subconscious. The smell of hospitals was one such trigger. Antiseptic overpowering the scent of human frailty; a vicious contention between the natural world and the unnaturalness of human innovation.

Renn's first experiences of hospitals had drawn a firm correlation between that smell and impending trauma so that every time he caught a whiff of that distinct aroma, a mixture of chemicals and putridness, his interior being flinched. But, after years of practice, he hid it well. Even his partner couldn't detect the shift in his demeanor as they moved through the corridors of the hospital. Renn figured doctors weren't all that different from him. They fought against death, just as he did. But, for them, it was death in a more abstract sense, while Renn faced death incarnate, with all the fallibilities of its human form. Nevertheless, at its base, the struggle was the same.

The early loss of his father had been Renn's introduction to hospitals. A barroom brawl had landed Ronald Renn in the hospital with a shattered eye socket, crushed sinus cavity, a punctured lung from a broken rib, and a crack in his skull, but it was the damage he sustained to his kidneys that finally did him in. Renn, the son, had been there when his father finally succumbed to his injuries the morning following the attack. His father's bowels immediately released their contents and the smell of human waste mixed with the antiseptic air. From that point forward, every time Renn's nostrils caught that distinctive hospital aroma, he always imagined he could detect the faint scent of shit underneath.

Ronnie Renn was a brawler who had been in more than his fair share of fistfights and usually came out the victor, except this once. The younger Renn believed a strange sort of justice had been delivered. Until that point, he had only seen the blueish-black markings on his own skin and that of his mother. A puffy red cheek, a purple bruise, a busted lip, young Richard had known them all. It was as if all of his father's sins were visited back upon him in those final hours of life. But intermingled with his sense of victory was fear. Ronnie Renn was an unmatchable force in his son's universe; to see him broken and bruised made Richard Renn very afraid that unknown forces capable of such violence freely wandered the world.

Maurice nodded to the officer on duty and knocked on the door.

A faint, "Come in," was heard before Maurice entered with Renn following behind.

He was almost grateful for the excess of flowers scattered across every available surface in Nicole Mason-Lambert's room. They filled the air with their own perfume that momentarily distracted him from his surroundings. Unfortunately, the illusion vanished quickly as the aromas mingled. Renn noted that Jonathan Lambert was absent. He had been present every time they visited Nicole during the previous week. Maybe, now that she was doing better, he felt comfortable leaving her alone for the night so he could sleep in an actual bed, not just on the cot the hospital had provided when he refused to leave her side. Renn felt sympathy for the young couple. They had unknowingly been drawn into someone's elaborate scheme for justice. To many, they looked like the victims. True, a lot of people were going to suffer for the criminal misjudgments of Southwest Resources and Jonathan Lambert was named director of that corporation, but he seemed like the least culpable in the decisions made by that board until only recently. Nevertheless, it was Jonathan and Nicole that suffered the most for the company's crimes. If not, of course, their child. Jude carried out a strange brand of justice.

"It's all a bit foggy, but I remember packing. I was looking for my shoes, my favorite heels; I mean, how ridiculous is that? Nine months pregnant and I'm trying to pack a six-inch pair of heels," Nicole explained as her fingers fumbled with the edge of the hospital blanket. "Jonathan did say that he didn't know how long we'd be gone, but still, I don't know why I thought I needed them. I went to ask Val where they were because I couldn't find them in the closet. I remember I saw her in the hallway by the kitchen. You know, that little corridor that leads to the kitchen? And then there was a hand on my mouth, and then nothing. But I remembered seeing Val. Surely, she must have seen who grabbed me, right? She couldn't have been more than ten feet away."

Maurice's eyes briefly darted to Renn's own. They had interviewed the maid, but she had not said a word about being witness to Nicole's abduction. They suspected Nicole might have gone out through the kitchen door for some reason, but now they knew for certain that Jude, or one of his associates, had gained access to the house directly. That had been considered, but if Nicki's memory was returning with a degree of accuracy, they might have somewhere to start, for once.

Jude didn't leave witnesses. He moved like a phantom, unseen and unheard, and he always seemed to know just a little more than Renn would believe was humanly possible. When Penelope Garland died and the local PD was called in to protect 8-year-old Jeremy Sutter until their team could arrive, the boy was snatched away during his school day. Renn had chalked it up to incompetence or corruption within the New York City police force, but now that he had been present for one of Jude's abductions, he understood things differently. The man was a ghost.

"She didn't say anything to you? Val? She didn't say anything?" Nicki asked, her voice beginning to rise. "Do you think she might have been threatened? Why else wouldn't she say anything?"

"We'll talk to her again. It's possible that she might have felt she was in danger. We certainly can't say, but please calm down, Mrs. Lambert. The doctor says you are still recovering," Renn said in a calming tone. He had learned that certain inflection patterns could present an air of calm authority that served to reassure victims. "Have you told anyone else about this? Your husband or one of the nurses?"

"No, I sent Jonathan home this afternoon. As soon as I remembered, I messaged Agent Whitlock. Have you made any progress on locating this Jude? Do you know where he's taken my baby?" Nicki's agitation immediately turned from Val to the child she hadn't been permitted to set eyes upon. Even Cadence McNeil's mother had been granted that much. Renn wondered if it would be easier for Nicki in the long run, to never have an image to attach to her loss. He worried that instead every infant would evoke grief for Nicki Lambert.

"Mrs. Lambert, as soon as we know something, I'll be sure to let you know," Renn tried to reassure her.

"Please call me Nicki," she reminded him once again, her voice giving away her exhaustion.

"Yes, Nicki, if we could go back to that night. I'd like to run through the details once again. Start at the very beginning, when the agents showed up at your house, before your in-laws arrived," Renn said, notepad in hand. Nicki began recounting the details from her initial alarm to the moment she started packing with Patricia Lambert while Jonathan and his father argued in the study. Maurice stepped quietly out of the room to make a quick call to their team to see that Val Cobar was picked up immediately and taken in for questioning, or so Renn accurately assumed. By the time Nicki arrived at the moment she entered the kitchen and felt a hand close over her mouth, Maurice reentered the room and offered Renn a curt nod to indicate that, yes, he had made the call about the maid.

They had already suspected that the kidnapper had gained entrance to the house through an unmonitored entrance. The front door had two surveillance cameras in place, one at the entryway and another in the grand foyer. The younger Lambert residence was not quite as extravagant as Wallace and Patricia's own estate. It did not, for example, boast its own gated entrance, but rather shared a gate with the surrounding community. That meant that the perpetrator had to have a key card or code to gain entrance to the neighborhood. It also meant they were able to monitor any vehicle coming or going that same evening. Unless, of course, Nicole's body was somehow carried to the back of the property and hefted over the wall. An expanse of desert sat on the opposing side, but Renn figured someone, or multiple someones, might have been able to carry her unconscious body to a vehicle waiting beyond the gates of the Desert Primrose Estates and its surveillance cameras. As far as they knew, no one unaccounted for had moved in or out of the gated neighborhood. Then again, two cops had been stationed in the backyard and they hadn't seen anything out of place, certainly not one or two unknown assailants carrying a pregnant woman.

With Nicki's newly recovered memories, they knew that someone had in fact been in the house, so her body needed to be carried, unconscious, beyond the perimeter of the property in order to make their escape. There hadn't been a trail left across the carefully manicured lawns, no indentations to mark the passage of feet laden with the burden of an additional body. If the perpetrator had disappeared out the back, he had stuck to the gravel pathways until he reached the xeriscaped area beyond the pool and gazebo. Renn remembered the cynical eye with which he had first viewed the Lamberts' backyard. Why hadn't they continued the grass to the edge of their property? The Lamberts controlled most of the water in the Valley of the Sun. A little showboating seemed to be in line with that.

By the time they left the hospital, Renn had the first glimmer of hope that they might be onto something: an access point to the victim. In all the other incidents involving Jude, no one remained to tell the tale of their abduction. They were never able to isolate, with any certainty, an individual who might have given the perpetrator access to the children even though they suspected there had to be at least one person close to the family who had assisted in the abductions. This time, they had someone. Valeria Cobar, originally from Guatemala, who had been in the employ of the Lambert family for more than twenty years. She had started working for the family when Jonathan was little more than a toddler and, once he established his own family with Nicole as his wife, Val had been gifted from the elder Lamberts to see to the newlyweds' household management. She didn't have any family, no children of her own or monthly money transfers back to her home country. She hadn't raised any red flags during their initial interviews. She expressed reasonable concern for Nicole and for her child, she didn't hesitate to offer information about herself even though she described her citizenship status as "pending," and she didn't once mention seeing Nicole Lambert being drugged and snatched away right in front of her.

Maurice's phone started to buzz and he removed it from the interior pocket of his blazer. From the driver's seat, Renn watched him hit the button for the speaker option and a voice piped into the interior of their car.

"Yeah, Rice, we got a problem," the voice said anxiously. Everyone who knew Maurice personally, including those down at the Bureau, called him Rice, pronouncing it "Reese". Renn disdained the overfamiliarity his partner seemed to encourage. Perhaps that's why the boss put them together. Renn could be described as distant, calculating, even cold, but it always surprised him to hear those words applied to him because he knew the fiery temperament that danced within his heart and mind. At the same time, hearing himself described as such also carried a measure of victory for him. The difficult journey he undertook in his youth to manage his own behavior had proved successful. He decided he just needed to work on adopting a warmer tone with colleagues similar to the one he used with victims, but altered slightly. He would listen with more care to Maurice when he talked to others within their department. People described his partner as warm and approachable. Renn decided he could be warm and approachable too. He just needed to work on it.

"What now?" Maurice asked, annoyance adding a slight growl to his voice. Renn imagined the agent on the other end cringing slightly wherever he happened to be at this moment.

"She's gone. Vamoosed."

"Cobar?" Maurice asked, alarmed. His alarm quickly gave way to anger. "She lived at the Lambert residence! I thought we had her under watch?"

"So did we, but she slipped out."

"Just now?" Renn interjected. "When was the last visual check?"

"Twenty-six hours ago."

Maurice hit the mute button on the phone.

"Fuck."

"How in the hell could he have predicted that?" Renn asked, alarmed. "I mean, come on, he leaves the maid there for five goddamn days and then pulls her out right before Nicole regains her memory? What are the fucking chances of that?" Renn's mind raced to figure out how Jude always seemed to be right ahead of them by one impossible step. He had never encountered a criminal so frustrating and, if he was being honest, so completely beyond the parameters of his understanding.

The agent on the line started to fill in the perceived silence on his end. "Listen, Rice, we're getting the word out to everyone. We already had her flagged for travel…."

Maurice continued talking over him and their voices ran together until Renn couldn't distinguish one from the other. He focused on calming his breath. How had Jude done it? How did he always know something *before* they did? Every single time they thought they might have a lead in the case, it was snatched away from them. Renn just couldn't understand it. He felt a need growing inside of him, gathering up the force of an epiphany. He needed to know Jude, who he was and how he worked. He felt it with a passion unlike any he had felt before. This was his case, he realized, *the* case of his career. As each new thought raced into his head, he felt it with the reverence of revealed truth. Jude would make a mistake and Renn would be there to use that one misstep to chase him down. He accepted this new thought with complete faith. The idea steadied him in the wake of the maid's sudden disappearance and, with her, their one lead.

17

Renn felt his new beliefs confirmed six hours later when they received a call that Val Cobar had been picked up crossing the desert with a band of known Coyotes. An agent called them with the news. Coyotes usually journeyed north across the border into the United States, not south into Mexico, with those that paid for guided passage, but it looks like they were making a special run. They must have been paid handsomely for such an undertaking.

Border Patrol agents were on their way from Southern Arizona with Val in handcuffs. Her escape seemed like a sloppy plan and Renn wondered optimistically if this was Jude's grave error or if this mistake belonged to the housekeeper alone. Only time would tell. He sat at the Formica countertop of one of Phoenix's few 24-hour eateries that didn't cater specifically toward the young and hip. He just wanted coffee and two eggs over medium on toast at half past four in the morning. Maurice had suggested they make a quick trip to the diner, a nearby spot in a chain of national, open-all-night restaurants that served decent coffee, if only tolerable food. Renn was beyond caring. Last night, he had been ready to end a long day with a few drinks when his partner received that message from Nicki Lambert that sent them scurrying to the hospital.

After they discovered Cobar's disappearance, Renn and his partner spent the next five hours trying to track down any information that might assist them in locating the missing housekeeper. By the time they had decided to discontinue their search until the following morning and returned to the hotel, they both got a message that Val Cobar had been picked up and was on her way back to Phoenix. The agents decided to stay at the hotel and rest for a couple hours before meeting up again at four in the morning to grab breakfast before heading back to the station.

As they sat eating their early morning meal, Val was still a couple of hours away. They wanted to begin questioning her as soon as she arrived. Hopefully, she had been unable to rest while en route to Phoenix. Her exhaustion might help move things along faster. Renn knew this could be the turning point in the case after two years and twelve kidnappings. That alone provided the energy he needed for the day ahead, but he added four cups of black coffee just to be certain. Maurice matched him cup for cup rather than adopting the slowly paced sips that he applied to his alcohol consumption. In his mind, Renn ran through the potential information contained within Val Cobar. He checked his watch frequently with increasing frustration. The passage of time in relation to anticipation was one of the grave annoyances Renn felt he had to endure as part of the human condition. The idle minutes vanished as quickly as they arrived and hours passed unnoticed, but as soon as a momentous event was placed on the horizon, time slowed to a dribble and the seconds laboriously dragged on.

The server, some pock-marked youth with blue hair, returned with their check. Maurice pulled some cash out of his wallet and dropped it on the table. Renn checked his coat for toast crumbs before rising from the booth and following Maurice back to their rental car. Renn always drove. He preferred it that way and, given that Maurice was the senior officer, it seemed appropriate to automatically take on the responsibility. In truth, he was uncomfortable in vehicles when he was not the driver. He knew this spoke to his issues with control and managed to hide his discomfort whenever he was a passenger, but he volunteered to drive whenever it was appropriate to do so. With Maurice, the responsibility of driving had naturally fallen to him and he was secretly grateful for this division of tasks.

Agent Garber and Marcado of the Phoenix division were already on hand by the time Renn and Whitlock arrived. They had prepared the interrogation room and had a fresh pot of coffee brewing. Renn suspected they were trying to make a lasting impression on their DC-based counterparts. Maybe they also saw this case as a career-changing moment, just as he did, but Renn wasn't interested in personal advancement. Since the day he started with the Bureau, all he wanted was that one case that almost outsmarted him; one he had to wrestle to uncover its inner workings. Sure, there had been cases that went unsolved, criminals that got away, but they didn't torment him with a complexity that eluded him like the puzzles he played as a child. Young Richard Renn would buy a newsprint book of logic puzzles from the supermarket every Sunday and furiously unravel them with a number two pencil during the week that followed. When he finished his degree at Georgetown and interviewed with the FBI, he said it was the violent death of his father that initially turned his eye toward law enforcement, but, in truth, he knew it was those puzzle games that fueled his interest—their simple, applied logic and the flush he felt when all the pieces came together after the slow distillation of the facts.

Val Cobar was the piece of the puzzle he had been waiting for; that one, invaluable piece that allows you to make your first connection. Renn felt a surging of emotion and realized it was happiness. Jude was just another puzzle for him to unravel, perhaps the most perfect puzzle Renn would ever encounter. He discretely watched from a distance as Val Cobar was escorted through the station to the interrogation room they had waiting for her. She had on a black, oversized, hooded sweatshirt and dark, army green pants. When Renn had met her at the Lambert residence earlier that week, and later questioned her, Val Cobar had seemed smaller than average with a delicate bone structure that made him think of birds even though he knew she was strong, the result of a lifetime of uninterrupted work. As Renn watched her move through the station, she seemed somehow reduced in size. Her shoulders crumbled inward and her neck curved downward so that her face was pointed directly at her own feet. Was it fear or shame that altered her posture? Maybe it was both. Once she was shut away in the interrogation room, Renn's senses returned to the world around him. Maurice was looking at him strangely but whatever he was feeling seemed to pass quickly and he nodded toward the Border Patrol agents who had arrested and delivered Val Cobar to them. Yes, they would need to talk to these agents first. Val would have to wait a little longer. That was good, Renn decided. Let her stew in the hopelessness of her situation for a few more minutes. It might make her more pliable.

18

Renn offered Val some coffee and one of the cigarettes he always carried into an interrogation. She nodded her head and accepted both. Maurice watched silently from behind as Renn took a seat opposite Val. She looked older than he remembered. Perhaps it was the absence of makeup or even sleep that had aged her in the course of a few days. More than anything, her eyes had taken on the look of world-weariness Renn often saw in the very old and, only occasionally, in the young. Usually only those who had known desperate circumstances took on this weariness early in life. In his profession, however, Renn had witnessed more than his fair share of people who wore out before their time. The light in their eyes always looked a little dimmer and their shoulders curved downward a little more, as if burdened by an unseen weight. Renn knew this woman was already broken before the questions started.

She saw escape as her last chance and that had failed. Now, she had nowhere to run. Renn suppressed a smile. Jude would be his now; Val Cobar was his missing piece. This woman would tell them whatever they wanted to know. Maybe not right away, but with the right amount of pressure, she would break apart. In confessing her connection to the kidnapping, the shroud that hid Jude from Renn's sight would begin to grow opaque. The chase could finally begin in earnest, not this perpetual waiting for some mistake to offer some clue.

"Ms. Cobar, would you mind telling us why you were picked up trying to enter Mexico? You had explicit instructions not to travel," Renn began in a calm, non-accusing tone. That might come later.

The older woman said nothing, just continued smoking her cigarette. Renn exchanged looks with his partner who, as usual, preferred to stand slightly behind him. When he turned back to the housekeeper, he prompted her once again, "Ms. Cobar?"

She stubbed out the cigarette with deliberation and began speaking.

"I should've left sooner. I needed to stay, to make sure that Ms. Lambert is all right. He promised me that she would be all right."

"Who? The man who kidnapped her?" Renn asked, feeling suddenly more alert than he had in days.

"I wasn't supposed to be in the kitchen. Ms. Lambert called my name and I just started walking toward her. I didn't think about it. I just went through the kitchen like I always do," she answered, her voice distant as if she wasn't in her body at all, merely projecting her voice to appear as if the words came from her mouth. She spoke English with perfect clarity, carrying only the faintest hint of another homeland as she rolled across certain syllables. Renn focused on the woman's thin, parched lips as they moved. He wondered if the Border Patrol officers hadn't offered her any water on the long drive back to Phoenix. Val Cobar had forty-eight years, but Renn would not have been surprised to learn that she was actually older. Sometimes, undocumented workers would misrepresent their age to appear younger and, thereby, stronger and more resilient for laborious jobs. It was possible that she had lied about her age, or maybe life just wore her down faster. Renn left space for silence in the hope that it would prompt Val to continue speaking. And she did.

"I went into the kitchen and I saw her and I know she saw me. When I heard she was in the hospital, I only felt relief even though I knew what it meant for me," she said as her voice cracked and he worried she was about to collapse into tears, but Val pulled herself together and locked a stony expression on her weathered face.

"You saw Nicole Lambert and her kidnapper? When you went into the kitchen, that's what you saw?" Renn asked. He knew she would talk, but he expected a little resistance. So far, she hadn't shown any. This might even be easier than he thought. "And you knew he was in there because you gave him access to the house?"

"To see justice done, you must be willing to carry out justice," Val said.

"Excuse me?"

"That is what he told me. 'To see justice done, you must be willing to carry out justice.' I didn't really know what it would mean, but I remembered it."

Renn sat back in his chair. Val would tell them everything. She was tired of hiding, broken down, and world weary. He pushed the pack of cigarettes a little closer to her. Let her tell her story however she wants, he decided. He would follow with questions. Val pulled another cigarette from the pack and lit it with the matches Renn had set out on the table beside her coffee cup and the ashtray.

"I gave these up when I started working for the Lamberts. Ms. Patricia asked me if I smoked and I thought it was best to say no. When I got the job, I had to quit so I wouldn't be caught in a lie."

Renn wondered what could drive this woman to hate her employers with such force that she would participate in a scheme to kidnap a baby straight out of his mother's womb? He ventured to ask as Val's thin mouth pulled another drag from the cigarette.

"This has nothing to do with hate. In war, you do not have to hate your enemy to know that you do not want them to succeed," Val said, exhaling a small cloud of smoke. "This is about sadness and anger. To be so sad and so angry, to wake up to that feeling every day and tell yourself it might be a little easier to bear tomorrow, but it never is. That kind of suffering tears out your heart.

Bitterness grows in the space left behind. No one cared about my family. No one mourned their passing, no one but me. We are nothing but cogs in a machine, meant to be thrown out and replaced when we start to show signs of aging. My sister, even as she was dying of cancer, would say to me, 'Val, you have a good job. You don't struggle to eat. You don't have to move from place to place in search of wages. You only complain about how unfair it all is because you left while you were still a child. America made you think everything should be fair, but that is just a lie they tell to children there.' And, you know, she was right. Fairness, equality, democracy, these are the lies we are told, to hide from the horrors of our own lives."

"So kidnapping innocent children somehow serves your sense of justice? That's what you're telling me?"

"This is not justice. This is retribution. For too long, those that kill our children go unpunished."

A knock sounded from the door. Renn turned back in his seat to look at Maurice again. Who the fuck would knock on the door at a time like this? Maurice turned around and opened the door a crack. He could hear a hushed exchange but couldn't make out the words. When his partner turned back around, he wore a masked expression that told Renn he was furious.

"Ms. Cobar, please excuse us for a few minutes. We'll be right back," Maurice said as he put a hand on Renn's shoulder to indicate that they both needed to step out for a minute. Renn didn't understand what was happening. This woman was ready to give a full account of her involvement. She'd practically handed them her confession. Renn worried that Jude had somehow found out about Cobar's detainment and sent a lawyer to intercede, but when he left the interrogation room and found the black suits waiting outside, he knew it was much, much worse.

The Homeland Security Association, or HSA, came into existence under a new infrastructure after the Department of Homeland Security and the Justice Department, merged a few years ago in response to the increased number of domestic terrorist acts. The NSA under the Department of Defense gave way to the HSA and their authority grew. Renn always wondered if their agents' propensity for mortician's black was strictly a personal style choice or if the HSA's guidelines required black suits.

"So, you guys have to dress in black, or what?" he ventured to ask. It didn't matter what he said right now. He knew what would happen next whether he wanted it or not.

They ignored the question.

"The HSA is taking over the case and requires that you remand custody of Valeria Cobar to us immediately," the first suit said from behind the thick framed glasses that perched on his beak-like nose. He stiffly stuck out his arm with a bundle of paperwork neatly clasped in his hand. Maurice took the papers and began shuffling through them.

"You have to be fucking kidding me," Renn began. He was rapidly moving past a manageable level of anger. Two years and no leads. The first person that could offer them a glimpse into the inner workings of Jude and his organization and the goddamn HSA shows up to commandeer his prize. Maurice shot him a reproving look before returning his eyes to the paperwork in front of him, but Renn couldn't stop the tide of emotions churning inside his torso. "Two fucking years I've been on this case and you just waltz in here and expect me to hand over everything? You can go fuck yourself."

"Renn, calm down." Maurice interrupted his tirade just as he was getting started. Renn tried to put his emotions in check but he felt his exterior crumbling like a wall and knew that any moment he would lash out if he wasn't careful. He sucked in three slow breaths. The suit with the glasses smirked at him and it was all he could do to not beat him bloody in the middle of the station. Maurice seemed to notice it and told him to take a walk. When Renn refused to move, he said, "I mean it, Ricky. Go take a walk."

Renn turned sharply on his heel and started toward the door. He thought about leaving and never returning, but he knew he probably just needed some air and things would begin to settle down once again. Technically, it wasn't even *their* case. They were only brought in to assist with the investigation. Maybe he could continue to work on the Jude investigation in that capacity: as a consultant. True, he hadn't made the best first impression on those suits back there, but they might understand his frustration. He and Whitlock had been working the case almost exclusively since Teresa Attel had been kidnapped from her father's New York brownstone. They had invested too much of their own lives in this case to just walk away now. Or so Renn was able to reason as the first blast of fresh air hit his face. It was only February now and already warm in Arizona.

Renn had no sooner put his foot to the pavement when

a commotion inside drew his attention away from the outdoors and the walk he was ordered to take. He turned around and saw people moving in alarm. Maurice darted into the interrogation room behind the two suits. Renn hurried back toward the source of the confusion. He pushed his way past the others to find his partner inside the interrogation room beside the crumbled form of Val Cobar.

"She's dead," one of the black suits declared, his finger on the absent pulse of Cobar's neck. Renn already knew that. There was a putridness in the air his sensitive olfactory receptors could already detect. The suit continued speaking, "Who had access to her? I need the name of everyone who had contact with Valeria Cobar. Border Patrol, local PD, your people, everyone."

Renn couldn't begin to formulate a response. He stood in stunned silence as he looked upon the corpse of the woman he had been speaking to only minutes earlier, the woman who held the missing piece that could have led him to Jude.

Patricia

19

The white sun threatened to melt her carefully applied foundation. Patricia could feel beads of sweat forming on her brow despite it only being February. Her driver had left the vehicle in the sun and, as a result, the interior temperature rose to a degree that Patricia felt wasn't safe for human occupants. She hated the heat in Arizona, even in the cooler winter months. Despite being born and raised within the confines of the Sonoran Desert, she had never acclimated to its blistering summer heat, but she could generally manage the rest of the year with few complaints. Assuming, of course, her driver remembered to park the car in the shade. Usually, Patricia preferred to spend the summer months abroad. When Jonathan was younger, he would accompany her on those trips while her husband remained behind to see to business affairs. That arrangement suited her fine. She was never particularly fond of her husband, Wallace. Not in the early days of their courtship, nor during the length of the marriage that followed.

Both parties saw it as a marriage of convenience and hoped that, for the other, it was something more. But it wasn't. Her mother encouraged the match. Patricia had been an introverted girl who grew into an awkwardly quiet woman without the attention of many suitors. When speaking with others, she had a way of pausing too long before responding that made people uncomfortable; like she was sizing them up before answering or, worse, like she was dim-witted. As an adult of wealth and stature, these long pauses were respectfully permitted without any mocking smirks or unsettled shifts of the eye. She knew that she now had a power that wasn't hers before and she knew that much of this power arose from her marriage to Wallace Lambert. Overall, she felt she had made the right decision all those years ago. She got what she wanted out of the deal: a continuation of the privilege she had known as a child and Jonathan, her legacy to carry on after she passed. And, for the past two decades, they had kept separate bedrooms and different lovers.

Whether her husband knew about her string of affairs, Patricia could not say. It didn't matter. She didn't feel the least bit guilty about her amorous dealings outside of her marriage. Wallace had embarked upon that path before her, probably long before her. He was the one who came home doused in his secretary's perfume. Estée Lauder's *Pleasures*, no less. Patricia didn't complain. She just packed up her things and took residence further down the hall. They had a happier marriage for it. Each was respectful of the other, their tasks were divided, and their empire grew.

If she had to venture a guess, she would say that Wallace remained unaware of her love affairs. He could be rather obtuse. He probably thought she had been celibate for the last twenty years. She shook her head at the thought. How the Old Bull could be so stupid and have such a keen nose for money, she would never know. Every investment he touched seemed to gush forth yields, like he was a goddamn golden goose or something. Whatever it was Wallace had, she had to give herself a little credit for possessing some of that magical sense herself. After all, she had chosen him. When all the girls in her sorority were chasing after athletes and frat boys, it was the smart-mouthed upstart in her father's company that won her attention with his persistent advances. He saw her as an opportunity for advancement and Patricia chose to look at him the same way. She had always been proud that she wasn't given to the sniveling romanticism she saw in other women.

And not just women. Men could be that way too. Look at Jonathan, for example. He should have never gotten married at twenty-five. There was no good reason for the wedding other than they *wanted* to get married. He was overly sentimental, like her own father. If only he had waited a little longer to settle down and start a family, maybe this whole thing could have gone very differently. But what was the use fretting over those decisions now that they were faced with the repercussions? Besides, this wasn't Jonathan's fault. That blame should be placed on Wallace. He was the buffoon that led SWR along this terrible path. Now the town of Harrison, and the rest of the country, was enraged. They wanted criminal charges brought forth against The Old Bull and she couldn't blame them. Good. When the newspapers started running stories about the water crisis, she would let the dogs have him.

Early retirement and the impending scandal had left its mark on old Wallace Lambert. He seemed to shrink in size right before her eyes and the last few wisps of hair on his head relinquished their hold and fell away. His skin was sallow except for the places where it was splotchy and red across his face, especially his nose. The faintly musky odor Patricia had come to associate with her husband had turned sour. He'd already suffered a heart attack and had undergone two surgeries, but it was being forced out of the company that he helped build that really crushed his spirit. Wallace just wasn't the man he used to be. Over the last six months, the old scoundrel had become rather pathetic: a figure to be pitied. A year ago, Patricia would have believed Wallace was going to barrel easily into his nineties, but today, she would be surprised if he made it to the age of retirement. It was as if a light had gone off inside of him, like he no longer cared about controlling the hands of fate as he had sought to do in the past. He would willingly accept whatever was doled out to him. It was a wise move to have Jonathan step in as head of Southwest Resources. Michael had been smart to suggest it.

As his name rose up in her mind, her eyes wandered over to the younger man seated beside her. Not as young as he once was, admittedly, but still as handsome as ever. He put time into his appearance. She considered it a worthy effort as she evaluated the results. He wore a suit well, but she also could call to mind the image of him unfettered by his clothing. The broad shoulders and shapely arms. The sculpted feel of his abdomen and the strong hands that sometimes left marks on her body when passion overcame him and he gripped a little too tightly in a rapturous moment. Patricia smiled again, recalling the looks she received from Stella and Julie in the sauna of their gym last time when they caught sight of the fingerprints left on her thighs.

"The Old Bull?" one of her friends asked with an expression somewhere between a sneer and smirk. Patricia didn't bother to respond. Let them think it was her husband or let them think she had taken a lover. The fact was, she didn't care what they thought. She would neither confirm nor deny anything. It was an impudent question to ask.

Michael felt Patricia's eyes on him and turned his head to smile in her direction. He could be warm, yes, but there was always something that felt fraudulent about his mannerisms. It was true that he didn't come from money. Instead, Michael had to study wealth in order to acquire it and, in doing so, he studied the wealthy. His behavior was learned; practiced. Exuding an air of wealth is far more involved than knowing the proper place settings at a dinner table. It is in the way you carry yourself. Perhaps it stems from having a certain level of comfort with the world; a sense of security denied to others. It exudes itself in a way Patricia always found ineffable. A person either had it or they didn't. Wallace didn't have it. He reeked of New Money. But, somehow, Michael Maestri had been able to identify and isolate this quality so that he could integrate it into his persona. Maybe that was what made him always seem fake to her. She knew his secret and knew the layers he wore to hide it.

The driver rolled down the window to punch in the gate code that would allow them access to Jonathan's neighborhood. Patricia suggested they move to a more secure location while they were at the hospital, one that didn't back an open stretch of desert. She could see that Nicole was willing to consider the option, but Jonathan would hear nothing of the matter. Patricia worried over the state of her son's marriage. A marriage, she refrained from mentioning, that she had opposed from the start. Just a few short years after the vows were exchanged and she would have to help the couple weather a storm. She didn't know how much more they could withstand. Michael's gaze had drifted from her back to the window and Patricia followed, taking in the sandstone-colored houses against the early morning sky.

20

They had agreed earlier that Michael would speak with Jonathan first while Patricia checked on the new maid. With his wife in the hospital, Jonathan didn't seem to mind that his mother took up the charge of replacing their housekeeper and restoring order to the disarray left behind during the abduction. This time, however, Patricia not only ran a thorough background check, as was done with Val, she also hired a P.I. to keep tabs on all the people on the Lambert payroll outside of Southwest Resources. If this recent experience had taught her anything, it was that the threat was everywhere and you could never let your guard down. The French Revolution, the Galician Slaughter, the Red Terror, the list went on and on. History was littered with peasant uprisings. The have-nots revolting against those who have more. Patricia could almost sympathize with their plight, but at the same time, she had her own family to think about.

So, she hired a private eye to keep tabs on the help. Patricia also paid the new housekeeper a little something extra to keep her updated on the internal workings of her son's home life. Nicole would need time to grieve. Honestly, Patricia wasn't sure her daughter-in-law would ever recover from the ordeal. Nicole didn't appear to be made of the strongest metal. And, while a period of grieving would be expected for anyone after this experience, Patricia didn't know how long it might take the young woman to recover. Especially now that any future hope of children was dashed.

Patricia always thought Jonathan had terrible taste in women: pretty and frail, always the damsel in distress. She did not think she was that way at all. She heard that men generally favored spouses that reminded them of their mothers, but it did not appear to be the case every time. Other than a slender frame and a tasteful sense of dress, Patricia shared very few qualities with her daughter-in-law. She had handled her emotional breakdowns, of which there were a few, quickly and, more importantly, privately. She woke up in the morning, got dressed, arranged her hair and make-up, and called Janice, her shrink, to schedule an afternoon appointment before Jonathan returned home from school. These things happen, but how you deal with them is what defines you. At least, that was how her own mother explained it to her many, many years ago. She was leaving for a "treatment center" yet again and explaining to Patricia, in a very grown-up fashion, that some people are just prone to fits of depression; that can't be helped. What you can do is find your way through them in a dignified fashion. It was probably the one good piece of advice her mother had always given her beyond, "If it fits just right, buy it in every color."

She found the housekeeper in the kitchen refilling a portable mug of coffee for a man Patricia didn't recognize.

This must be one of the guards Michael hired to keep watch at Jonathan's house, she decided. A three-man security team with each person working an eight-hour shift had been arranged. Patricia wondered what good it would do. Afterall, Nicki had been snatched away from a house teaming with law enforcement. Nevertheless, she felt more comfortable with guards in place round the clock.

"Good morning, Mrs. Lambert," the housekeeper said. "Would you like some coffee?"

"No, thank you. Is Jonathan awake yet?" Patricia asked.

"I have not seen him this morning," she answered. The security guard nodded his head in acknowledgement to Patricia and then again as thanks for the coffee to the housekeeper before beginning his rounds again.

"How has my son been sleeping?" she inquired once the guard left the kitchen.

"Not well, I'm afraid," the housekeeper said with a nod to the windows that overlooked the pool. "This morning I found him there. He's still there, I think."

Patricia walked over to the windows and saw Jonathan asleep in a lounge chair outside. His arms dangled over the sides, along with one leg, in what looked to be an uncomfortable sprawl. It was then Patricia caught sight of Michael Maestri opening the glass doors off the living room to make his way over to Jonathan. He needed to wake up and get ready. The water contamination story broke wide open on the day he would be taking his wife home from the hospital. The optics right now were crucial and Jonathan had a key role to play.

21

Patricia walked back to the living room. The wall-to-ceiling glass of the window granted her a breathtaking view of the desert from an air-conditioned climate. She knew why Jonathan didn't want to give up this house. You would be hard pressed to find a better view than the one Camelback Mountain offered. Still, in a marriage, concessions must be made. If Nicole needed to find a new home, one that didn't contain the memories of her brutal abduction, Jonathan should acquiesce on that point. She would bring it up with him. Maybe suggest he agree to look for a new house if Nicole agrees to counseling. Give and take, that's what gets you through the rough patches.

Michael had left the doors ajar to the backyard so she could hear their voices before her arrival was noted. The two men were exchanging words. The tone sounded casual, friendly even, but Patricia could hear a sharp edge hidden in their conversation. She wondered if it just had to do with being roused from sleep and told to hop in the shower by a subordinate. Or was it something more? She did not dare think there was something more to it, something that might involve her. Her husband discovering her romantic trysts was one thing. Jonathan learning of them was another matter entirely. Patricia was horrified at the thought. Throughout it all, she continually strived to present Jonathan the best possible image of herself. She wanted him to see her as a beacon of calm, of strength and respectability, exactly opposite of the way her own mother had presented herself when she was a child.

Patricia paused a moment longer, listening, gripping

the pearl pendant that hung around her neck in her hand.

"Hey, Patricia asked that I make sure you find your way to the hospital on time this morning," Michael said, in a tone that suggested boredom, if not mild irritation.

"Well, *Patricia* is going to have to wait for me to take a shower. I'll drive myself down afterward," Jonathan answered as he stood up to look Michael in the eye. He was a good three inches taller than the man, which he felt made up for the fact that he was eight years his junior.

"I hope I'm not interrupting," Patricia said as she burst out the doors, obviously interrupting, "but I need you to speak to the housekeeper for me, Michael. I can't seem to understand her." The housekeeper, of course, spoke perfect English, though accented. In truth, she spoke Spanish, English, Italian, and a little French in addition to Portuguese, her native language. Patricia, upon hiring her, asked her to downplay her English skills so Jonathan and Nicole would feel more comfortable speaking freely in front of her. It served to make them feel more at ease in their own home and helped pave the way for an open flow of information from their lives to her.

As Michael turned back toward the house, Jonathan rose from his lounge chair and brushed the remnants of some weed from his t-shirt. Patricia noticed a tin box on the ground next to where her son had been sleeping with several neatly rolled joints inside, but the man was almost thirty. It was hardly the time to have a conversation about the effects of marijuana.

"Today's an important day for us," Patricia began.

"You think I don't know that," Jonathan growled. "Christ, first Michael and then you. Can't I at least get some coffee and a shower before you both come down on me?"

"Fine," Patricia said in her iciest tone, "but hurry. The news cameras can't tell what you smell like but they can see if you are standing beside your wife as she is released from the hospital today in the wake of this tragedy."

And without another word, she marched back to the house. Not too fast, as if angry, but at a steady pace, as if righteous. Let him think about how he spoke to her with such audacity. Patricia knew her son and he would soon be cowed by shame. For the rest of the day, he would bend to her, trying to appease her, willing to do whatever was best for the company and the family. That was right where she needed him.

22

"We want to thank the press for respecting our privacy at this difficult time," Jonathan began. "The loss of our son and my wife's resultant health issues have left our family shaken. We are trying to move quickly past our own grief to continue addressing the issues that have affected the town of Harrison. I took over operations at Southwest Resources to resolve these matters and I can promise I will continue to usher in a new era of transparency as we move forward. But today, I need to focus on my wife who will be returning home. Tomorrow, I will be meeting with the executive board to determine a plan of action for resolving the issues with the water supply in Harrison. Thank you for your patience and understanding."

Jonathan finished his speech and Patricia watched as

the hands flew into the air in hopes of being allowed an opportunity to ask him questions. Michael Maestri hurried onto the platform that temporarily served as their stage for the press conference. He put one hand on Jonathan's shoulder and, with the other hand, guided him away. Nicki was waiting in the corridor, seated in a wheelchair. After his little speech, he was supposed to push her out the glass doors of the hospital in full view of the press and help her into the car that Michael had arranged to have waiting at the curb. As Jonathan made his way back into the hospital to retrieve his wife, Patricia could tell that Nicole was not happy with the arrangement. The young woman looked tired and a little frightened. Patricia wanted to remind her to stay strong. She needed to hold it together. Right now, the press was watching. They had to continue through the motions that had been laid out for them. Once Nicole was in the sanctity of their own home, she could collapse into a pit of despair and wallow for as long as she needed.

Patricia picked out the nightgown Nicole wore for her exit from the hospital. She selected a high-necked nightgown made from stiff material that hid Nicki's form underneath its pastel floral pattern. It was matronly in the figure, but soft and feminine with its rosebud pattern. It reminded Patricia of the type of house dress her own mother would have selected to wear home from the hospital after giving birth. She was certain Nicki hated it, but the house dress would serve its purpose well.

Jonathan leaned forward to whisper in his wife's ear as he took hold of the wheelchair's rubber hand grips. "It's almost over now."

Patricia wondered if that statement was in any way true. Now was not the time to think about it, she decided, as the doors slid apart and she followed Jonathan and Nicki toward the waiting vehicle.

Audra

23

Cherie's supposed to be here by now, Audra thought as she watched the minutes slouch by on the analog clock that hung over her desk. She had been up and dressed an hour before she was required to be at the station. That gave her enough time to pick up Cherie's iced latte on her bike ride into work. Today, she had selected a teal A-line frock and paired it with an electric orange belt. Audra tugged at the hemline as she sat down in her office chair. Cherie would have some snide remark to make about her color palette, but Audra didn't care. She was used to the animosity of squares. She wore their disdain like a badge of honor. They were straight on all four sides, but they couldn't tell you which way was up. No thank you.

Besides, what did it matter what Cherie Rodgers thought of her wardrobe choices? She was all kinds of boring wrapped in two layers of bitchy. Even though, lately, Cherie had been scoring loads of character points with Audra in her relentless pursuit of the truth behind the Lambert case. Officially, there was no case. There was no report of Nicole Lambert's kidnapping or of a missing infant. According to all the records, Nicole Lambert suffered a miscarriage at home. They knew that wasn't true. Marv offered to hack into Nicole's medical records to see if different information was recorded elsewhere, but Cherie objected. That was a clear violation of the law. She was still trying to get to the truth of the story playing by the rules. She still didn't seem to understand that just by researching a story on the blacklist, she was already breaking the rules.

Audra shook her head and turned her attention away from her thoughts, back to the clock on the wall. Cherie was supposed to be here twenty minutes ago. The ice in her coffee was probably melting. If she didn't show up soon, Audra was going to have to make another trip to the coffee shop for a fresh latte. No matter how indispensable she had proven herself to be during the past week, Cherie still ordered her about like she was her minion. That was fine. The Channel 9 News at 6 was just a stepping stone for Audra. Her internship would end with glowing recommendations; a first from Cherie Rodgers. Audra didn't want to work in mainstream media anyway, not in a country that maintained a government-controlled blacklist. She wanted to subvert the mainstream. She took this internship just to prove she could do it and do it better than any of those plastic broadcast babes willing to spit back whatever script they were fed.

Cherie was probably one of those types back in her college days, Audra thought as she looked to the clock again. Twenty-three minutes late. Audra started looking through her emails, hoping to distract herself until Cherie's arrival. An instant message from another P.A. popped up on her screen: GET OVER HERE! CHERIE IS GETTING ICED!!!!!

Audra hopped to her feet and darted through the corridor. She could hear the voices before she turned the corner toward their executive producer's office. She slowed her stride to a reasonable pace so no one would detect her alarm. The assistant wore a troublesome look of self-satisfaction that split into a full smile when she caught sight of Audra.

"Oh my god, they're going at it," she said in a giddy half-whisper. Audra felt her brow knot in confusion, her ears reaching to distinguish words in the argumentative tones emanating from the closed door of the office. She continued, "He caught her in the parking lot this morning and brought her straight into his office. I don't know what's going on, but from the sounds in there, I think she's getting canned."

Once again, Audra didn't respond, but focused on the door and the noise behind it. Suddenly, the door flew open and Cherie burst out of the room. She looked livid. Her face burned red and her hair had begun to drift from its careful coifing. Audra remembered that Cherie typically moved her head around a bit erratically when she yelled. In the past, it reminded her of a pecking chicken and she would struggle to suppress her laughter at those moments. Right now, nothing seemed particularly funny about the tendrils of hair shaken loose around Cherie's haggard expression. It wasn't just anger that burned in her eyes. Audra could also sense fear.

Cherie's expression changed to surprise as her gaze fell upon Audra. She looked like she might say something but then her eyes moved on to the secretary's delighted face and Cherie seethed.

"Screw you, Becky," Cherie snarled. "He's been fucking some girl from wardrobe and everyone knows it."

Without another word, Cherie marched away, leaving Becky fuming in her seat. Audra watched the exchange in a daze and her eyes continued to follow Cherie as she stormed off down the corridor, her navy-blue heels clicking with each angry stomp. She stared a moment too long and didn't notice that the producer had stepped out of his office. In fact, neither woman noticed the sudden appearance of their boss until he cleared his throat to alert them to his presence. Audra spun around, wide-eyed and startled. Becky, on the other hand, refused to budge from the direction she was facing. She seemed to still be processing the information Cherie had imparted to her before leaving. Audra wondered if she meant to continue ignoring her boss or cause some sort of scene at the station. Becky was probably deciding that right now. Audra didn't really care. All she wanted to do was run to the bathroom, lock the door, and call Cherie to find out what happened. The producer's fixed gaze held her in place, however.

"Audrey, right?" he asked.

"Audra."

"Yes, of course. My apologies, Audra. It seems we're going to be facing a change in staff. I believe you were assigned to Ms. Rodgers for your internship?"

"Yes," she answered, wondering if she was about to be dismissed.

"If you wouldn't mind packing up her office for me today. Security will come by later to retrieve her possessions. I'll have a new assignment to you this evening before the show so you can finish your internship with the station," he said in a cheery tone meant to reassure her that everything would continue along as before minus one small part: Cherie Rodgers. She did not feel reassured. She wondered, for the moment, if she should storm off after Cherie. After all, she felt like they were partners in something more important than just this station. With

Marv, they were seeking to uncover a conspiracy to keep a number of high-profile kidnappings out of the public's eye. Maybe storming off after Cherie wasn't the best idea. Maybe it was good to keep someone on the inside if Cherie was suddenly ousted from the broadcasting community. She wouldn't know until she talked with her. Audra acquiesced with a nod of her head and turned back toward her desk.

She was barely ten feet away when she heard the producer ask, "Rebecca, is there a problem?"

On another occasion, she would have paused to hear Becky's response, but not today. She wanted to lock herself away in Cherie's office so she could call her cell phone and find out what happened. And to ask how she should proceed. The good thing about serving as Cherie's intern, a lowly position if ever there was one, is that no one would believe she had any sort of personal relationship with the woman. Cherie was hated by every intern that had ever been assigned to her. Her boss probably believed she'd take a gloating pleasure in being granted the privilege of packing up Cherie's shit when she got the boot. Admittedly, a couple weeks ago, that would have been true, but everything was different now.

24

The hours ticked by slowly, painfully. Audra couldn't remember a longer day in all her history: not the last day of school before summer break, not Christmas Eve, not anything. She poured through the contents of Cherie's office: the knickknacks and keepsakes, the papers and files, the pictures and awards on the walls, the odds and ends that created a portal into her professional life. Cherie kept a bottle of gin in the bottom drawer of her desk behind an arsenal of beauty and personal hygiene products. It was embarrassing to pack up such items knowing that they would be reviewed by the station's security team and maybe even the executive producer himself. She considered stashing the bottle in her satchel, but decided against it. She was already risking quite a bit sneaking out certain documents that pertained to their private investigation. Maybe Cherie had once offered the producer a drink from that secret bottle of gin and he would notice its absence amongst her other personal effects. That would be the thing that would tip him off that Audra and Cherie had dealings outside of the station. No, it was better to leave everything where it was and just take the crucial items.

It only took her an hour to pack up 16 years' worth of work-related bric-a-brac. Most of the items in Cherie's desk served a specific purpose. Pens, hair spray, endless notepads, a couple reference books, paper clips, a tape recorder, and so on. There weren't the little personal markers of the woman who occupied this space for so many hours of her week. Audra had little touchstones all over her workspace to remind her of who she was when she wasn't at work. There was a green-haired Troll doll she called Merriweather on her computer monitor, a Snoopy Pez dispenser amongst her writing utensils, at least a dozen varying shades of both lipstick and eye shadow, and a first edition Charizard card encased in plastic that her older brother had gifted to her in 2004 and tried to steal back in 2009 to accommodate his growing drug habit. Marv and Audra would joke about the great Pokémon caper in Jason's bouts of sobriety, but the topic was definitely off the table during his periods of relapse.

Audra preferred to keep the card at her place of work rather than in her own home in case Jason returned to his earlier ways of feeding his habit. And it served as a pleasant reminder every time she opened the desk drawer where it was tucked away of Jason before the drugs had addled his mind and his concept of morality, back to the time when he had just been her cool older brother who listened to Rage Against the Machine and forged their parents' signatures so he could get a tattoo before his eighteenth birthday. Jason had been integral in the shaping of Audra's character. Through him, she'd discovered the wealth that lay hidden beneath the phrase "counter-culture" and also learned that every human has limits that, once transcended, can make the occupation of human form far more trying than it need be. She steered clear of hard drugs and found her own path toward disrupting normative standards.

Cherie, by contrast, had very little by way of mementos. She kept her desktop free of clutter. No family pictures competed with the images of Cherie interviewing some famous industrialist or shaking hands with a governor. There were awards, all from local or regional organizations, that stood out in unembellished frames of brushed chrome. Audra wondered for a moment if the incident that took place earlier today would end up costing Cherie her career. She pushed the thought out of her mind. Audra wouldn't know what actually transpired until this evening. When she called Cherie, the woman dismissed her with a curt, "We'll talk later," before she disconnected the call. In her view of things, it was better to be positive until you knew you were in hot water. No sense in worrying, but, in spite of this sound reasoning, Audra couldn't stop her thoughts from returning to Cherie even after she'd finished her task and returned to her own desk to await her summons.

Audra finally received word that the producer would like to speak with her. Audra drummed up her courage and set off toward his office for the second time that day. Becky was stationed exactly as Audra had left her earlier, but her eyes were red and puffy from some barely concealed show of emotion. She didn't even smile at Audra, but simply informed her that she was expected and should let herself into the office. Audra put her hand on Becky's arm ever so briefly before she continued on her way. It seemed like it was just going to be a shit day for everyone. Audra couldn't help but feel a measure of sympathy for this woman. They were of a similar age, although maybe Becky was a couple years older, and both had known heartache. At her gentle gesture, Becky found a new store of tears that she began to quietly shed as Audra moved past her and opened the office door.

Jeremiah was seated in a casual posture with both feet propped up on the edge of his desk while his office chair leaned back in a recumbent arch. He had his cell phone perched between his shoulder and chin while he laughed with a boisterous air.

"All right, I gotta go. Later," Jeremiah said as he ended the call. Audra wondered briefly if "later" was an affectation he commonly used or if he was trying to pepper his speech with hip terms to appeal to Audra's youthful sensibilities. In her experience, people would often try to incorporate more slang into their speech than they were generally accustomed to using when in conversation with her, like they were trying to make friends with the cool girl in grade school by using the newly acquired word "cock" three times in four sentences. People often did this around her, probably in response to her outward appearance, but Audra could almost always detect the shift, the slight hesitation before interjecting an uncertain word or phrase into their regular speech pattern. Audra was offered two chairs that sat opposite the producer with a wave of his hand and she selected the one on the left, carefully tucking her dress under her as she sat down.

"Thanks for stopping by," he began much to her annoyance, as he pulled his feet off the top of his desk and planted them on the floor beneath it. She always hated when supervisors applied a false gratitude with those in their employ. Here was her employer, thanking her for stopping by like it was an afternoon visit for tea rather than a mandatory conversation between boss and bossed. Audra didn't respond. She stared at his lavender tie, admiring the color. It was a shade she would select for herself. Of course, she would throw in fuchsia tights and her turquoise cardigan. That would certainly liven up such a demure shade. "As you've probably surmised, Cherie Rodgers has been dismissed and is no longer a part of the Channel 9 news team. We're going to put out a call for a replacement, but in the meantime, Haley Roth will be filling in for Cherie. She'll be needing an assistant. Any interest in completing your internship under Ms. Roth? She's newer in the field, but that might help you understand the groundwork for establishing a broadcasting career."

That idiot weather girl was going to take Cherie's place? It might be only temporary, as was being suggested, but it might not be. Either way, Cherie was going to flip her fucking lid when she found out and Audra didn't want to be anywhere around her when it happened. Only trouble was, Cherie would probably find out tonight, right in Audra's own living room when the 6 o'clock news started. Marv needed to be warned. She extended her silence too long and the producer once again spoke up, "Audra? Your thoughts?"

"That would be fine," she blurted out. She often felt like she was trapped in a current that kept moving her around without design. This was one such moment and she did what she always did. She went with what felt right.

25

Audra pedaled down her block in the cool evening air. The sun was setting behind her and it cast an array of colors in the sky above. Rabbit-eye pink, goldenrod, and tangerine against pure powder blue. The horizon would soon give way to an inky night. Not too much longer now and it would be too hot to ride her bicycle to and from the station. She would have to go back to driving her clunky, old Corolla. Not that she was complaining about Lucille. That car had carried her everywhere she needed to go since she was sixteen years old: to oceans and music festivals, from the Grand Canyon to the Gulf of Mexico. She couldn't roll down the windows in the back and the left headlight shorted out every now and again, but Lucille had always gotten Audra to her destination. Hopefully, she had another summer or two left in her.

In the driveway, behind Lucille's bruised bumper, sat Cherie's silver SUV. A BMW, of course. Audra noticed that Marv's Vespa was parked along their stone walkway. She momentarily entertained the thought that she might walk in to find them engaged in some lover's tryst, but then she laughed off the notion. Cherie was definitely not Marv's type. She was all pinched and painted. Not to mention, Marv had pretty much identified her as the enemy since day one. Cherie was the epitome of corporate news or, in other words, vapid and corrupt. She didn't care about the blacklist until it impeded her own path to glory. Even her interest in this story, Marv argued, expressed her gross sense of entitlement. She felt the story *belonged* to her, like God handed her the lead or something, instead of that Haley Roth chick stumbling upon the story out of sheer dumb luck.

Haley Roth. Just the thought of her name brought on a wave of discomfort. Audra had been sent home for the day early, much to her dismay. She was hoping that the 6 o'clock news would air before she began her trek back to the bungalow she shared with Marv and, for the past couple weeks, with Cherie too. No such luck. He let her go before the sun had even settled in the sky. That gave Audra plenty of time to get home and talk to Cherie before the news segment started. She would have to tell her. She would have to explain that Haley would be filling in for her tonight. Cherie would figure out the rest. She was being replaced by a younger, dumber, blonder, *weather girl*. The one she continually referred to as "Little Miss Warm

Front" when she launched into her all too familiar tirades.

Audra pulled the sherbet-colored bicycle she called Sandra to the side of the house and chained it to the fence that divided the front yard from the back. She took a deep breath as she made her way around to the front of the house and, after a long exhalation, opened her front door. Much to her relief, only Marv was in their living room, standing next to the floral couch they'd bought at Goodwill, flipping a record over on their turntable. Joy Division. He listened to that record at least a dozen times every month. When he put the record on repeatedly, flipping from one side to the other and then back again, she knew it was a bad day. Judging from the haggard look in his eyes, she could guess that this wasn't his first time listening to *Closer* today.

"Where's Cherie?" Audra asked. She was nowhere to be seen but her car was parked in their driveway.

"She's out back making calls. She's been making calls all day."

"Angry calls?" Audra asked tentatively, although she already knew the answer.

"Oh yeah," Marv answered in drawn out syllables. He'd had just about enough of Cherie Rodgers. Audra was beginning to wonder how much longer his patience would hold.

She dropped her satchel on the floor and offered Marv a brief and perfunctory hug before hurrying along to her back door to try and eavesdrop on Cherie. Audra wondered if she should tap on the window to let Cherie know she was home early, but she decided against it. Maybe she'd keep talking right up to the 6 o'clock news, maybe even later, but Audra didn't think it likely. She gave up on trying to listen in and returned to her living room where Marv had settled back into his regular seat on their floral couch, his laptop propped open in front of him. Above him, the findings of their search were tackled to the wall—computer print-outs and index cards affixed with a colorful assortment of pushpins. All they needed was some thread looping all the notes together and it would look like a scene in some crime show drama, the one where they find where the serial killer is hiding.

"Did she tell you what happened at the station?" Audra asked him.

"About getting the axe? Yeah," Marv replied.

"Did she seem upset?"

"What the hell do you think?" Marv asked, irritation burrowing in his forehead. "Of course she's upset. She's fucking pissed. Seventeen years and she's given the boot because the goddamn Lambert family complained that she wouldn't leave them alone."

"I told her it was a mistake to try to talk to Nicole again. The family is keeping her under lock and key," Audra mumbled as she flopped onto the sofa in exhaustion. The past ten days had passed in a flurry. Every day, she returned from work to start her *real* investigation with Cherie and Marv into Jude and the strange workings of his organization. Ever since that first night when she returned home from the station with Cherie to find Marv entrenched in his research, he was able to identify four additional names; four other high-profile kidnappings that occurred right around the time some corporate indiscretion was made public. That gave them seven names in total. Now, more than a week later, they were up to nine. Nine children missing and a total media blackout on the topic.

Something in her had always suspected that corruption ran deep in contemporary society. She knew things were not the way they were portrayed in the media, but now that she was faced with an actual example of that corruption, she still found it difficult to believe that such nefarious dealings were taking place. Rather than leaving her with a sense of satisfaction in the knowledge that she had been right all along, the alignment of Audra's beliefs with her reality left her disquieted. It was all too real now. A commotion at the backdoor alerted both Audra and Marv that their houseguest was about to return.

"Can you fucking believe this shit?" Cherie's voice entered the room before she did. "I mean, they won't even take my calls. I've been trying to reach the executive producer over at Channel 15, but she's been in and out of meetings all day. I mean, she's been trying to get me to jump ship for seven years now, but, apparently, I don't even rank low on her list of priorities today."

Cherie threw her phone on the couch beside Audra with such force it ricocheted off the cushion and struck her in the leg. Cherie didn't notice. She began pacing the narrow strip of carpeting that wasn't encumbered by piles of books or furniture. Her hair, which was usually so carefully arranged, affixed with products to achieve seemingly impossible volume, was now an unkempt mass held together with a hot pink scrunchie. A fucking scrunchie. Cherie was losing it.

26

Somehow the topic of Cherie's replacement didn't come up in the conversation before the start of the Channel 9 News at 6, much to Audra's relief. Cherie was far too entrenched in her own woes to even notice that Audra had returned home early. She spent twenty minutes pacing their small living room before storming out the backdoor once again to scroll through her contacts. Marv and Audra could hear her barking into her phone a few minutes later. Apparently, someone bothered to answer.

Cherie rushed through the house after her call. Audra listened to her engine start in the driveway and watched as Cherie's silver SUV navigated away from their house. Marv had moved from the record player back to the couch where he now sat beside Audra, delving through missing persons reports from North Dakota. He was moving through the states alphabetically, looking for potential correlations to their case. The moment Cherie's car vanished from view, however, Marv stopped typing and turned to look at Audra with a sly grin on his face. That was one of the first things she'd noticed about him all those years ago: that insinuating smile of his. He had seemed like such a shy man, not really more than a boy, nineteen and awkward. He had long, lank hair and was dressed entirely in black except for the colors of the band logo emblazoned on his t-shirt. Audra, at the time, had waist-length hair dyed a pale shade of blue that she spent nearly an hour styling every morning in an attempt to look more like an anime character than an actual human being. Most humans, in her opinion, were gross. Oily, slovenly, *boring* creatures devoid of empathy or even basic manners. At least, that was her opinion at seventeen. Over the years, she had softened a bit. Marv had helped in that capacity. And now she remembered; it all started with that grin.

Marv transferred to her high school as a senior. Word got around that he had been expelled from his last school for hacking into the vice principal's email account and releasing a photograph of her with the football coach in the off hours. They weren't naked, but they were drinking, afterhours, outside the presence of their spouses, in noticeably close proximity to one another. The school agreed not to press criminal charges if Marv went quietly. He took the rest of the year off and then transferred to Cactus Shadows, Audra's alma mater. She had skipped ninth grade and began high school as a sophomore so at seventeen she found herself sitting next to Marv, two years her senior, in the same advanced English course. He seemed dull, *normal* even, despite his propensity for all black attire. Until one day, he made a joke under his breath for Audra's benefit alone. The joke didn't stay with her, but the smile did, that wry twist of his lips, the same one she was looking at now.

Of late, Cherie had granted them very little alone time. And what time they did have together was usually spent sleeping in a fit of exhaustion. In addition to her full-time internship with the station, Audra was also completing her last two required courses for her undergraduate degree. Thankfully, one was an independent study and the other, Spanish 202, could be completed online. Marv worked full-time coding for a software company. He only went to college long enough to get his foot in the door somewhere and, once his job was secure, he quit school. He was more of an autodidactic person anyway. He taught himself Japanese and he was now learning Mandarin. And he taught himself the ins-and-outs of all things powered by a plug. Even though he had more free time than Audra, his hours were being eaten up by Cherie's struggle to connect Jude and his crimes. It wasn't just her story anymore. It was consuming them all.

Marv's grin reminded Audra that they hadn't been intimate with each other since this whole fiasco started. Without another moment's hesitation, they closed their laptops and hastily removed their clothing. After four years of cohabitation and five years of coital partnership, the initiation of sex just took a certain look. Audra hoped she would be gone for the night, but Cherie left without a word so there was really no way of knowing. They didn't take their time. They tore into each other in an act that was desperate and wanting, denied for what felt like an eternity even though it had only been a couple of weeks. They were dressed and appropriately placed on the same couch where they had just defiled each other quite happily outside the bounds of marriage and, as timing would have it, ordering yet another pizza when Cherie returned. Their tryst had left a pleasant glow on both of them and Marv had finally consented to a new album on the turntable. Joy Division was returned to the shelf.

Cherie barged in just as abruptly as she'd left. She smelled like whiskey. Audra had learned to discern the scent of various alcohols from her mother. Vodka made her cry, gin made her sleepy, and whiskey made her angry. She wondered who Cherie had met at a bar and just what was said that set her off so badly. Maybe it was just the accumulation of the entire day's events. This woman, whom she had held in such contempt for so many months, was now falling apart right in front of her eyes. Audra couldn't bear to watch the undoing. She wanted Cherie to assume heroic proportions in facing this adversarial situation. She wanted her to sober up, toughen up, and fight the bastards to the bitter end, but it didn't look like it was going that way. She looked like she had a one-way ticket to total self-destruct. Audra had seen this all before.

In her absence, Audra had told Marv that Haley Roth would be standing in for Cherie during the evening's newscast. They both held a moment of silence in the hope that she wouldn't return before the news shows began, but there she was at 6:07, bursting through their front door. They only locked the door when no one was at home, but Audra was now beginning to rethink that policy. Cherie looked even more haggard than before. Her blouse was slightly asunder and her lipstick worn away as you moved inward from the rim of her mouth. And, of course, there was the aforementioned scrunchie which Audra thought she would remove before exiting their house for the world at large. No such luck.

Cherie's eyes flew around the room, pausing to take in Marv and Audra innocently beside one another on the floral sofa, each invested in the contents of the laptops in front of them. Her eyes moved to their vacant television screen.

"Why don't you have it on already?" Cherie snarled. Marv and Audra exchanged looks, but said nothing. This was not the time to push Cherie any further. Marv reached for the remote and turned on the box. Neal Doran was still delivering his piece. Audra exhaled the breath she'd inadvertently been holding in since Cherie's arrival. Maybe Jeremiah had already warned her, maybe not. Neal talked about the efforts to correct the problems in Harrison and shifts in the managerial structure within Southwest Resources before handing off the coverage to their onsite reporter, Haley Roth.

There she was, in a baby pink suit jacket and matching mini skirt, speaking to none other than Jonathan Lambert himself. Cherie's mouth parted in shock and remained open for the duration of the segment. Audra watched Cherie's face as her mind struggled to process what she was seeing through the sludge of alcohol.

"So tell me, Mr. Lambert, what changes can we expect to see from Southwest Resources in the coming weeks?" Haley asked with her candy-colored smile, just a shade brighter than her suit.

"Please, call me Jonathan," he answered with an equally warm smile. "The first two things on my list have been the people of Harrison, of course, and the restructuring of the company. It seems like it's about time we put some old bulls out to pasture and got some new blood on the board: innovative thinkers with their eyes focused on the future."

He cracked another winning smile for Haley and the viewers at home. Jonathan Lambert could have had a career in Hollywood. Something told Audra he'd probably make a killing staying right here in Phoenix as the good guy who swooped in to save Daddy's company and a town sick from tainted water. This Lambert kid was PR gold. No wonder Cherie hunted him down so tirelessly. A tearful plea from that face for his kidnapped child might rip apart the media blackout by generating enough internet attention. That's really the only way around a blackout. Get your facts straight and go rogue with the story, hoping that enough people in the right places see it, and start demanding answers. An interview with Jonathan Lambert might have been enough to get their story the attention it deserves, but that honor was now being given to Haley Roth.

Audra realized that this must have been part of the agreement that cost Cherie her job. Get rid of Cherie and you can have exclusive access to Jonathan Lambert. The producers must have jumped at the chance. Rules were rules and Cherie got busted breaking the blacklist. One of Audra's teachers had discussed the blacklist in their ethics class, although the topic did not appear on their syllabus nor in their exams. Only within the past couple years did word of its existence get out to the public. Previously, it operated completely under the table, but a Danish reporter had released the story of a media blacklist controlled by the Homeland Security Administration that existed in total opposition to the notion of free press a couple years back. The story was leaked to the American public through social media websites. Audra expected outrage, rioting in the streets even, but nothing happened. Some stern letters to politicians were written, public sentiment was against the HSA, as it usually was, and petitions were circulated online against the blacklist, but, eventually, people just moved on to other topics. The attention span of the internet generation, her generation, sometimes kept Audra up at nights worrying. Tragedies occurred one day and were forgotten the next. What's to stop history from repeating itself if no one remembers what happened last week?

Audra knew that this was a moment that would live in her mind forever—Cherie, slack-jawed and staring at her bubbly, twenty-five-year-old replacement on the evening news questioning Jonathan Lambert about the future of Southwest Resources. Cherie's face began to redden with rage. Her head swiveled on her neck and her green eyes locked on Audra.

"Did you know about this?" she sneered.

Audra shifted uncomfortably, deciding how to answer.

"I knew that Haley was asked to fill in for you tonight. That's all I knew."

Cherie turned on her heel and barreled out the front door. Audra stood up, trying to decide if she should stop Cherie or just let her leave. Maybe she was just going for a walk to clear her head. The start of the BMW's engine told her otherwise. By the time Audra reached the door, Cherie's tires squealed out of the driveway and she was on her way down the street at a menacing speed.

27

After Cherie's angry departure, Audra and Marv decided to call it a night. They hadn't retired to their own bedroom before midnight in quite some time and the lure of extra hours of sleep pulled them away from their ongoing search. Cherie would be back, Marv argued, as soon as she sobered up in a day or two. Audra hoped he was right and the woman wasn't dead in a smashed-up SUV on the freeway. She almost wanted to call the police. Cherie was in no condition to be driving, but she knew

Marv would just remind her that they were not the type of people who called the cops. Instead, she prayed to no one in particular that Cherie got home without causing anyone injury. She knew she would feel responsible if Cherie hurt herself or someone else, but this was one of those gray moral areas, the kind she hated wading into. Driving drunk is bad, but calling the cops is also bad. She decided to bank on luck and hope the fates didn't make her eat it in the end.

Audra settled into bed beside Marv, eager for a full night's rest. Eager, that is, until Marv shut off the lights and she was alone with her thoughts. She listened carefully to Marv's breathing to see if he had already established his sleeping rhythm which was marked by a slight wheeze on the inhalation followed by a strange guttural sound as he exhaled. She knew these sounds as well as she knew his face. From the steady, silent breath beside her, she knew Marv was also awake.

"Hey Marv," she began quietly.

"Yeah," he responded, even though his voice carried the want of sleep.

"You think Cherie's all right?"

"The odds are with her," he mumbled dismissively.

"Marv?"

"Yes, Audra?"

"What do you think he does with the children?"

Marv let out a long, exasperated sigh and turned over onto his back. He knew her well enough to know when her mind was racing. Slumber was almost impossible before she had hashed out all of her questions.

"I don't know really. Maybe they're all living on a farm together in Bolivia."

"Why Bolivia?"

"I don't know. It was just the first place that I thought of. Maybe he takes the children of American industrialists and gives them a Third World upbringing. Maybe they'll all be brought back here in twenty years to take over for their aging parents."

"Do you really think that's what's happening?" she asked, a tinge of hope on her voice.

"No, probably not," Marv answered. He always told Audra the truth. It was one of their agreements. "But it could be."

Audra didn't ask any more questions even though they kept filling her mind. After a few minutes of silence, Marv spoke up again.

"At least this guy is doing *something*. I mean, he's going after these bigshot assholes and making them pay for what they've done. That's more than any of those other so-called activist groups out there. They should just call them protest groups, not activists. They're not active, they're passive. They make noise, they sign petitions, but they don't really *do* anything. They're not out there making the evil-doers accountable for their actions, not like this Jude guy."

"You think it's some sort of justice to kidnap children? Can you imagine what these kids must be going through?" Audra asked, appalled.

"Revolutions are never easy. I think Jude might be working on something even bigger. This might only be the beginning."

Marv leaned over and gave Audra a kiss on her cheek. She remained silent, allowing the thoughts to roll unmitigated through her brain space. She knew now that if sleep came at all, it was still hours away. No sense in dragging Marv into her restlessness. She waited for his gentle wheeze and soft grunts that signified slumber before she quietly got up from bed. She secretly kept a pack of cigarettes and a few grams of weed in the back of the freezer in a box of peas that she had emptied out and re-taped. Marv didn't approve of smoking in any form. He felt it dampened the revolutionary spirit. Right now, however, Audra needed some dampening of the spirit. Her internal fires were burning through her mind. She needed to calm the fuck down. Something that Marv said hadn't sat well with her, but she couldn't put her finger on what it was.

The night air was still cool but the days were noticeably warmer. By the end of the month, winter would be over even though it wouldn't yet be spring by any standard calendar. This place seemingly had only two seasons: the hot one and the not-quite-hot one. The shift from one to the other could be brutal. The blow from Mother Nature was only softened slightly by the scent of orange blossoms on the night air. Sure, the desert would turn into a living hell in a couple of months, but the perfumed breeze assuaged the threat during early Spring until it seemed no more than a distant promise. Audra smoked two cigarettes and then returned the pack to their hiding spot in the freezer.

She walked quietly to the bathroom to brush her teeth for the second time that night and crawled back into bed with Marv. He was still out like a light and, therefore, took no notice of her absence. Audra felt calmer now, more centered. She knew it was just the effects of the nicotine, but she hoped the feelings stuck around long enough for her to drift off to sleep before the next wave of anxiety hit. Thankfully, sleep came quickly this time. Audra fell into fitful dreams and, when she woke late in the morning, she was alone and almost as tired as when she laid down to rest the night before. Looking at the clock, she realized she must have forgotten to set her alarm which was pretty out of character for her. Maybe Marv knew she had trouble sleeping and shut it off for her. That was more likely.

Marv had to be at work early in the morning and she usually got up with him so she could squeeze in some school work before she had to get to the station. Marv was already gone. Audra decided she could just go back to sleep or catch up on her school work before she needed to be at the station. The thought of working under Haley Roth was just about as distasteful as anything Audra could imagine. She considered giving up her internship at that very moment. Instead she decided to buy herself one more day. She picked up her phone and called the station to tell them she was feeling under the weather. Audra said it was probably just a bug and would pass by the morning, totally uncertain if the ominous feeling that settled into the pit of her stomach would pass by tomorrow, but hoping it would.

She would take a break today. Maybe read a book and drink tea until Marv got home. He'd be pleasantly surprised to find Audra still there. She knew he hated the long hours that she was forced to keep for the station, but it was only a few more months until graduation. Then she would probably move to a more normal 9-5 at one of the local print publications.

With her call to the station taken care of, she then sent Cherie a text asking her to call so they could talk about what had transpired last night. Audra felt guilty that she didn't force the conversation of Cherie's replacement earlier, but she knew that she had been hoping for an out. Cherie didn't ask about the show so Audra didn't say anything. Now that she had time to think about it, that seemed like the cowardly way out and she wasn't proud of it. Cherie was probably still out cold, but in all likelihood, she would find the message when she woke up and give Audra a call. That is, if she wasn't sleeping it off in a drunk tank downtown.

Audra watched the hours of the day pass by slowly, peacefully. She drank chamomile tea to steady her nerves which, for some reason, remained all aflutter throughout the afternoon. Marv usually arrived home between five and six, depending on his choice in transportation for the day. His Vespa was parked outside which meant he'd opted for the public transit system today. She should expect him closer to six. Audra dug through the kitchen and found the ingredients required to make a tuna noodle casserole. She hadn't made Marv dinner in quite some time. During the week, she was always down at the station. On the weekends, they would meet up with friends or, sometimes, with Marv's family for dinner. She probably hadn't prepared a meal with her own hands in well over a month. Marv was the one more likely to crack some eggs and whip up an omelet for the two of them anyway. Audra had a deep-seated animosity for any task deemed domestic, but on occasion, she was willing to make one of the three dishes within her repertoire: tuna noodle casserole, lasagna, or cheesy chicken.

The casserole was sitting on the small table in their kitchen at half past six. Audra ate a few defiant bites around seven so the dinner she prepared didn't go entirely to waste. She convinced herself that Marv was caught up in an affair. That it had probably been taking place for several months now, only she didn't notice because she's been working all those evenings at the news station. Her sorrow turned to anger thirty minutes later as she thought about what a rotten scoundrel Marv was to hide this from her for so long. Another half an hour passed and, by eight in the evening, Audra had forgotten all about the affair and began to worry about the wellbeing of her lover. Why wasn't he home yet? Why hadn't he answered her texts inquiring as to his whereabouts? At nine, Audra called Marv's parents to make sure the hospital or the police hadn't been in touch to say there had been an accident. They weren't married so Audra often worried she wouldn't be notified if something happened to him. And Marv's parents, in their grief, would probably forget to call her and let her know that something was wrong.

His parents had no idea that anything was amiss. Ray, Marv's stepfather, assured her that he probably just had a rough day and work and needed to walk off some steam. Ray was constantly accusing his stepson of getting too "steamed up" about things. Audra wanted to take Ray's words at face value, but something kept gnawing away at her. Something wasn't right and she knew it. She waited up all night for Marv to return home, but he never did.

Part 2: July

Patricia

1

Patricia found Nicole entombed in the master suite with the curtains drawn against the daylight. She had pulled back her hair in a ponytail and she was wearing a pair of flannel sleep shorts and a weathered t-shirt. Nicole had previously been so meticulous about her appearance. It was one of the few qualities Patricia had found redeeming in her daughter-in-law. She even had matching sets of workout clothes that she wore to the gym Monday through Friday. Meticulous. That was gone now. The weight she'd gained during pregnancy remained and it looked like Nicole had added several more pounds in the months that followed. And, judging from the odor in the room, Patricia would assume that daily showers were also too much of an encumbrance as well. She paused before pushing the doors open to the master bedroom further and searched herself for sympathy. Jonathan loved this woman, he married this woman, and a child had been stolen from her in an act of savagery.

"Knock, knock," Patricia said as she pushed the doors open.

Nicole moved quickly to adjust the covers on the bed around her, but she realized that the room was in shambles and gave up. Patricia knew she exuded an air of judgment, one of superiority, but she hoped it would serve her on this errand, rather than prove an impediment. Perhaps Nicole would see her as a beacon in the dark. A guiding light to help her through this difficult time. She could fill that role this once, for Jonathan's sake. Patricia sat beside Nicole and took the woman's hand in hers.

"We're all worried about you, Nicki," she began. She disdained nicknames. Jonathan was always Jonathan, never "John" or "Johnny". Her husband called her Patty and, like all shows of affection from the man, it only served to irritate her.

Nicole's eyes began to well up with water and Patricia suddenly felt the urge to slap her across the face, to shake her by the shoulders, and demand that she pull herself together, but that wouldn't do any good. The girl's state was tenuous at best. The last thing they needed was another family incident to play out in the papers, like a divorce. Patricia remembered her goal for the day. She was here to help Nicki reach the decision to move past the trauma.

"I know you've been through an unimaginable ordeal," Patricia recited the words she practiced in her head earlier, "but we all want to see you pull through this and we know you can."

Nicole sniffled and offered a vacant nod of her head.

"Now, my mother always said a good shrink is a wife's best friend," Patricia said as she removed the business card from her pocket. The card was a soft gray with indigo blue letters embossed, boldly yet elegantly, across the front. "I think you just need to talk to somebody. Maybe get out of the house a couple times a week. It will be good for you."

The gentle sniffles turned into full waterworks. Patricia offered the younger woman an affectionate pat on the hand and set the card on the nightstand, already littered with pill bottles and used Kleenex. It must have been an Eight Tissue Night, as Patricia liked to call them. She had those herself, but she still managed to get up and dressed every morning. That was how you got through life. Whether a day was good or terrible, you had to wake up and face the next one. Sure, she had sympathy for Nicole and her situation, but six months was six months. It was time to start moving on.

She rose up from the bed and moved toward the door. Behind her, she could hear Nicole stifling her tears to say something before she left. Patricia paused to give her a moment more.

"Thank you, Patricia. I'm trying," Nicole said in a half-hearted voice.

"I know, dear, but try harder." And, without another word, she left Nicole alone to cry until she fell asleep again. Sympathy was one thing, but she had found that a strong word can be much more effective. Nicole lost a child, that much was true, but if she didn't get herself together, she was going to lose a whole lot more.

2

Patricia walked back down the stairs to look for Michael. He was locked in conversation with Jonathan in the study. From what she could hear, they were talking about Southwest Resources. Something about another hit to their stock. Michael had been explaining that to her earlier. By eliminating certain water sources, they were forced to pay a higher price for access to other ones.

Michael was trying to explain that the rebuilding of the corporation would be a long-term venture, not something that could happen overnight, but Jonathan was interested in diversifying the family holdings and investing in other industries or resources to expedite the process. Patricia felt an unexpected measure of pride. Jonathan knew what he was talking about. And, besides, water in the Southwest was going to dry up anyway. They needed to think about other sources of income if they were going to take the family from "rich" to "dynasty".

Patricia listened for a moment. Her approach hadn't been noted. That was partly thanks to the thick carpeting beneath her heels. The carpet had been part of her housewarming gift when Jonathan and Nicole purchased the house. Patricia, and by extension, Wallace, paid to have the house repainted, inside and out, and they threw in the cost for new flooring as an unexpected surprise for the newlyweds. Nicole had selected a plush white carpeting throughout the interior. It would need to be replaced every few years, but she didn't give much thought to such things. Not a year in the house and the signs of age could already be noted in certain areas. Jonathan and Nicole were at far too social a time in their lives to accommodate such low-traffic carpet requirements.

Judging from Michael's tone, he was chafing a little under her son's newfound authority. That was to be expected. Michael would just have to adjust. Her son was born to lead this family. Michael was a decent lay, maybe even more than that, but when it came down to it, he was just some guy from nowhere. If he played his cards right through this transition, he would be Jonathan's second-in-command, but that's as far as he could go: second.

This time, Patricia knocked before entering.

"Did you go see Nicki?" Jonathan asked, returning to his seat behind the desk. Patricia chose to remain standing rather than sit opposite her son.

"I did." She looked over to Michael as she answered, who quickly set down his drink and started for the door. Her son should know better than to launch into such personal matters in front of an outsider. Even one as close as Michael Maestri.

"And?" Jonathan asked impatiently, once again before the door to the study even closed, extending his hand in want of elaboration.

"And what? She's not doing well, but I don't know if you're doing any better. A few ounces of scotch before noon just to get the day started? That doesn't sound too healthy," Patricia tried to keep her tone light. She had always enjoyed an open rapport with her son, more playful and teasing than openly authoritarian.

"Will you come off it? You barely waited for the school bus to pull away before you were back inside tying one on."

Patricia stood there stunned as if she had been slapped across the face. How could Jonathan even know that she would have a drink when he left for school? Could one of the servants have told him? Maybe Val, that snake in the grass. Patricia wished the woman hadn't killed herself so she could do it with her own hands, slower than whatever killed her in that interrogation room. She swallowed some pill and, with it, devoured any hope of discovering where her missing grandchild might be. Patricia thought Val's suicide was her last affront to their family, but now she knew that wasn't true. This latest offense left her standing there in pained silence. Did Val, one of the *servants*, dare to speak ill of her to her own son? How else could Jonathan know that she was partial to a swift, strong kickstart to her day? Her face burned from a mixture of shame and anger. She hoped her foundation hid the flush while her stony face masked the tumultuous emotions coursing through her.

Jonathan noticed a slight change in his mother's demeanor and changed his tone. "My wife won't even get out of bed. If I want a drink, that's my business."

Back to playing the tragedy card, Patricia noted, with a certain degree of gratitude that the focus had moved away from her. She needed time to think, to decide if she should have a heart-to-heart with Jonathan about her wayward moments. She always feared this day would eventually come and, lately, she had begun to feel it approaching with eyes fixed upon her. But, today need not be that day. Patricia always felt close to her son. At least, closer to him than she was to anyone else. Wallace spent most of his time at the office. Working late nights and weekends was part of his regular routine, but she didn't mind. It gave her more time with Jonathan, and time alone once Jonathan was in school. However, it was only natural that a son would assume a certain distance from his mother as he grew into adulthood. Patricia felt disappointment that this distance should assume a chill now. Then again, so many others saw her as cold, perhaps she was wrong to think she could convey warmth to anyone, even to her own child.

"Have you heard anything else from the HSA?" she asked, trying to push the conversation further from herself.

"Nothing new in months. Nothing new is going to come up. It's over for us."

"Then it's time to move on. If Nicole can't continue living here, it's time to find a new house. You owe this marriage at least that much."

"I think we're already past that."

For the second time that day, Jonathan managed to shock her into silence.

"Aren't you going to say something about how you were right all along? That you knew we wouldn't make it?" Jonathan asked, taunting her again. He was just being cruel today. She would have liked to attribute this trait to Wallace, but she knew that Jonathan's cruelty came from her. Her husband could be selfish and demeaning, but he was never cruel.

"Of course I wasn't going to say anything like that," Patricia finally answered. "I'm just sorry things aren't working out like you wanted them to."

Her voice was reproachful enough that Jonathan's eyes veered away from hers. He knew he had taken it too far today.

"I'm just past the breaking point with her. She's not even trying to get through this. I have my hands full with the company and then I have to deal with all of this when I get home. It's too much." Jonathan put his elbows on the desk and buried his head into his hands, his hair tangling around his fingers. It all seemed a little melodramatic for Patricia's taste. Her son was just trying to win her sympathy on the matter with a great show of distress. He had stumbled into this marriage professing endless love and now, not even three years later, he was trying to worm his way out of it.

"I gave Nicole the name of a doctor. If she calls to set up an appointment, you should stick it out a while longer. She's been through some unimaginable tragedies, but she could come back from this. If she doesn't, divorce her. What do I care? I just hope you don't start collecting a string of alimony payments."

Patricia didn't wait for the hurt to register on Jonathan's face. She turned on her heel and left the room in search of Michael. There was a man who didn't want or need her sympathy. Michael could handle himself. The scotch on Jonathan's desk told her he had no intentions of heading into the office today. Let him stew in his thoughts for the remainder of the afternoon.

3

Wallace had donned his blue robe for dinner this evening. Last night, it was the burgundy robe. At least he's changing his pajamas regularly, even if he hadn't put on a real pair of pants in six weeks. Retirement did not suit The Old Bull, Patricia noted. A favorite occupation of his newly acquired idle hours was complaining. He could watch the morning news and find enough fault with the world to keep him talking until the ten o'clock news. At which point, he promptly retired to his room for eight to ten hours of sleep before rising in the morning to a new litany of complaints. Patricia took on additional responsibilities in the organizations she was active with in order to limit the amount of time she was expected to be at home. She moved from fundraising committees to council meetings on public art to luncheons with the Ladies' Association for Architectural Preservation. Wallace could find someone else to listen to his grumblings. She simply wasn't interested.

At dinner, however, she would have to listen to his most pressing lamentations. The local media was still talking about Harrison. He would have thought it was old news, but no, they kept harping on the matter. In Wallace's opinion, it was the media that kept the water poisoning in the public eye, not the subsequent hearings to determine liability or the ongoing health issues of those impacted. It was all she could do to maintain her composure. High society used to conduct itself with dignity. Where had that gone? From her husband to her son and his wife, everyone around her was behaving in a decidedly undignified fashion. There was no sense of self-respect anymore. No one seemed to feel the least bit ashamed acting like a simpering fool. Patricia thought, and not for the first time, that she should have been born to a different era. The modern world simply had no class.

The housekeeper served roast lamb for dinner. It was far too hot outside for such a heavy dish. Patricia made a mental note to speak with her later about the evening's menu. Perhaps you could get away with lamb in spring, but no later than Easter, and summer in Arizona was far too hot for such fare. She usually preferred a salad and maybe a little fish during the warmest months, although Wallace complained if they weren't served heartier dishes every now and again. If he had his druthers, it would be red meat with a side of starch every night of the week. Maybe she should give him his way. The doctors warned them that another heart attack could be the end of old

Wallace Lambert. Patricia was beginning to look forward to her years as a widow. She certainly wouldn't cause any direct harm to prematurely end her husband's life, but if allowing him to make his own dietary choices might expedite the matter, she couldn't see the fault in that.

"What did you do today? Did you speak with Jonathan?" Wallace asked, taking note that his wife seemed unusually distracted this evening.

"I stopped by their house earlier. Michael had some papers for him to sign. I went along and spoke to both him and Nicole," Patricia dutifully recited. "I got a bite downtown and stopped at the bank. Then I returned home."

"How is Nicki doing?" Wallace asked. Of all the Lamberts, he seemed the most concerned about Nicole's wellbeing which surprised her. Her husband had never been mistaken for a sympathetic creature. Patricia believed it was because he felt guilty for the actions of his company that brought on the attention of the vigilante known as Jude. She wondered if he felt the same guilt when he thought about Cadence McNeil or any of the other people whose lives were affected by his gross misjudgments. Probably not. He felt bad about Nicole because she was connected to his family. He was personally affected by her suffering, unlike the nameless others in Harrison. She wondered if Jonathan's thoughts on the matter were similar.

"Same as before. I left her the number for a psychiatrist. Hopefully, she'll make the call," Patricia said, leaving off the part about Jonathan considering divorce. Wallace would find out in due time if it came to pass. She didn't want to watch him get worked up even if it did carry the possibility of ending his life. This week was far too busy to plan a funeral in addition to everything else. She was hosting a fundraiser on Friday at some new Scottsdale restaurant that would officially open its doors to the public on the following day. The event was to help provide instruments for school music programs. Or was it for breast cancer awareness? She toyed with the pearl pendant she often wore as she tried to remember. The jewel had been passed down to her from her mother and from her mother's mother before that. Her grandmother ordered its creation and even helped with the design, right down to the selection of the pearl, in order to replicate a pendant that once belonged to Marie Antoinette. Patricia's mother claimed that her grandmother carried some "fashionable spiritualism" and believed herself the reincarnation of the once queen of France. Of course, Patricia thought with mild amusement, her grandmother hadn't envisioned herself a tavern keeper's daughter or a blacksmith.

Patricia's mind wandered back from the nostalgic shift of her thoughts to the man seated across from her, feebly pushing a piece of lamb onto his fork with a butter knife. His hands shook a little, the result of medication. Once he had succeeded in assembling a respectable bite on the end of his fork, it would begin its tremulous journey toward Wallace's mouth. Only half the food would arrive, making dinner an event that took twice its normal time. Patricia only ate at home in the evening a few times a week. Tonight, like most others in recent months, Patricia finished her meal before her husband. It's funny how the tables had turned, she thought. For years, Wallace was the one missing dinners or gobbling up his meal before everyone else at the table. Patricia was the one home with Jonathan, asking about his day, making sure their child ate properly as he grew. Wallace popped in and out, but Patricia made sure she was home every night. Well, almost every night. Occasionally she attended events and, once or twice a month, she might be overcome with a "headache," which was her secret way of saying she wasn't feeling capable of confronting the world, or even her child. At least she didn't need to remove herself to treatment centers every couple of years for a month-long holiday. She just needed a night or two to herself to sink into depression with a bottle of gin. Every time, she'd pull herself through in a couple of days, call Dr. Barnstone, and get back to her old self. If only Nicole could learn to do the same, she'd make a good wife for Jonathan.

As it stood, it had been years since Patricia relied on the regular services of her therapist. She would stop in once every few months when she was in town to keep Janice Barnstone apprised of her general wellbeing, but she didn't feel apprehensive if she canceled a session here or there. Patricia felt like she had finally found a comfortable stride in her own life. Even the recent media scandal and the loss of her grandchild did not shake her into a relapse. She remained strong throughout the entire ordeal. Michael had been invaluable in helping her through such a difficult time. She wondered, for a brief moment, if it was love she felt for him, but she quickly dismissed the idea. It wasn't love. It was gratitude. Michael was young and attractive, but more importantly, he was accommodating. He was the one person in her life that didn't ask anything more than she offered. He asked how *she* was doing. A temptation rose to confess her affair for the first time in Patricia's life. She ignored the urge, but a smile rose to her lips as she looked at Wallace, imagining his response.

"Are you remembering something funny?" Wallace asked. Patricia realized that he was watching her as he ate. Usually, he concentrated on moving bites of food from the plate to his mouth.

Patricia's brow scrunched in confusion.

"You were just smiling. I asked if you were remembering something funny. I could use a funny story. The news today was so goddamn awful," Wallace said. Patricia looked at her husband with her head cocked slightly to one side. He was lonely. She could see that now. Patricia felt a flutter of sympathy, but then it was gone. Had this man reached out to her when she was struggling? Not when she lost their second child nor when her mother died and loneliness consumed her for months on end. No, he didn't care about her until he realized that no one seemed to care about him. That wasn't love. That was justice.

"Nothing, just something one of the girls said at the salon."

For the remainder of the meal, Wallace focused on the movement of his fork while Patricia silently sat, spinning a tumbler of gin and tonic and slowly draining its contents.

Renn

4

The light in his kitchen was on, but it was supposed to be at this hour. Renn set the lights to a timer to help discourage potential burglars. He spent a lot of his nights away from home. "Home" was now an efficiency apartment with a small kitchenette. It should probably be furnished with a couch aimed at a television and maybe a small table for eating, but it wasn't. Renn had turned the cramped living room into the headquarters of his investigation. A desk from IKEA sat littered with documents next to a TV tray holding a printer and a beat up loveseat. Renn took a moment to pause and observe his domicile upon entering to see if anything had been moved around in his absence. The apartment was attached to another unit on the north, part of a duplex. The windows faced east and west. When he first moved in, Renn didn't consider how brutal the summer sun would be when it poured in through those windows. He forgave himself this misstep. After all, it was his first summer in Phoenix.

Besides, he didn't spend much time at home anyway. He shared an office space with a P.I. downtown. After he quit the Bureau, Renn lived off his savings for a couple months, but he quickly realized that without an income, he'd be flat broke before the end of the year. He got some help putting together a website and, before long, he was getting pretty steady work. He couldn't ask clients to meet him in his shithole apartment not too far from the Melrose

Curve, but thankfully, he found Gerald Williams, another P.I. that was looking to share his office space, through an ad online. The setup with Gerry was working out nicely. If Renn was swamped, he could throw a case Gerry's way and vice versa. Renn said it was bad luck that kept him in Phoenix when Gerry asked about it, but even he had to admit, his luck didn't seem half bad since he'd decided to stick around. The money was good, better than he expected, and he didn't have to answer to any sort of bureaucratic chain of command. Renn was surprised to discover that he actually seemed better suited to the life of a private investigator rather than that of an FBI agent.

Once word got around to the local PD that he had a background in behavioral analysis, they took to consulting him on the rare occasion. Four months since he'd received his P.I. license and he'd already consulted on two separate cases, and once a detective brought him an old file just to see if he might be able to provide any new insight. Sure, P.I. work was mainly cases of infidelity, but the job gave him a certain amount of freedom he didn't have at any other time in his life and he found that he enjoyed it. Of course, most of that free time was devoted to Jude and uncovering the inner workings of his organization. Renn would stay up through most of the night trying to drum up new leads or researching the dark web for new posts about the vigilante group.

Jude was the reason he stayed in Phoenix. Val Cobar was their best lead and she died in custody from what was an apparent self-administered dose of cyanide. One of two things happened: either Val had that dose on her all the way from the border to Phoenix or a law enforcement agent gave it to her after the HSA arrived. Either way, it was their fault she died before they had been able to extract any real information. If she had the capsule on her and didn't take it on the long drive up to Phoenix, it was because she had something to say before she died, something she was starting to say to Renn before they were interrupted. She might have just kept going, unveiling clues to Jude's organization; but no, she was stopped. Then she decided her silence would continue forever.

Nevertheless, she was an access point to Jude. The organization had used her to help carry out their plans. Renn had scrambled for months to draw a connection between Val Cobar and Jude, some point of contact. Thus far, he had come up empty-handed. He also struggled to connect Val or Jude to an underground smuggling operation, the one hired to sneak the housekeeper across the border. Of the three men traveling in her company across the southern desert, two were shot dead by border patrol agents and the third was killed in prison before his preliminary hearing. That didn't stop his search, even though it seemed like the well had run dry. Something inside tugged at him. He knew the missing puzzle piece was here in Phoenix. He could feel it. He just needed to stay focused and he would find it.

Renn finished his scan of the apartment and decided that everything looked to be in order. Even the mug with a used teabag dangling its small paper tag on the counter remained where it had been earlier today, with its handle pushed exactly parallel to the edge of the counter. Renn relaxed a little and moved to his coffee maker, the remains of his morning pot still collected inside its glass confines. He rinsed the pot and dumped the contents down the sink before refilling it with fresh water from a jug on the counter. As soon as the machine was busy percolating, Renn took off his tie and coat and draped them over his desk chair in the living room before moving into the bedroom to change his remaining clothes.

When he returned to the kitchen, a fresh pot of coffee was waiting for him. Renn searched out a clean mug, but a noise at the door made him pause. There was a gun in the kitchen drawer a foot to his right. He waited, silent and unsure. A key slid into the front lock and Renn relaxed a little. He heard the click of the tumblers giving way and the door opened. The front wheel of the bicycle pushed its way into his apartment before its owner stepped in beside it. A melon-colored cruiser with a lime green stripe and a white basket, the sort of bike a nine-year-old girl might choose, but Audra wasn't nine. She was twenty-three. That was legal by any nation's standards. Still, Renn felt a tinge of guilt every time she pushed that damn bike into his apartment.

Her pixie mop of blonde hair was especially disheveled this evening, but her face split into a grin when she saw Renn standing in the kitchen. He offered her a quick smile back and then turned his attention to the coffee and the mug.

"How was your day?" he asked over his shoulder once he'd filled his cup to within an inch of the brim with the black liquid.

"Long. I'm glad it's over," Audra answered as she leaned her bicycle against the wall near the door and made her way into the kitchen. She took the kettle from the stove and began filling it with water. Once the kettle was in position on the stove, she leaned over and gave Renn a kiss. She was wearing a cherry red shade of lipstick today. He rubbed any remnants off his mouth and walked over to his desk. Audra's voice floated toward him from the kitchen where she was opening a tea bag in preparation for the boiling water, "I thought Cherie was bad, but Haley is getting worse by the day. I might spike her green tea with some acid before the six o'clock news just to see what happens."

"At least you're getting paid to be there," Renn reminded her. After Audra completed her undergraduate degree in the spring, she was offered a full-time position at the station. Her graduation was marked by little celebration. Audra refused to attend the official ceremony, but she had allowed Renn to take her out to dinner to mark the occasion.

"Not enough," Audra half-joked in response.

"You could always start shopping your resume," Renn offered. He hadn't asked Audra if she'd completely abandoned her earlier career plans in the wake of Marv's disappearance, but he knew she hadn't been looking for another position. Judging by the silence that fell over the room, he was guessing that the resume would have to continue to wait. He worried she might be floundering, caught in the moment of Marv's disappearance, and unable to move forward with her life.

Audra only shrugged in response to him as the tea kettle started whistling. Renn let the matter drop. Afterall, he was in no position to point fingers.

5

The sun rose early in August and Renn rose with it. He had never been inclined toward lingering in bed as the morning hours frittered away. Audra, on the other hand, remained sound asleep beside him. He turned to look at her in the dawn light. She looked much younger asleep than she usually did. Renn felt that tinge of guilt that festered in him. She was more than ten years his junior. Then again, she had sought him out. Audra had been his first client. She'd found him shortly after he quit the Bureau and explained that her boyfriend, Marv, had gone missing while investigating Jude and his organization. She needed help locating him, but, despite his best efforts and a few called-in favors, the man was still missing.

Renn hoped his investigation into Marv's disappearance might prove useful in finding more information about Jude, but after a couple months, he realized that this lead would be as useless as all the rest. When Audra described her boyfriend as a "rebel looking for a cause," Renn knew she suspected he left of his own volition to join Jude's ranks. Marv's bank account remained untouched. If he traveled by plane, he did so under an assumed name. That was assuming Marv did leave on his own accord, without a word to his girlfriend or family, and without any additional resources than what he had in his pockets. To Renn, that suggested foul play. Maybe Marv uncovered something and was killed for it. Only Audra's belief that Marv was still alive somewhere kept Renn from dismissing the idea entirely.

Then again, maybe rage was easier to deal with than

grief. Audra's belief that Marv was still out there kept her angry; angry that he'd left without a word, without taking her with him. Maybe that was still easier to process on an emotional level then the loss she would have to address if she knew he was murdered. Even now, asleep, Audra's brow crinkled with tension; her pale eyelashes pushed against her cheek with the force of eyes held shut rather than delicately grazing the tender swell of flesh. That first night they spent together, Audra had been aggressive, vengeful. She had practically torn off his clothes. Renn tried to talk her out of it, to remind her that loss wreaks havoc on your emotional state, to suggest that the hurt Marv caused her was leading her to act out with another man. She told him to "shut the fuck up and strip."

He considered holding his ground. It seemed like the honorable thing to do, given her state, but he was drunk on both the freedom of no longer being encumbered by the Bureau's rules and quite a bit of scotch. She won out in the end. Their affair had stretched on for months now. It was Audra who suggested taking up P.I. work and Audra who helped him build his website. In the evenings, he would drink coffee while she sipped her tea and they would continue to search out Jude. When they grew tired, or a lead dried up, they would screw and then pass out until morning. There was rarely any tenderness involved. Every act was needful and hurried. Renn knew what they had would never evolve into a relationship in a long-term sense. One day, they would just slip out of each other's lives as easily as they came together. Their bond arose from the need for some mutual release, a burst of endorphins amid the pain and turmoil burrowed down inside of them. He didn't plan on trying to hold onto her, but he also didn't expect to leave Audra worse off from another heartbreak. He was an abeyance for her and, when she was ready, she would move on from him.

Renn looked at the clock. It was not quite six and the sun was growing warmer in the sky. He got up and started the coffee maker so a fresh pot would be ready by the time he was out of the shower. He drank at least two pots of black coffee a day. Audra warned him that he might someday be forced to pay for this addiction with ulcers and other stomach ailments. He politely reminded her that cigarettes would get him first. Renn had taken up smoking regularly after leaving the Bureau. He considered quitting every week when he bought a carton of Marlboro Reds out on the reservation, but it seemed to suit the new P.I. image of himself he had constructed in his mind. Black coffee, cigarettes, and only shaving every few days rather than every morning, sure as the sun will rise. Life after the FBI was suiting him just fine.

His work gave him enough free time to pursue his investigation of Jude which, after showering and getting dressed, Renn sat down at his desk to continue. He took a tentative sip of his coffee, testing the temperature, and lit his first cigarette of the day. Audra hated that he smoked inside. He could see it in her face and the way her body subconsciously shifted away from the smoke in aversion, but he didn't care. If she hated it so much, she could go home. Audra was allowed to keep a toothbrush in the bathroom and a box of tea in his kitchen. Everything else he strictly forbade. He didn't want her to get comfortable here. It was important, for her own sake, that she continue on with her life when the time was right.

Renn booted up his computer while his thoughts

roamed over the investigation. Every lead had come up dry. He needed a new angle. Renn started thinking about the children, the real victims in all of this. What was Jude doing with those children? Could he be selling them on the black market? That was a horrifying thought and it didn't seem to fit with the moral impetus behind these kidnappings. Maybe he actually was relocating them to some remote spot and indoctrinating them with some form of liberation theology, like Audra speculated. It seemed far too idealistic to believe that these children might someday be returned to their parents, even brainwashed. No, Jude was dealing out his own twisted brand of justice, not proselytizing. If that was the case there would be more notes, more sermons. This was justice, swift and exacting. An Old Testament brand of justice. Renn felt the coffee in his stomach sour.

6

The day dragged on and on with no end in sight. Renn was hired by a seventy-two-year-old man to spy on his forty-eight-year-old spouse who he believed was having a tryst with their twenty-three-year-old pool boy. This meant a Thursday afternoon spent waiting for the pool boy to arrive. Thankfully, he did, at 12:06 p.m. A certain Mrs. Daubson met him poolside in a fuchsia bikini, they fucked on the cool deck for seventeen minutes, then she laid in the sun on a chaise lounge while he cleaned the pool. Afterward, she slipped him a folded-up bill into the pocket of his pants and sent him off with a kiss. It all seemed so matter-of-fact that Renn didn't want to tell Mr. Daubson about it. His old lady had a right to a decent screw every once in a while, didn't she? She had been careful in arranging the pool cleaning service to coincide with her husband's physical therapy appointments each week and she didn't drag the pool boy inside to her marital bed. Nevertheless, the old man was his client and this little afternoon dalliance would put more than a grand in Renn's pocket. A job was a job.

He had slated the whole afternoon for this sting. Thomas Daubson's appointments stretched from noon until three in the afternoon. He usually took time afterwards to see to any additional errands he might have scheduled for himself and not assigned to his younger, more mobile, wife. Thomas Daubson normally called on his way home to see if his wife, Lauren, needed anything from the marketplace. The pool boy usually arrived during this two-hour window, but sometimes he ran late. Thomas was initially alerted to the possibility of his wife's infidelity when she was unusually irritated one afternoon when the pool service truck arrived at half past four. Thomas watched Lauren as she went outside to speak to the pool boy. Apparently, a recent haboob had ravaged many pools on his route. When he inquired about his wife's anger at the boy's late arrival, she snapped at him, "Our pool is dirty too!" The following week, Thomas Daubson had an appointment with Richard Renn arranged to promptly follow his physical therapy session.

The coming Thursday, he would hand over a stack of dirty pictures to the old man. That was the embarrassing part of the job, witnessing the moment a person realizes that they have been betrayed. Sheila always came to his mind in those awkward moments. When he'd abandoned his life in D.C., he hadn't given much thought to the woman he left behind. Sheila had been his on-and-off again girlfriend for more than six years, but things had never solidified between them. Renn was surprised when she showed up at his front door in Phoenix, but not nearly as surprised as she was to find Audra, fifteen years her junior, curled up on the floor in one of his sweatshirts with a laptop perched on her knees. The hurt and anger that registered on her face as she silently took in Renn and Audra told him that she had placed a different sort of value on their relationship. Renn felt guilty, sure, but Sheila had never said anything to him to indicate the inner workings of her heart. He couldn't be blamed for failing to protect what he didn't know was entrusted to him. He watched her storm away, even went so far as to chase after her, but she hopped into a car, a rental judging from the sticker on the back, and drove away into the night. She wouldn't take his calls or return his emails. After a couple of weeks, Renn gave up trying to apologize. Audra, thankfully, didn't ask any questions.

With the afternoon suddenly open to him, Renn decided to return home and pick up where he'd left off earlier that morning. The missing children. Fourteen, by his count. Who knows how many more the HSA knew about now? He tried dropping Maurice a line once or twice, but his old partner always told him that, as a civilian, the case was no longer within his jurisdiction. Renn stopped writing. Audra had arrived with her own leads: a hidden website that asked for prayers for the victims of corporate crimes and a list of names longer than anyone in the media had been able to provide. Not as long as his list, but still, it revealed something of her unique capabilities. With her help, he was able to discover a new victim, Diane Nereus, kidnapped in retaliation for Anwar Bata's death, both seven years old. Bata died due to a toxic interaction of medications, one not reported by the pharmaceutical company despite clinical findings to suggest a likely toxicity. His parents were eventually lumped into a larger class action suit against the company, but the legal costs, even when charged with fraud, paled by comparison to the dividends brought in by the drug's release. Diane Nereus disappeared in June, four months after the Lambert incident, from Los Angeles. Renn's new Phoenix address gave him easy access to the City of Angels, just a five-hour stint on the I-10, but the local PD was hesitant to share details, especially after the Homeland Security Administration showed up and spread a thick layer of threats over the department.

Renn drove back to Phoenix the next day, empty-handed.

7

When Renn returned to his apartment after the poolside affair, he discovered the front door was unlocked. His hand automatically went to the gun he wore at his hip. The day he surrendered his badge and his firearm, he purchased a new weapon at a gun show. He had to give it to Phoenix. They kept the spirit of the Old West alive when it came to guns. Concealed carry and no waiting period before purchase left Renn with a sneaking suspicion he could be shot any time he was in a crowded, public place, but it made it easy for him to procure a couple of firearms. Arizona didn't even require gun owners to register with the state. With his gun in hand, he slowly pushed open the front door. Suddenly, he felt very much alone. Maybe that was one thing he missed about the FBI: the backup. If he stumbled across the same key piece of information that he believed Marv had discovered, knowingly or otherwise, would he be killed and his body discarded without a trace? After all this time, he still didn't know who or what he was dealing with and that only infuriated him further.

Whatever was waiting for him, he decided he was ready. Renn pushed the door open wide and moved into the apartment with this gun drawn. There was a figure standing beside his desk. His eyes struggled to adjust to the dimmer light indoors. The man was facing away from him. Renn knew he could shoot him in the back and claim defense against an intruder, but he didn't. He really didn't want to kill anyone today unless it was absolutely necessary. He stepped forward, positioning himself at the threshold of the living space where his research lay strewn about in what seemed like disarray.

Renn kept his gun trained on the man as the stranger turned around to face him.

"First you abandon me to finish up all the paperwork from the Lambert case by myself and now you point a gun at me?" Maurice said with false offense before his face gave way to a smile.

Renn lowered his weapon, but did not put it back in the holster. His voice betrayed his vexation, "I would have called first."

"And I would have, but where is the fun in that?"

Maurice quipped and crossed the room to pull Renn into a brief, and unexpected, embrace. "I suppose you know that threatening a federal agent with a weapon is a serious crime. Not to mention that failing to register your new address with the HSA upon moving is an offense that could land you on a watch list, at the very least."

"I thought I earned a spot on that list the minute I clocked one of their agents."

"Maybe, but I can't say they didn't have it coming. No one likes to have a case stolen away from them, especially not one they put years into working. They could have been a little smarter in their approach. Might've saved them a busted nose," Maurice said.

"You managed to keep your anger in check." Renn began to feel he was being ever so slightly patronized and wondered what Maurice was doing here in the first place.

"Me? I'm always in check. Six years you spent as my partner and you never figured that out? Maybe the BAU was wrong to accept you in the first place."

Renn swelled with anger and waited for the wave to wash over him before responding.

"Maybe I just focused my attention on the criminals rather than the other people in my department."

"No, that isn't it. You were brought onto the team for another reason," Maurice explained. "You, better than anyone I've ever known, have an uncanny knack for noticing the most obscure details hidden in a crime scene. Remember the Belini murders? If you hadn't pointed out that missing photograph, we would never have caught Rachman."

"That was easy. Dust patterns on the dresser gave it away," Renn said dismissively.

"Local PD and agents from the FBI both missed it, but you walked into that room and saw what no one else could. That was the case that got you on the team."

"What are you doing in Phoenix?" Renn asked, cutting through the chase to get straight to the question on his mind.

"Never one for small talk. I almost admire that about you. It would seem that Jude is back on your turf," Maurice revealed the information with a casual air, like he was telling Renn there was a forecast of cloudy weather for the weekend. Renn stood there stunned for a moment.

"What? Who's the target?" he asked, when he was sufficiently recovered.

"The Kaine family, we believe. They own a pharmaceutical company that relocated to Chandler two years ago and they have a son about the right age."

"Pharmaceuticals? Like the Nereus case? Two in a row might suggest he's narrowing his field."

Maurice looked surprised for a moment that Renn was aware of the case before responding, "It wasn't two pharmaceutical companies in a row. Jude abducted another child in July, this one in conjunction with an agricultural chemical incident."

"One child a month? He's moving a lot faster than he used to."

"We suspect he's expanding his organization with each strike."

"Who would choose to be complicit in the abduction of children?" Renn asked. The question was directed toward himself rather than Maurice. "These can't just be normal, everyday people. Normal people don't hurt children or take them away from their parents."

"I think you might be wrong there. Everyone has a limit, a point where they've been pushed too far. These people can be brought around to think of heinous crimes as some form of justice if they've been denied any other form for too long," Maurice speculated. Renn could feel the other man's eyes scrutinizing his responses, trying to determine just how much he knows, and probably trying to assess his current mental state.

"We vetted the families of the victims in the McNeil case and others. There was never any reason to suspect that they had any involvement leading up to the abduction," Renn argued.

"Ah, Renn, always thinking too small. You're always focusing on all these little pieces and failing to see the bigger picture." Maurice smiled again and plopped himself down into the computer chair stationed in front of the desk. There was also a lumpy loveseat in the room purchased from a thrift store after Audra spent a couple of nights seated cross legged on the threadbare carpet of his apartment. Renn chose to remain standing.

"How do you know all this information about Jude now? I thought the FBI was off the case?" he asked Maurice.

"I kept my mouth shut when they pulled it from our department and then I asked to be brought in as a consultant. So, temporarily, I am working in conjunction with the HSA."

Renn finally decided to move over to the sofa and took a seat. He pulled a cigarette out of the pack he kept in his pocket.

"Can I have one of those?" Maurice asked. Renn tossed him a cigarette, lit his own, and then also tossed Maurice the lighter. His former partner took one long drag and, as he exhaled, he continued, "You should have done exactly that too, but you had to fly off the handle and knock that agent in the head. What did you expect to happen?"

"I wasn't thinking about the future. I was thinking about the two years of my life they wasted when they interrupted that interview to flout their authority," Renn answered, suddenly feeling rather tired, his anger spent.

"That's your problem. Well, that's one of your problems."

Renn considered tossing Maurice out of his apartment on his ass. He didn't need a lecture now and certainly not from him. Instead, he continued smoking and listening as Maurice went on, "You see everything in black and white, right and wrong, but the rest of the world lives in the grey areas. That's why you don't fit anywhere. You just don't get people because you don't know how they look at the world."

"I knew them well enough to land a spot in the BAU," Renn countered. He forgot what a real dick Maurice could be when he was trying to get a point across.

"Bullshit. You remember facts. You can walk into a room and analyze the space like no one else, but when it comes to people, you can be obtuse."

"Is this what you came here to talk to me about? My insufficiencies as an agent of the Bureau?" Renn's voice carried an unintended fluctuation that gave him away to his ex-partner. He was as irritated with himself as he was with the man sitting across from him in his dive apartment in the wasting heat of the Sonoran Desert.

"No, I was just in the neighborhood and wanted to see how your investigation is panning out."

"Well, I assume you had time to poke around before I got here. You probably have everything you came to find out."

"Except for how *you're* doing, yes," Maurice replied, his eyes honing in on Renn's own red-lined orbs.

"Splendid. Never better."

"And the job?"

"No dental, but no boss either," Renn answered.

"Sounds like a fair trade to me."

"What's your evaluation, Special Agent Whitlock?" Renn asked, prodding Maurice a little by acknowledging his true intentions.

"Too little sleep and too much caffeine, but otherwise of sound mind."

Renn gave a short laugh and Maurice smiled again. They fell into a comfortable conversation. Maurice gave him updates on his former coworkers and his own family. His wife, Angie, recently found out she was pregnant once again. Maurice already had two children, a sixteen-year-old daughter and a twelve-year-old son, so a new baby was neither expected nor exactly welcome. But Angie was excited so Maurice realized he was six months away from changing diapers at the age of forty-four. After a half an hour of idle chatter, Maurice announced he had to get back to work. He'd only stopped by briefly to "catch up," but Renn suspected he was also there to see if he had made any useful discoveries during his investigation.

One thing kept bothering Renn. How did Maurice find his residential address? He had intentionally avoided registering the change in residence with the HSA. He even listed his office address on his driver's license and used an alias when signing his lease agreement. He thought he had been careful in hiding his location. Of course, Maurice could always exploit company resources and trace his cellphone's most frequent locations. He should get rid of his contracted phone and just use disposables.

"Hey, how did you find my place?" Renn asked before he left.

"I work for the FBI," he answered smugly.

"No, seriously, I've been keeping it underwraps." Maurice might be able to fool some, but Renn knew what he was doing when he covered his tracks.

"You know, Sheila was pretty pissed at you," Maurice said with a chuckle. "I can't believe you asked her to forward your mail if you were trying to keep your location secret. If someone showed up there and said they wanted you dead, she would probably draw them a map."

Haley

Haley looked over to the stories slated for that evening. Another child drowning in Glendale. What was it going to take for people to learn? Growing up in Arizona, she saw this same story on the evening news every summer. Now that she was responsible for delivering the nightly news, she realized this same report had played out three times since she'd made the jump from weather girl to newscaster. It was too much. She wondered, after she had a couple decades under her belt, if all the news stories would start to feel redundant, even the multiple homicides and tales of political corruption. Haley felt a surge of anxiety at the thought, but she pushed it aside when Audra popped her head into her office, formerly the office of Cherie Rodgers.

"Make-up in ten. Do you need anything?" her assistant asked.

"Another latte would be wonderful," Haley replied with a camera-ready smile. She thought she detected a slight roll of the eyes before Audra slipped from view. Her smile immediately vanished. She didn't know why Audra hated her, but she knew it was true. Haley could feel the contempt pouring out of her assistant every time they spoke.

She was probably just jealous. After all, Haley was of a similar age to her assistant, but she had moved through the ranks to the position of newscaster while Audra was still fetching coffee for barely more than minimum wage. Yes, Audra was most likely jealous.

Haley thought working for her would have been considerably better than working for that bitch, Cherie Rodgers, but Audra's behavior suggested otherwise. Haley remembered the day she moved into her new office. She'd picked up cupcakes at Gigi's on the way to the station to mark the occasion. Audra had looked at her and the cupcakes with disdain before announcing, "I'm vegan." Haley was left standing alone holding a ridiculous box of baked goods, like she was celebrating her own promotion all by herself. Haley found her assistant outside the executive producer's office, chatting with another secretary who also seemed to despise Haley for some inexplicable reason, later that same day. She had been on her way to complain to her boss, but she continued straight past his office, pretending she had some matter to attend to with the wardrobe department.

Later, she sent her producer an email asking if it was possible to find a new assistant. His response was prompt and disappointing. He reminded her that Audra managed to see to Cherie's needs efficiently enough and proved herself by holding onto the position longer than any of her predecessors. He also pointed out that Haley was newly promoted to a position many people at the station thought would be better suited for someone with more experience. If she started "showboating," his term, then the animosity toward her might grow. So, apparently, everyone at the news channel hated her. At least she now had a private office she could retreat to when she needed to unleash a torrent of tears, which was happening with alarming frequency.

The best part of her day came when the news ended and Haley could return home. She had a new boyfriend and things felt like they were starting to get serious. He was married, sure, but his divorce was imminent. Or so he claimed. Did she have a thing for unavailable men? This wasn't the first time she'd found herself the secret addition to a sworn union. Haley made a mental note to bring it up with her therapist later in the week.

She gathered her notes and hurried over to makeup. The station's head make-up artist did not like to be kept waiting. She chewed out Haley the first, and last, time she showed up late for her scheduled time slot. Haley knew the make-up department would never have dared to aim a critical word at Cherie when she was still around, but Haley was apparently an easier target. Ever since then, she made sure she was on time in hopes of avoiding another embarrassing confrontation. She took her place in a chair facing the wall of mirrors with three minutes to spare.

"Be right with you!" Jayci called over to her from where she was finishing up Neal's makeup. Haley focused her eyes on the notes in her lap in fear that she would give herself away with her expression. Sure, *she* couldn't be a few minutes late, but Neal Doran could waltz in any time before the show and expect to be accommodated. Neal was her co-host on the nightly news, but he continued to treat her like she was a child who had been invited to tour the set as part of a school project. When she'd made an embarrassing slip of the tongue back in May, Neal gave her two gentle pats on the hand as he rose up from his chair after their segment ended. That patronizing gesture made her embarrassment all the more searing.

Haley couldn't stand Neal with his repulsive,

surgically-enhanced face and roaming eyes. When she had been an intern assigned to the station, he had given her a few inappropriate pats on her rear when she set his coffee mug in front of him. Once she made it to the status of weather girl, those unwelcome caresses abruptly stopped, probably out of fear of legal retribution more than gained respect from her upward shift. Jayci moved away from Neal Doran, taking one final moment to pause and admire her work. Under her careful artistry, wrinkles retreated and age spots vanished entirely. Haley would be lucky if she could last as long as Neal had managed in this profession. Aging women were usually shunned from the public eye while men of a similar age were praised as wise or virile depending on their body's ability to resist the weathering of time.

Jayci moved to Haley's station and began fussing with her brushes while Neal rose up from his seat and pulled off the paper protectors shoved into the collar of his shirt to prevent any makeup mishaps.

"You hear about the Kaine kidnapping?" Neal asked Haley. She was startled that he addressed her directly. Usually he refrained from speaking to her entirely unless it was to share a lewd joke he heard in the few idle minutes they shared on set before going live. When she recovered from her surprise, Haley shook her head.

"It's another one on the blacklist. Just got the word on it today," Neal added. "Wasn't there another one of those just a while back? That one Cherie was all fired up about."

"I think so," Haley said, although she knew perfectly well that the Lambert case was hushed up by that damned blacklist only six months ago. She supposed she should be grateful. If Cherie hadn't insisted on destroying her career by pursuing a blacklisted story, Haley wouldn't have been offered her job. Still, it chafed her that the first big story of her career had been deemed off-limits by the HSA.

"That's a bit of a coincidence, don't you think?" Neal asked in an off-handed manner.

"Sure do," Haley answered, but her mind was already somewhere else. No, she didn't think it was a coincidence at all.

9

"Daisy?" Haley called out to her cat as she hurried to switch on the light in her kitchen. She forgot to leave on a light for the cat. Retribution would be swift and spiteful. Haley moved from room to room of her newly acquired condominium. Sure enough, Daisy had pissed on the comforter of her bed. Haley swore under her breath and yanked off the covers. She had her old bedspread shoved in the closet of the guest bedroom. She would retrieve it as soon as she threw the sheets in the washing machine and fetched another set. The comforter would have to wait until tomorrow. She could drop it at the dry cleaners on her way to the station and send Audra to pick it up before they closed for the day. Having an assistant, even a surly one, had its perks.

Haley had only finished reassembling her bed when she heard the culprit meowing from inside her walk-in closet. She flipped on the light and saw the fat British longhair staring back at her with hostility. Next time she would get a dog or forgo the whole pet-experience entirely. It might be lonely for a time, but at least she wouldn't need to remember her lint roller every time she left the house. Haley was busy scolding Daisy, who didn't seem overly concerned with her owner's displeasure. She didn't hear the front door open or the footsteps along her carpeted hallway. She did hear the casual, "Hey," as she leaned forward to scoop up her pestilent animal. Haley screamed and immediately dropped Daisy, who darted out of the closet and under the bed. She spun around and found Jonathan standing in the doorway to her bedroom.

"Jesus Christ, you scared me!" she yelled before giving him a playful swat on the arm. Jonathan Lambert rubbed his bicep as if enduring some great injury and laughed. He had a great laugh; it rose from his chest in a deep chuckle. Haley immediately forgave the fright he gave her and moved into his arms.

Only afterward did Jonathan ask about the disheveled bedding.

"Daisy peed all over my bed. I guess I forgot to leave a light on for her," Haley explained, still nestled against Jonathan's exposed chest.

"Oh shit, that might have been me. I forgot my cell phone here this morning. I might have switched off the light as I was running out. I guess I didn't realize you left it on for your cat," he said, shifting his weight out from under her and moving to the edge of the bed. Haley suddenly felt irritated, but she reminded herself that Jonathan had enough to deal with at home these days. Nicki, his wife, was getting worse by the day. He sat up on the side of the bed and reached for his boxer shorts. "I can get you a new comforter," he added, sensing a change in mood.

"No," Haley began. "It's not a big deal. I'll just run it by the dry cleaners tomorrow. It's only a couple months old anyway." Haley didn't remind Jonathan that he'd bought her the comforter in the first place. Jonathan had also bought her new sheets at the time to go with the king-size bed he insisted she upgrade to when she moved into her condo. In truth, he was the most thoughtful boyfriend she'd ever had. Too bad she couldn't introduce him to her friends. At least, not yet anyway.

Jonathan rose up from the edge of the bed and left the room. As he moved down the hallway, he called back to her, "Do you need any water?"

"No, but could you make sure Daisy has some in her dish?" Haley answered. She heard Jonathan release an exaggerated groan. He wasn't a fan of her temperamental familiar. Oh well, she thought, by the time his divorce went through and they waited a respectable period of time for appearance's sake, say a few months or so, Daisy would be thirteen, maybe even fourteen. She probably wouldn't live very many years after Jonathan and Haley finally moved in together. That should make Jonathan happy, but the thought caused Haley a rush of anxiety. She clicked her tongue against the roof of her mouth to call Daisy to her. The cat appeared at the door of her bedroom and unleashed a meow of acknowledgement, but darted away again when Jonathan reappeared.

She hoped he would be staying the night, but she knew better than to ask. His wife's abduction six months ago and the kidnapping of their newborn son had sent her into a downward spiral. Jonathan also had his own stress to deal with in addition to the emotional collapse of his wife. He had taken over his father's company and faced down the scandal surrounding Southwest Resources and its contaminated water supply. Haley had been sent to interview him a couple of weeks after the kidnapping when the water contamination story broke open to talk about the new direction of the corporation for a segment on the 6 o'clock news. Haley apologized to him for the unpleasant scene at the hospital with Cherie Rodgers and Jonathan, in turn, apologized for having her forcibly removed from the ICU. From there, things evolved rather quickly.

The next weekend, she and Jonathan were sharing drinks as he confided in her about the disintegration of his wife's mental wellbeing in the wake of the attack. Haley felt a wellspring of sympathy for the young husband of Nicki Lambert, forced to take on so much responsibility while facing his own grief. They ended up at her apartment and the rest, as they say, is history. Sure, she felt a measure of guilt about Nicki at home in the throes of depression while she and Jonathan cavorted around their desert city, popping into questionable establishments where they wouldn't be recognized for the first couple months, before forsaking public life entirely for the privacy of her new condominium.

Since that time, they had fallen into a comfortable pattern. Haley worked late and, by the time she finally made it back home, Jonathan was usually planted in front of her large screen television, another gift, with a beer or a scotch in his hand. The drink he chose signaled to Haley what sort of a day he'd had. Scotch meant something went wrong at work or there had been another incident with Nicki. A beer meant that the playful, adoring Jonathan was present. Tonight, she had beaten him home. She wondered what might have held him up but decided not to ask. Sometimes Nicki stayed up late on the couch, but most of the time she didn't come down from her room at all. She and Jonathan had kept different bedrooms for months now. That first night together, he joked that he was celibate. First the pregnancy and then his wife's precarious mental state had put their sex life on indefinite hiatus. At the time, Haley felt relief. She was not the cause of their marriage's breakdown. Some unseen and maniacal force called Jude had been responsible for the death of Jonathan's marital union, not her.

At the thought of his name, Haley remembered the conversation she'd had earlier in the makeup room down at the station. Another kidnapping on the blacklist. She rolled over to look at Jonathan who was sitting beside her, drinking from a water glass.

"Hey, I heard something weird at the station today," she mentioned as casually as she could.

"Oh yeah?" Jonathan asked with interest. He always tried to appear involved in the conversation when she started talking to him. It was something she really appreciated after other men she'd dated. Sometimes she wondered how authentic his interest was, but at least he was willing to put on a good show for her sake.

"Yeah, Neal was talking about another kidnapping case in the Valley that was blacklisted by the HSA." Haley waited silently while Jonathan processed the new information she had given him. She didn't know how he would respond. He never talked about Nicki's abduction in relation to the child he lost. He only spoke about his wife's troubles in the aftermath.

Jonathan stood up abruptly and reached for the pants he'd carelessly discarded earlier.

"You didn't think about telling me this earlier?" he growled at her. Haley was surprised. She thought there might be some display of the hurt he felt, or even anger that the vigilante was free to strike again, but she didn't expect that any of that anger would be directed at *her*.

"Well, you sort of distracted me," she answered playfully, trying to remind him of the passion that encompassed them both.

"What the fuck, Haley? This is serious. Did you find out anything else? Like who was kidnapped or if it had anything to do with Jude?" Jonathan pummeled her with questions.

"I don't know. I mean, I thought it did just because the story was blacklisted like..." she was about to say "like the other one was," but she stopped herself. That *other one* was Jonathan's child, his son.

"Did you get a name at least?" he asked, his anger continuing to mount.

"I don't remember," she began as Jonathan reached down to grab his shirt, "I could probably ask Neal tomorrow if he knows anything else. Or maybe even the producer."

Even though she offered those concessions, going so far as to promise to speak to her boss about a blacklisted story, Jonathan stormed out of the room. A moment later, she heard the front door slam.

10

The following day, Haley asked around at the station. They were only able to give her a name: Vanessa Kaine, five-year-old heir to Kaine Health Solutions which had only recently relocated to the Valley of the Sun. She texted the information to Jonathan, but he didn't respond. Getting through her day became an arduous undertaking. She was tormented by her fight with Jonathan the previous night. Did he go home after he left? She worried he did not. His home no longer held any comforts for him. He probably went out drinking. Did he find someone else to spend the night with? Someone who hadn't reminded him about the worst tragedy he'd ever faced?

Even Jayci had noticed Haley wasn't her usual chipper self as she touched up her eyeliner when her eyes misted over at the thought of Jonathan in the arms of another woman. Thankfully, she asked no questions, she merely reminded Haley that, "No man was worth ruining good mascara." Haley had only nodded and strengthened her resolve to make it through the program without dissolving into a sea of tears. That would have to wait until later.

By the time Haley left the studio, all her hope hinged on whether or not she would find Jonathan at her condo. She didn't even notice the strange figure in the parking lot until someone said her name. Haley turned abruptly. This time she managed to suppress her scream only to find Cherie Rodgers standing there. She looked much changed since the last time Haley had seen her. Greying roots were visible beneath the bottle blonde. Her face looked like she had aged a decade in only six months, or maybe that was the effect of the dingy streetlight that struggled to illuminate the parking lot.

"Sorry to startle you," Cherie began. Haley immediately realized the changes were more than skin-deep. Something about her was different. The old Cherie Rodgers would never have apologized for an offense, especially something so trivial as startling her.

"Uh, that's okay," Haley replied while her hand continued searching in her bag for her keys. "Waiting on the boss? I think he's working late on something."

During the first couple months following Cherie's dismissal, their producer received no less than thirty voice messages and emails from the woman demanding, then pleading, for her job back. She had even gone so far as to go over the heads of the producers to contact the owner of the news station in hopes of a meeting on more than one occasion, but Cherie was rebuffed at every turn.

"No, I'm here to see you. I just received a tip that another kidnapping story was added to the blacklist," Cherie explained. Haley couldn't believe her luck. This Jude guy was really starting to annoy the shit out of her. "I thought you might have a name."

"Check the missing persons' reports," Haley suggested, her fingers finally encircling the key ring at the bottom of her handbag. "I really don't know anything."

"Well, I can believe that," Cherie replied in annoyance. Haley couldn't believe this woman. Here she was, standing before her in a dreadful state of self-care, insulting *her*. It was more than Haley could bear.

"What's your problem, Cherie? Jealous? That someone so much *younger* could so easily step in and replace you?" Haley raged.

"No, just that I was replaced with a halfwit who would do whatever the higher-ups said without a word of argument. Someone so stupid she wouldn't pose any threat of breaking a *real* news story," Cherie said with a sneer.

"Jesus Christ, Cherie, just look at yourself. No wonder the station wouldn't take you back no matter how much you pleaded with them," Haley snapped back. She knew she had struck a chord when the woman didn't immediately offer a retort. Cherie stood quietly, shocked and embarrassed, while Haley unlocked her car door and climbed into the driver's seat. She'd replaced her red Prius with a silver Mercedes, a convertible, two months ago after she put a down payment on her condominium. Jonathan had helped her cover the initial costs of both, but it was her job at the station that paid the monthly bills. She was proud of her car, proud of her job, and she reminded herself of both as she backed up and drove away from the station, leaving Cherie Rodgers alone once again. There it was, that glimmer of guilt. She shoved it aside and steered her vehicle down the road, toward her home, and, she hoped, toward Jonathan.

11

The door was unlocked. Jonathan must be inside, Haley decided with an overwhelming sense of relief. He always forgot to lock the door behind him, even after a stranger came into his home and kidnapped his pregnant wife. She tried to gently remind him about locking the door and he always promised to be more mindful, but he never was. She would forgive this lapse if only they could pretend like last night never happened. More than anything, Haley just wanted this terrible day to be over and to find Jonathan returned to his normal, charming self, not the angry man who'd stormed out of her bedroom the night before. She found Jonathan sitting on the sofa, a bottle of tequila perched on the table in front of him with half its contents drained.

Haley panicked. She knew scotch meant a bad day, but what did tequila mean? A breakup? She took a few breaths to steady herself before speaking.

"Hey, babe. Long day?" she asked, pretending their skirmish never took place. Maybe, if she was lucky, he would play along. Her parents had a long history of ignoring fights. It seemed to work for them. Jonathan roused from the half-stupor he was in, probably the effects of intoxication, Haley decided.

"I called over to Alec Kaine's office. He's out on a family matter. I can only assume that matter has something to do with his daughter's kidnapping," Jonathan said, his words blurring together a little in the haze of alcohol. "I tried calling that guy Renn for more information. Turns out, he's no longer with the FBI. I got his partner though. And, wouldn't you know it, he's right here in Phoenix investigating another kid's disappearance. I doubt it'll do them any fucking good. They didn't turn up jack shit when my kid was sliced right out of Nicki."

Haley cringed, the image of Nicki on the side of the road flashed in front of her and then vanished just as quickly. She'd never seen Jonathan like this. Haley didn't know how to comfort him. She dropped her bag on the ground and curled up next to him on the couch. Jonathan pulled her closer and buried his head in her chest. At first, she thought she was going to have to submit to his drunken groping from which she would likely derive little pleasure, but then, much to her horror, Jonathan began to sob. She ran her fingers through his hair and made a shushing sound that her own mother made when Haley would cry as a child.

Through his tears, Jonathan began talking, "I didn't know where to go last night. I just drove around for a while and then I went home to Nicki. She was still on the couch watching TV, just like she was when I left. I tried to talk to her, to tell her that there was another kidnapping, but I couldn't bring myself to mention it. We hardly ever talk anymore."

Haley remained silent, tenderly brushing his hair as his words tore into her with renewed anxiety. Jonathan continued, "I tried kissing her, saying I was sorry, and I was thinking to myself, 'This is your wife, the woman you married.' I tried to go through with it, but when she took off her shirt and I saw that scar, I couldn't. Nicki started crying and then she was yelling and then she said she was going to kill herself. I told her that was fine by me. I just couldn't stop myself. I hated myself and I hated her too."

Jonathan stopped talking as his tears gained force. Haley didn't know what to say but she knew she was supposed to say something.

"You can't blame yourself. You went through something really horrible. Seeing that scar probably brought it all back to you," she offered.

"What's it like for Nicki? Every time she has to take a shower, she's got to look at where they cut her open. She can remember hearing him cry."

Jonathan began sobbing again until, worn out, he drifted into a slobbery sleep on her chest. Haley let out a long sigh. Here she was comforting her boyfriend about his wife. This was a new low in her life. Maybe it was a bad idea to get involved with Jonathan Lambert. She knew going in that he was married and that his family had recently faced a staggering series of tragedies. That's not a great starting point for a new relationship. Add to that the fact that everyone at the station hated her and probably thought she was an imbecile. And, she might be because she'd somehow managed to fall in love with another woman's emotionally scarred husband. What was wrong with her? Haley searched her brain for an answer until, tired herself, she pushed Jonathan aside and watched as he curled up against the armrest completely unaware that she had moved away from him. She reached for the tequila and, not finding a shot glass nearby, opted to take a swig straight from the bottle.

Haley awoke on the couch alone with a devastating headache. She hurried to the bathroom and vomited the contents of her stomach. It didn't look like today was going to be any better than the last. She brushed her teeth and ran a comb through her hair. She needed a shower in a very real way, but first she had to make sure Daisy had food and water, as per their agreement. Haley clicked her tongue against the roof of her mouth as she made her way to the kitchen. The cat must be hiding. Daisy was probably upset that she didn't receive any attention when Haley returned home last night. She clicked her tongue again and she picked up the cat's dishes from the placemat she kept on the floor of the dining area. Still no Daisy. As she went into the kitchen, Haley noticed the front door was slightly ajar. Not much, but wide enough to permit the passage of a small creature. Jonathan had not only forgotten to lock the door when he left, but he also forgot to make sure the latch clicked.

Haley slammed the door and locked it. Then she tore through her condominium in search of Daisy, but to no avail. Finally, she ventured into the hallway in search of her cat. Daisy couldn't have gotten very far. As Haley rounded the corner, she noted that a moving truck was parked outside and someone had the door propped open as they maneuvered a dolly full of boxes through the narrow entrance.

"Have you seen a white cat?" she inquired, trying to contain her apprehension.

"No, sorry, lady," the man said as he steered around her.

Haley hurried past him into the blinding daylight. She looked down the street in both directions, but she knew it was no use. Daisy could have wandered off anywhere. She marched back to her condo and closed the door before succumbing to tears. When she felt she could compose herself enough, she called Jonathan. The phone rang several times before the answering machine picked up. She almost began to cry again at the sound of his voice, but she held herself together until the beep.

"Jonathan, you're an asshole and I don't ever want to see you again," Haley said in a curt tone. Then she disconnected the call and began to weep for the second time that morning.

Audra

"Latte?" Audra asked, pushing open the door to Cherie's office. Except it wasn't Cherie's office anymore. No, the office in question was now assigned to Haley Roth, former weather girl recently promoted to the ranks of newscaster. A feat Haley no doubt considered an illustrious accomplishment, but for Audra, it served to only reinforce her belief that the mainstream media was for the corrupt and their puppets. And Haley wasn't even clever enough to be corrupt.

"Uh, thank you, Audra," Haley answered as she fumbled with some papers atop her desk.

Audra pushed the door open further and made her way across the room.

"Green tea latte, iced and dirty," Audra said as she set the cup on Haley's desk. She'd worked in a coffee shop when she was in high school. These moments that started her day, the ritual of coffee that carried over from Cherie to Haley, made her feel as if all those years spent in college had brought her no further in life than where she'd been at seventeen. The pay was moderately better, but not quite a livable wage. Still, the work was "in the industry" and would help her on the way toward her true calling. Or so she told herself every day when she walked into the station.

Audra looked at the scattered papers, photocopied inquiries for a missing pet. A fluffy white cat named Daisy.

Shit, Audra thought, trying to ignore the sudden burst of sympathy growing inside of her. Fuck Haley and fuck her stupid cat, she decided and turned back toward the door, but it was too late. *Know thyself*, Audra reminded herself. She had a bleeding heart. Try as she might, she couldn't ignore the red-rimmed eyes and simpering thanks from her idiot boss as she unsuccessfully tried to hide her misuse of the office photocopier.

Audra turned back.

"That your cat?" she asked. Haley looked up at her with woeful eyes and immediately erupted into tears. From the puffiness of her face, Audra determined that most of Haley's morning had been spent in tears.

"Yes, she got out this morning," Haley sniveled. Audra was torn between a compulsion to hug her and smack her at the same time. She opted out of both and remained where she was, standing a prudent two feet from Haley's cluttered desk.

"Do you want me to put up a flyer in the breakroom?" Audra offered. It only minimally assuaged her guilt, but she reminded herself that she didn't even like Haley in the first place. If only she could extend that malaise to pets, she thought, but her heart had other notions. Haley looked honestly touched that Audra would extend any offer of assistance beyond her job description. She stuttered a thanks and handed a few copies of the flyer over to her assistant.

"I can fax it over to the nearby animal shelters, too," Audra added, immediately wanting to kick herself. Haley began to cry once again.

"Thank you," Haley said when she'd collected herself enough to speak, "it really means a lot to me."

"Yeah, no problem," Audra said dismissively. She was doing it for the cat, not for Haley.

"I don't know how I'm going to go on the air tonight," Haley confessed. "My face must look like it was stung by a bee."

Audra almost agreed, but she stopped herself. Haley did look like a ragged mess. Suddenly, she had an idea.

"Give me five minutes," Audra said and darted out of Haley's office. She returned in seven.

"Here you go," she said as she handed a narrow tube across the desk to Haley. Her head drooped to read the label, then she looked back to Audra with surprise.

"Hemorrhoid cream?" Haley asked.

"Just use it on the red parts and you'll be sprugged up in no time," Audra explained. "Neal Doran's assistant has to keep it on back stock. She sold me a tube for twenty bucks. Price gouging for sure, but what can you do?"

Haley's face lit up. She rose from her desk and rushed around it to wrap Audra in an uncomfortably tight embrace.

"I'm sorry," Haley apologized although Audra wasn't sure why, unless she was apologizing for the torrent of tears she'd released into the shoulder of Audra's dress. "It's just that my boyfriend and I had a fight and then he didn't make sure the door latch caught when he left so Daisy got outside."

Audra suppressed her grimace. When Haley finally released her and stepped back, Audra saw fresh tears glazing her eyes and forced a smile. Haley might represent everything Audra saw as wrong in the world, but she was still a human being, even if she was a stupid human being. Everyone deserves a little kindness when they're having a shit day.

"Thank you for everything, Audra," Haley said and offered up her best camera smile.

"No trouble," Audra said as she started to make her way to the door with the Lost Cat flyer in her hand. At the last moment, she turned back, "Haley?"

"Yes?" she replied as she took a seat once again on the correct side of her desk.

"You owe me twenty bucks." Kindness was one thing, but twenty bucks was twenty bucks. She wasn't going to pay the exorbitant amount Molly demanded for one lousy tube of cream from her boss's hidden cache. Haley was a newscaster now. She could afford it.

Audra rode to her place first after work. She always went home to shower and shove a change of clothes into her backpack. She knew she was still harboring hope she would one day find Marv sitting on her couch as if nothing had ever happened. She liked to imagine different ways she might respond, from calmly and coolly insisting he explain what'd happened to smashing him over the head with the plaster bust of Artemis she kept on top of the bookcase by the front door. She'd run different scenarios as she made her way home. Each scenario began with opening the door to find Marv working on his laptop while Porgy, their cat, napped beside him.

Porgy's companion, Bess, had been hit by a car last year when she'd managed to escape through a torn window screen. She tried not to think about Bess while she was at the office earlier faxing the image of Daisy to the local animal shelters and hospitals. Later on, she tried not to think about Daisy or Bess or Haley or even Marv, for that matter, as she pedaled down the familiar street where her bungalow waited in darkness. No lights. That told her there would be no Marv either. Audra tried to ignore the familiar sense of disappointment as it washed over her. She felt foolish. The disappointment reminded her she was carrying hope that Marv would return to her. No matter how hard she tried to kill that lingering thought, she felt it swell anew each time she approached the house she used to share with him.

Once inside, she fed Porgy and jumped in the shower. The cat seemed annoyed to see her. She couldn't blame him. He spent most of his time alone these days. She'd been passing her nights at Renn's apartment. She came home for a while on the weekends, but during the week, her hours were usually divided up between the station and Renn's place. She rebuked herself for being a neglectful pet parent. Audra decided she would tell Renn not to expect her for a couple of days. She could use some time to herself anyway. Once she was dressed, she spent a few minutes petting the cat before bidding Porgy farewell and locking up her bungalow. Renn was only a few miles away and Audra enjoyed taking in the night air on her bicycle, even in the sweltering summer heat. And, besides, her Corolla crapped out on her in June. Riding her bike calmed her even though it left her sweaty. She usually didn't make it to Renn's apartment until close to nine, but she knew he would be up for hours still.

No matter what time he went to sleep, Renn would wake up promptly at half past six. Old habit from his bureau days, she supposed, but after six months as a private dick, she would have thought his body would transition to his new schedule. He didn't seem to need much sleep anyway. Audra couldn't function properly unless she had at least seven hours of rest although she preferred a full eight. Sometimes, when she had the day off, she wouldn't get out of bed at all. She and Marv passed many an afternoon in their pajamas, eating cereal and watching Japanese cartoons until the sun settled back into the Western sky. Audra pushed the memory from her mind, pedaling faster until she was stopped at Central by the Lightrail.

13

Renn was seated at his desk when she let herself into his apartment. He didn't turn to greet her. Audra, once again, thought of Marv and the excitement on his features whenever she returned home after a long day at work. She pushed down the thought. Renn was nothing like Marv. That counted for a lot in her book right now. Renn had been employed by the FBI for almost a decade while Marv hated anything and everything associated with the federal government. Renn had a tough guy air from his five o'clock shadow, no matter the hour of the day, to his hard, precise eyes while Marv gave off the appearance that a stiff wind might get the better of him. Marv described himself as a card-carrying pacifist, but a revolutionary at heart. Those two components always stood at odds in Audra's mind. She thought revolution, violent revolution, might be the only way to enact change in the current capitalist regime that held power in this county. It was Marv who'd taught her about peaceful demonstrations and alternative ways of drawing attention to important issues that didn't involve violence.

Although she had never discussed such things with Renn, she definitely saw him as a man who had known violence. He carried a holstered gun at his side and kept another discreetly hidden at his ankle. Even when he was in the sanctity of his own domicile sitting in an undershirt so his white button-up wouldn't wrinkle, he wore a holster holding his Smith & Wesson 9mm Shield.

"Hey there," Audra said from the kitchen area. Chinese take-out sat in containers on the counter. She put her hand against the side of one of the boxes: still warm.

"Hey, if you're hungry, there's food," Renn called back. He still didn't turn around. Something must really have his attention. He wasn't what Audra would call a thoughtful boyfriend, not that she considered him her *boyfriend*, but he usually granted her the small courtesy of a smile when she said hello. Tonight, he didn't even look at her once as she set about making herself some tea.

What they shared wasn't love. She wasn't so naïve as to believe that, nor was that something she was seeking from Renn. They took comfort in one another when they needed it. That was all. And, more important than any shared comfort, they were unified in their quest to uncover Jude. When Marv vanished, Audra thought Cherie would be her partner in the struggle to reveal the truth, but the journalist seemed to lose all semblance of reason when she lost her job and, later, the respect of the broadcasting community. Never had Audra before seen someone fall so far so fast.

Cherie shopped the story to every news outfit in the

country. Continually rebuffed, she turned to some of the less credible news providers and, eventually, even to alternative websites that claimed to run the stories other stations were afraid to touch, but they all said no. No one was willing to go against a direct order from the HSA. Cherie was left ranting on barstools to anyone who would listen about the media blacklist and Jude and even the Channel 9 News Team. It was ridiculous. Cherie even went so far as to suggest that Audra access the station's feed to splice in a report that they would produce themselves about the missing children.

When Audra refused, Cherie accused her of sabotaging her career. That was it for her. She'd had enough. She told Cherie she was a fool. That this one story wasn't the only "big story" out there. That every single kidnapping they investigated was in response to a "big story" that didn't receive the attention it deserved. Contaminated water poisoning communities, drug companies knowingly releasing false data, safety standards ignored, corners cut to save costs that ended up costing lives. So many people dying in the name of profits and no one held accountable. Cherie was so focused on the kidnapping she didn't even care that the town of Harrison still didn't have access to clean drinking water or that Jonathan Lambert seemed to be shuffling assets to divest from Southwest Resources before the financial fallout of legal action. Audra realized it wasn't about justice for Cherie. It was about Cherie.

Audra stopped returning her calls and, finally, Cherie stopped calling. Cherie did her best, however, to keep in touch with Renn. He informed her that he was no longer working with the FBI, but she insisted on calling every couple of weeks to see if he'd heard anything new about the case. He never gave her anything, but she kept calling. Audra wondered if Cherie's interest in Renn went beyond strictly professional, but she didn't care. He seemed like a man of singular focus. Actually, he didn't seem all that much interested in her either, Audra realized, but they shared the bond of similar goals and that united them, if only for the time being.

The water finished boiling and Audra poured a cup of tea for herself. Renn preferred copious amounts of black coffee to fuel his day. She placed a saucer over the mug so the tea could steep for a few minutes and walked over to Renn where he sat at his computer.

"What are you looking for?" she asked, her eyes focusing on the digital newspaper archives on his screen.

Renn ignored her question as he continued scrolling. Frustration began slowly building inside of her. Renn could be so damn annoying when he was caught up in his thoughts, which happened rather frequently. He would act like Audra wasn't even there. Until, that is, he needed something. Needed her to crack into police records or once even peek into the FBI database to see what new leads his former coworkers might have discovered. The latter incident didn't prove of much use. After the case was transferred over to the HSA, the Bureau had to relinquish all of their files: physical and digital. In fact, the only mention of Jude that Audra could scour up came from a contact form instructing all agents to direct any information that pertained to Jude to the HSA. She wouldn't dare break into the HSA's database. Nothing would land her in jail for hacking faster than to attempt to break into their system, not the Department of Defense or the FBI or any other computer network maintained by the

Federal Government. Renn seemed frustrated with her outright refusal, but he accepted that the official files on Jude were simply out of their reach. Hell, if Renn wanted to see Putin's personal emails, she would consider that effort as having a greater likelihood of success. The HSA was off-limits.

After Renn's refusal to respond, or even acknowledge her, Audra took her tea over to the lumpy loveseat they had procured for twenty bucks from a nearby Goodwill a few months back. She set down her tea and pulled her laptop out of her backpack which, until that moment, she had still been carrying. She completed her degree back in May without ceremony or celebration. The certificate was sent to her home and remained on the counter in its envelope. The Channel 9 News moved her from the position of intern into an official role as Haley's personal assistant. The job was basically the same except a meager paycheck popped into her bank account every Thursday. It wasn't much, but it was something. Renn would kick her some cash when she assisted him with a case he was working on as a P.I. Sometimes all it took was a little Facebook stalking and you could learn enough about a person to piece together all their dirty secrets.

Audra had sought out Renn a couple weeks after Marv disappeared. She called Marv's parents again after forty-eight hours had passed and let them know he was missing. His stepdad, Ray, was characteristically unconcerned. He thought Marv probably went on some "vision quest" and they would be getting a collect call from Moab any day now. His mother, on the other hand, launched into a panic and called the Phoenix Police Department to file a missing person report. Audra faithfully answered the cop's questions when he came to her door, but she did not bring up Jude or their research into his organization. She did not want to land on an HSA watchlist. The cop confiscated his computer, but Audra had already wiped the files pertaining to Jude. There were so many passcodes on his computer anyway, she didn't expect the PD would get very far. She didn't believe Marv was dead. She knew he had made some headway in his research and hadn't shared it with her. Instead, he'd left her behind and joined Jude's organization. She didn't have any evidence to support her beliefs. She just knew it was true in the same way she knew her own name and she hated him for it.

They'd found each other during their last year of high school and, after a few short months, they were inseparable. As soon as they started college, they moved in together in the small bungalow she still called home, one of her father's rental properties that he would later sign over to her. He only offered her the rental after he found out Audra had been living in some shithole studio in a crime-ridden stretch of town. Initially, her father seemed reluctant to allow Marv to move into the bungalow with her, but she said it was all or nothing. Now she could better understand his initial reluctance. The house, *her* home, served as a constant reminder of her abandonment. The squeaky latch that announced Marv's return from work. The bed they slept in together. The table where they shared their meals. Even that damned cat, Porgy, echoed the loss she felt. This was Porgy's first home too, brought here as a kitten with his sister, Bess. Now, his life partner was lost to him just as Marv was to her.

Audra decided she preferred to sleep at Renn's place. It was like the shithole she swore to her father she would keep living in years ago if he didn't let her boyfriend move in too. Marv, that fucker.

14

Renn was back at the computer in the morning, exactly where Audra had left him the previous night. She waited until two a.m. for him to share the furious inner workings of his mind, or maybe take her to bed, but she remained ignored. When she finally grew tired, she crawled into bed without Renn. She didn't mind. At least, not too much anyway. She remembered that she was going to tell him that she wouldn't be coming by for a couple days so she could spend some time at home straightening up, attending to bills, and providing Porgy with some much-needed attention. Audra decided it would serve him right if she just didn't show up for a couple days. If he even noticed, that is.

Audra got ready for work and, as she walked past Renn towards her sherbet cruiser, asked, "Ready to tell me what you're looking for?"

Renn seemed initially startled to hear another voice in his apartment, but then he remembered Audra and turned toward her.

"I've been thinking about the kids. The ones Jude takes," he began. "What is he doing with those kids? I mean, where can you hide that many children?"

"Bolivia? The Yukon? Who knows?" Audra replied. "Marv thought he probably set up a camp for them somewhere where they could be indoctrinated with some sort of anti-capitalist propaganda."

Renn stared at her for a moment. Audra shifted uncomfortably as he scrutinized her face. She always felt like he was sizing her up in these moments, breaking down the nuances of her character and analyzing the details to see if what she'd said matched up with what she was thinking.

"I don't think that's it, Audra," he said with a firm undertone that told Audra he had a different theory entirely.

"Where do you think he's taking them?" she asked, annoyed. Why did he always make her draw information out of him? Why was he so reluctant to confide in her?

"I don't think he's taking them anywhere. I think he's killing them."

Audra's body tightened, inside and out. She realized the source of Renn's hesitancy. It was her. He could read her and he knew how deeply she felt everything. That was her biggest problem as a journalism student: assuming an appropriate distance from the tragedies she covered. She was too empathetic. A bleeding heart. She knew she needed to toughen up and she thought she felt her skin thickening over the past six months, but she was wrong. The faces of all those children started shuffling through her brain one by one. Lacey Hardgrove. Caleb Babcock. Jeremy Sutter. Diane Nereus. And all the other ones known and unknown to them. All this time, she thought they were dealing with some form of vigilante justice, but if Renn was right, this wasn't justice. How can you execute a child for the crimes of its parents and call it just? And then Audra remembered Marv.

"There's no way Marv would sign on for something

like that," she contended. Renn drew in a deep breath.

"Audra, we have to consider the possibility that Marv is dead. He might have found out something he wasn't supposed to. Or maybe he even decided to go after a lead and got himself killed," Renn said. "I'm really sorry to have to say it, but chances are, Marv is gone. One person is murdered every minute in this country. It might have just been his minute."

"He's not dead. I would know if he was dead."

"Would you? Tell me how that works, Audra," Renn asked, his voice taking on a slightly snide air. Something was bothering him and he was taking it out on her.

"I just think I'd know," Audra answered honestly. She was suddenly tired. Sorrow in the blood had an exhausting effect on the body. She was beginning to grieve for all those missing children whose files she had poured through for the past six months. She knew each of their names, their ages. She worked laboriously to seek out their brethren, other children born to wealth and snatched away from their families as some form of revenge. The children the media ignored in order to maintain some flimsy hold on the status quo. She thought of the ones not kidnapped, but dead anyway; the ones killed through corporate malignance brought on by greed. Malcolm McDonald whose autopsy report included an ulcerated digestive tract in addition to his failed liver and kidneys. Amber Williams with her skin covered in blisters from the sulphuric acid even though it was the inhalation of the chemical that ultimately did her in. Tiny Cadence McNeil in her small white casket. Curly-haired Penelope Garland mangled in a car crash that also killed her father when their anti-lock brakes failed two months before the official recall. And Renn believed Marv should also be added to Audra's grief, but it didn't feel right. Something internal whispered to her that he was still breathing out there somewhere. Not dead and in the ground like that sea of ghost children that rose up around her.

Renn didn't say anything more to her. He just turned back to his computer and launched into his research again. *Yes*, she thought to herself, *maybe I could use a few days alone*. Audra pushed her bike out the front door, not bothering to lock it behind her. Renn had a gun. He'd be fine. Her backpack was firmly affixed to her back. It held her laptop, a change of clothes, and her sundries bag which included a respectable array of lipstick shades. If she needed to, she could pull a grand out of her bank account and flee the country. The idea surprised her, but she indulged the fantasy for a few minutes as she rode toward Central Avenue and the television station. Thankfully, there was a coffee shop located kitty corner from work which made it easier to keep a steady flow of lattes and other caffeinated beverages to the news team through the capable hands of their personal assistants. Audra had started a text message group just for coffee orders between herself, Becky, Molly, and a few others on staff frequently tasked with making coffee runs. That saved on a lot of time in the long run.

The Lightrail, the public mass transit system for the Phoenix metro area, slowed to a stop in front of her. Audra's eyes rolled over the people on the platform lined up to board. One face stopped her. A young man in khaki pants and a navy-blue shirt. He had short, light brown hair, but it was his face that made Audra feel like a bucket of ice water had suddenly been dumped over her head. The face was aimed right at her: Marv's face. Audra dropped her bike and rushed forward onto the crosswalk, but the man turned and stepped onto the Lightrail car as if he hadn't seen her. But she knew he had. Audra stopped running as she watched the doors close and the train take off again. A car horn brought her back to her immediate surroundings. She was standing in the intersection, blocking the southbound traffic when they had the green light to go. Audra hurried across to the Lightrail station and pulled out her wallet. She bought a ticket on the next train and began pacing the walkway. Fifteen fucking minutes before the next train? What are the chances she would be able to catch up to Marv? She didn't know what stop he would get off at nor did she know where he would go once he left the train. She suddenly remembered her bicycle and looked across the street to where she had dropped in on the sidewalk. Gone. Sandra, the sherbet-colored cruiser, was out of her life. She didn't care. She just wanted to find Marv again.

15

She rode the Lightrail until sunset and then Audra set off, on foot, toward her own little bungalow. Thankfully, it was only a few miles away from the station. The walk gave her time to clear her head. She had been right all along. Marv was alive. He just left her without a word. Five years together didn't warrant a word of goodbye. She was done looking for him. He didn't want to be found. But, still, she couldn't help wondering what he had been doing at that particular stop this morning. Had he been seeking her out and found her encamped at Renn's apartment? Could he blame her for shacking up with someone else after he disappeared six months ago? Did she care if he did? It seemed like too much of a coincidence that Marv had been at that stop around the same time she rolled her bicycle out of Renn's front door.

The bungalow was dark when she arrived. If he wanted to get in touch with her, he knew where she lived. Audra let herself in and turned on the lights in the living room. The same empty floral couch. The same stacks of books on shelves and on the floor. Porgy popped his head in from the hallway. He had probably been napping on her bed. She dropped her backpack and went into the kitchen to make sure the cat had food and water. Audra picked up the kettle to start some tea. Now that she had seen him, maybe Marv would finally make an appearance tonight to explain why he disappeared so suddenly back in February. There it was again. That sliver of hope burrowed in her heart. She didn't want it there. Fuck Marv. He was a bastard like any other bastard. It just took him half a decade to reveal his true self. She was done worrying about him.

Audra looked down at the grey cat that snaked around her legs.

"Sorry, Porgy, not tonight," she said and walked out of the kitchen. She grabbed her backpack and went into the bedroom to swap out her change of clothes. A few minutes later, she was back at the front door. She scooped up the spare keys to Marv's Vespa out of the dish on top of the short bookcase by the door. Audra turned off the lights and locked up the house before she walked over to the scooter covered by a dark green canvas tarp. She pulled off the cover and unlocked the seat where a special compartment held the helmet. Soon she was racing down the street at a speed never achieved on her bicycle, but the Vespa provided a similar sensation. The hot air rushed around her with a cooling effect. The world flew by as she sat unencumbered by the metal confines of an automobile. The scooter used gasoline, but not very much. She thought of the years she'd spent with Marv and released them one by one as payment for his Vespa. It was black, of course, but Audra began to wonder just how much her friend Andy would charge her for a paint job. Maybe she would make it sea green or bubble gum pink. Some bright shade that would make it hers.

Renn was home and he had a guest. Audra believed this was probably the first guest to come into his apartment besides her. It was true that a woman had shown up at the door a few weeks after he'd moved in, but she left abruptly, never to return again. Audra didn't ask him any questions about her. Renn never asked her about her history if it didn't pertain directly to Marv or his disappearance. She assumed he would appreciate it if she granted him the same courtesy. This stranger today wasn't as tall as Renn nor was he as narrow. Both men looked at her as she walked through the door.

"Where's your bike?" Renn asked her.

"Gone," she answered without explanation. She made her way into the living room where they were both seated, Renn on the chair by his desk while the stranger perched on the small sofa.

"Audra, this is Maurice Whitlock. We used to be partners over at the Bureau. Maurice, this is Audra," Renn offered the introductions and then paused for an awkward moment before adding, "She's a friend."

Maurice rose up and extended a hand toward her. Audra gave it a firm shake while offering the stranger a brief smile.

"If you don't mind, we're just finishing up in here," Renn began to explain.

"Oh, I'm sorry," Audra exclaimed, realizing she had interrupted a private conversation. "I can come back later."

She turned back toward the door, but Renn stopped her, taking her by the hand.

"You don't have to leave, but maybe you could just give us a couple minutes alone," Renn said as he nodded to the bedroom door. Audra took his meaning and headed off in that direction. She closed the door behind her but left it open a crack. She probably didn't even need to do that much. The walls were so thin here she could hear the neighbors every time they fought or fucked. It was a nightly drama that played out through the walls.

"You old dog," she heard his partner say once she was out of sight.

"Shut up, she's a nice girl."

"Girl, yes. Woman, not quite."

"She's twenty-three and she came on to me. Can we just get back to it?"

Audra could feel her cheeks reddening. She was glad she was in the bedroom where they couldn't see her. She was irritated but she realized that Renn probably knew she could hear every word they were saying. He wasn't trying to be snide; he was just telling it like it was.

"Right, this theory of yours."

"I'm telling you. This is where you're going to find them. You just have to look."

"And I told you that I'm on a 10 o'clock back to D.C. Phoenix is all washed up for us now. They didn't even call us in until the girl was gone. I don't know what they expect us to do now. Nearly half a million kids go missing every year. They expect us to pull out all the stops when it's a rich kid."

"This is more than a couple missing kids. This is a goddamn conspiracy. Who's thinking too small now?"

There was a long pause.

"And just what do you expect me to do with this information you seemed to have gleaned out of the air like a fucking premonition?"

"I'm asking you to catch the morning flight. Tonight we can go out and check Brandy Romero's grave. Do you know how many of these kids were cremated? I mean the national average is somewhere above a third, but it looks like less than half of them were given a traditional burial. Brandy Romero is one of them. Right here in Phoenix, buried just two days ago. We can go look tonight."

"I'm going to need to run it through the department. Get an order to exhume the body. That could take weeks."

Audra listened to the men go back and forth. So Renn wanted to dig up Brandy Romero's grave? Six-year-old Brandy was prone to tonic-clonic seizures for which she was occasionally given Depakote. The drug interacted with another experimental medication she was given to prevent seizures which caused a heart attack that ended her young life. An activist hacker group released emails that revealed the drug company was aware of the dangers, but failed to note the potential toxic interaction before releasing the medication to the public. Brandy was not the first victim, but she was the youngest and the only one under the age of fifty to die as a result. In retaliation, Jude kidnapped Vanessa, the five-year-old daughter of Alec Kaine, the head of Kaine Health Solutions. She was the latest kidnapping, snatched right here in Phoenix from her bed while she was sleeping.

"We don't need an order. Let's just go down there, you and me, and have a look. Maybe talk to the grave digger. See if he noticed anything amiss."

"And this is all based off some hunch you have?"

"It's more than a hunch, Maurice. I found a report from Anchorage police claiming the grave of Malcolm MacDonald had been disturbed. I looked into it. The police didn't exhume the body then. They just took a written report from the funeral director after their groundskeeper noticed the soil looked unsettled. I don't know why the police didn't contact us at that point. We were already working the case."

"You want me to miss the plane for that? Come on, Ricky, you're reaching."

"Listen, Whitlock, I got a feeling about this one. Are you going to come with me or am I going by myself? I don't have a badge anymore. I might get arrested poking around the cemetery at night. Can't you do me this one favor? For old time's sake?"

There was a drawn out pause while Renn, and secretly Audra, waited for a response. Finally, Maurice spoke up. "All right, fuck it. I'll go with this one time, but just because you threw away your whole career over this one case."

Renn let out a laugh. A minute later he pushed open the door to his bedroom and looked at Audra, who had obviously positioned herself in such a way that she could overhear everything being said.

"I'll be back later," he said. Audra nodded and watched as he slipped through the door. A minute later she heard the front door open and close. She had the place to herself. She considered making a cup of tea, but she was tired and a dark feeling had descended upon her. She didn't have the energy to get up and walk to the kitchen. Instead, she laid back on the bed still wearing her clothes from the day. The image of Marv standing on the Lightrail platform burned in her mind. She was quickly claimed by sleep.

Jonathan

16

Jonathan sat in quiet contemplation over the two files on his desk. One was a portfolio for an upstart drug company that was gearing up to launch a new treatment option for rheumatoid arthritis, one that their CEO termed "a real game changer". The other file contained information about a digital communication company that worked with gas-and-oil operations, connecting tankers around the world to offices in Texas and New York. He had several million dollars in investment capital ready to secure a controlling interest in one company or the other. The question was, which one? He considered consulting his father on the matter. The Old Bull enjoyed being brought up to speed on the family's investments, but Jonathan decided he wanted to make the decision on his own. This move was going to be his first big step toward the large-scale diversification of their financial portfolio and toward his big plans for the future fortunes of the Lambert family.

The phone rang, distracting him from the quandary on his desk, and Jonathan looked at it in annoyance. He'd told Stephen, his office assistant, to hold all his calls, but he must have forgotten. Jonathan reached for the phone and hit the speaker button.

"What is it, Stephen? I said to hold my calls," Jonathan said, noting the irritability in his own voice.

"I know, Mr. Lambert, except it's a Special Agent

Whitlock from the FBI on the line."

Jonathan's stomach turned. Did they finally know something?

"Put him through."

There was a pause followed by a beep, then Jonathan spoke up again.

"Agent Whitlock?"

"Yes, Mr. Lambert the younger, correct?" the voice on the line asked.

"Yes, Jonathan, please."

"Jonathan, we were hoping to come up and speak to you. Is now a good time?"

Jonathan shook his head. Did it matter if it was a good time or not when you were dealing with the FBI? Besides, what could be more important than this?

"Of course, I'll clear my schedule. What time can I expect you?" he asked.

"We're in the lobby now. See you in a few minutes."

Jonathan wondered what could be so important that the FBI had come all the way out to his office just to speak with him. Did they manage to locate this Jude? He didn't dare hope that they had found his child. He had given up that idea some time ago. It was too much to hold onto. Just look at what it was doing to Nicki. Jonathan tried to clear his mind as he collected the papers on his desk and returned them to the appropriate folders. That decision would have to wait a little longer. A knock at the door alerted him to his visitors' arrival.

"Come in," he called out.

Stephen opened the door and stepped through to admit two men. One was Maurice Whitlock who Jonathan remembered from the incident back in February. The other was unfamiliar. He was shorter in stature than Jonathan, but he had a muscular build that filled out the fabric of his black suit. He wore a crisp white shirt, a gunmetal grey tie, and the somber air of a mortician.

"Special Agent Whitlock," Jonathan said in acknowledgement as he rose to shake his hand.

"Jonathan Lambert, this is Agent Truitt of the Homeland Security Association," Maurice said by way of introduction.

Truitt nodded as he shook Jonathan's hand.

"Won't you both please have a seat? Can I get you anything to drink?" Jonathan asked in his customary way. The two agents sat down, but declined the offer.

"We won't take up too much of your time. There's been a development in the case that we felt you should be made aware of," Maurice began. "Another kidnapping took place in Phoenix recently. It appears to be the work of Jude."

"Alec Kaine's daughter, right?" Jonathan asked. The two agents exchanged looks. Even with a media blackout in place on Jude word still got around in certain circles, powerful circles.

"Yes, well, it appears his daughter was taken in retaliation for the death of Brandy Romero, a six-year-old who died when a toxic interaction of medications caused her heart to stop. We exhumed the body of Brandy and found a second corpse in the grave. We were able to confirm that it was the body of Vanessa Kaine," Maurice kept his voice level and calm, but his words struck Jonathan like a violent gale of wind, chilling him to the bone and threatening to knock him off his feet even though he was already seated. He didn't know how to respond, but the agent began speaking again, filling the silence. "We asked for permission to exhume the body of Cadence McNeil. A second corpse was found there as well. DNA tests are currently underway, but we believe that the infant was yours."

His son was dead. For the past six months, he told himself that his son was dead, but now that it was confirmed, Jonathan felt a hollowness forming inside of him.

"Does Nicki know yet?" Jonathan didn't know what else to say. His mind reeled, trying to accept this new information.

"We contacted you first."

He was supposed to tell her. Maybe they knew she had fallen into a state of emotional instability and decided to approach him in place of her. He knew he would have to go home and deliver the news that their child was dead, buried in another infant's grave.

"Have you been able to find out anything about Jude? Like who or where he is?" Jonathan asked. His sorrow was suddenly shifting toward anger. Neither the HSA nor FBI had been able to locate this vigilante who murdered children. How was it possible to hide in the 21st Century when everyone had a cell phone that tracked their movements and overheard their conversations? When satellites and drones could detect a heat lamp for growing weed in someone's bedroom closet and surveillance cameras monitored every public space? How could someone, or an entire organization, remain hidden for years?

"The investigation is ongoing. This new information will hopefully provide us with some additional leads," Special Agent Whitlock answered. The man's level tone grated on Jonathan, both coaxing yet stern, but he maintained his demeanor without revealing his irritation. As if some internal clock had struck its appointed hour, both agents rose simultaneously from their chairs. Jonathan still had one more question.

"When can we have the body back?"

"Excuse me?" the agent in the black suit asked, speaking for the first time since their brief introduction.

"My son. I'd like to give him a proper burial."

"Of course, Mr. Lambert. I understand," Agent Whitlock replied. "We'll have someone from our team get in touch with you as soon as forensics is complete."

Jonathan hit the button on his phone to signal Stephen, who was already opening the doors to allow them exit by the time the two men crossed the room. The man in black slipped through the doorway first with Whitlock in tow. Just before the agent stepped out of view, Maurice turned back to Jonathan and said, "Thank you for your time, Mr. Lambert. I am truly sorry for your loss."

Stephen looked to Jonathan with a confused expression, but said nothing. Jonathan dismissed his assistant with a wave of his hand. He picked up his cell phone and found Michael Maestri's name from his list of contacts. After two rings, he answered.

"Maestri," he said.

"Michael, I need to see you in my office."

"You have to be fucking kidding me, Jonathan. Do I have to remind you that you sent me out to the water treatment center to review the new specs in person?"

"They found my son. He's dead. I need you to get back here."

17

After Jonathan got off the phone with Maestri, he poured himself two fingers worth of scotch and sat at his desk. He stared at his phone wondering who to call. He should tell his parents, but he needed to tell Nicki first. She wasn't going to take this well. In fact, this might prove to be the proverbial straw that breaks the camel's back. No, he couldn't make that call. He would need to tell her in person to make sure she didn't do anything drastic in response to the news. Everyone, it would seem, would need to wait until this evening when he returned home. He would tell Nicki and then he could call Patricia. His mother could tell The Old Bull that his grandson was dead because of him and all the years of bad decision-making he'd made at the helm of Southwest Resources. Maybe a heart attack would finally do Wallace in this time. Jonathan could only hope.

Maestri didn't wait for Stephen to signal to Jonathan that he had a visitor. Instead, he just barged right into his office without knocking. Michael was wearing a lightweight Brooks Brothers suit in a soft blue, a nod to the stifling summer heat.

"Have you told your parents yet?" Michael asked as he took a seat across from Jonathan. He assumed a casual posture like they were two old friends catching up rather than employee and employer.

"No, I have to tell Nicki first," Jonathan answered. He noticed his scotch glass was empty and stood up to refill it. The crystal decanter that held the amber liquid had his initials etched on the front, a gift from his father when he took up Wallace's former office. It contained Macallan Rare Cask Highland Single Malt Scotch initially, but Jonathan had drained its contents within a month's time. By then, he'd developed a taste for that particular drink and ordered the same one every time the decanter got too low. He rarely offered Maestri a drink at the office, but he did today. The man accepted and Jonathan brought him a glass before he took his seat behind his desk once again. He looked at Michael, at the ruminations showing on his face. It didn't take a genius to see he was wondering why Jonathan asked him down here.

"So, explain to me how all this works," Jonathan began. Michael didn't understand his meaning and the confusion clouding his eyes expanded.

"I'm not sure what you…" he began but Jonathan cut him off.

"You. Explain to me what it is you can do exactly. I know my father valued you above everyone else at this company. He probably values you even more than me. There has to be reasons. So far, I've only heard hints. Insinuations. Now, please, outline for me what it is you did for my father beyond the normal parameters of your job description," Jonathan explained then he took a drink from his scotch glass and set it on the desk in front of him. He languidly twirled the glass while waiting for Michael to formulate his response. Even though Maestri had become quite adept at controlling his facial expressions, the extended silence told Jonathan that the man was trying to decide just how much to reveal about his dark dealings on behalf of his father and Southwest Resources.

"I guess you could say that I handled an array of assignments that went beyond the traditional scope of my official title. Everything from assisting in the negotiation of land and water rights to researching competitors. Anything your father didn't have time to see to personally went to me. I either assigned the responsibility within the company or I handled the situation myself using personal resources based on what was appropriate to Mr. Lambert's needs," Maestri answered while a slight smirk turned up the corner of his mouth. He was enjoying this, dancing around the answers Jonathan was looking for, forcing him to state his purpose in no uncertain terms.

"Thanks for the public relations version. Now tell me what you can actually do," Jonathan grumbled, shifting forward slightly in his seat. Maestri mimicked his movements and straightened his slouch before answering.

"Anything and everything."

"Murder and espionage?" Jonathan joked.

"If need be," Maestri answered, the smirk wiped from his face. The firmness of his mouth and the forward lock of his gaze told Jonathan he was serious. Jonathan leaned back in his chair and took a long drink from the tumbler in his hand. He'd always suspected Maestri conducted some dirty dealings on his father's behalf, but now he had his confirmation. His initial response was one of disgust, but that quickly gave way to intrigue. Michael Maestri might have his uses, after all.

"So how does this usually work?"

"We usually talked price and then your father would give me two numbers: what he thinks he should pay and what he's willing to pay," Maestri explained. "I usually come back somewhere in the middle."

Jonathan looked at the amber liquid in his tumbler and gave it a gentle swirl.

"If I wanted you to look into Jude and his organization, would that fall into your skill set?" he asked.

"I don't know how much I could turn up that the HSA hasn't found out already," Maestri admitted. He deflated a little before Jonathan's eyes. The first special order of business Jonathan had for him and he couldn't give a better answer. "I can look into the matter, but I can't promise results. How much are you in for?"

"I'd like to keep it under a hundred grand for information, but I'd go as high as two million if there's proof of death," Jonathan plainly stated.

"That's a pretty expansive gap." Maestri's eyes narrowed before disengaging his stare to drain the remainder of his scotch.

"Let's just see what sort of results you come back with," Jonathan replied. "Like I said, for the two million, I want proof of death."

18

Jonathan returned home as the sun was settling in the west. Beyond the haze surrounding Phoenix's urban center, the sunset burned watermelon and tangerine. He paused in the comfortable surroundings of his own living room, watching the Cimmerian night settle. For a brief moment, he willed the sun to never rise again, to freeze out the world and everyone on it. He thought of the son he would never know, buried in another child's grave. Womb to tomb, as they say, in a matter of hours. It was hard to grieve for a child he had never set eyes on, a child that only existed as an idea to him, a hope for the future now lost forever.

He could hear the faint buzz of a television program from Nicki's room upstairs. Lately, she had taken to turning up the volume to an alarming level. Patricia said it was a cry for help, but that didn't stop it from grating on Jonathan. Maybe his wife was losing her hearing along with her interest in life. Whatever the cause, he didn't care. Nicki had pushed him beyond the point of caring. She swore an oath to be his partner in life yet she'd tossed in the towel after the first challenging years they faced together. Sure, she lost an infant in an unjust reprisal for a crime she didn't commit, but so did he. Jonathan wasn't given the option of squandering his days with daytime dramas and Xanax, however. He became responsible for the family business and, resultantly, for the family's fortune. There was no one left to manage their affairs if he was suddenly overcome by tragedy.

At the thought of Nicki, Jonathan remembered the news he was tasked with delivering. He fixed himself another drink before he began his journey up the stairs. It was his fifth of the day. Usually, he kept it under two until he got home, but today had been an unexpected trial. He needed a little lightness on his feet to see the day to its end. As it stood, the world was weighing too heavy on him. Jonathan downed his drink and fixed himself another to carry upstairs to Nicki's room, the room he'd once shared with her. The sounds of the television grew louder as he climbed each step. Jonathan stopped outside the master suite and rapped on the door a few times. No answer. Jonathan pushed the door open and poked his head in to find Nicki dozing, half-seated and half-laying, against a throne of pillows on their bed. The room was dark except for the flashing hues from the television screen. Jonathan moved over to the bed and took a seat beside his wife. She woke with a start, her arms thrust forward to stop an imagined assault. Something began stirring inside of him and, for a moment, Jonathan longed to pull Nicki in close to him, to tell her everything was going to be alright. He didn't. He waited for her to recognize her surroundings as familiar. Nicki calmed down and reached forward to grab the remote control that was sitting beside her on the bed. She hit the mute button and the television went silent. The images continued to flash, filling the room with an eerie, erratic light.

"Agent Whitlock came to see me today with an HSA guy," Jonathan began. "Our son is dead. They found his body."

"What?" Nicki asked, suddenly alarmed. "Where?"

"In Cadence McNeil's grave," he answered, shifting slightly away from Nicki as he answered. He remembered the tumbler of scotch in his hand, but didn't feel it was the appropriate time to take a drink. Instead, he began counting in his head, waiting for Nicki to respond. They hadn't discussed Cadence McNeil or the crimes of Southwest Resources, but Jonathan knew Nicki had watched enough of the evening news in the past six months to be aware of both. He expected her to cry or to launch into a fit of hysterics, but she didn't do either.

After a minute of silence, Jonathan's discomfort began to show on his features. He tried to wait out the quiet, studying his wife's face as her mind struggled to process the news that her son was dead. Nicki had a delicate nose that turned up slightly at its tip. Jonathan always thought her nose gave her narrow face the look of a woodland fairy. Since the pregnancy, those delicate features were lost in the widening of her face as her body also thickened. Jonathan knew it wasn't the extra pounds that repulsed him. It was that jagged scar on her abdomen where she had been cut open and robbed of the life she was made to safeguard. His visceral response to that scar made him feel ashamed and his shame turned to anger in the unbroken silence of the room they'd once shared as husband and wife.

Finally, Nicki spoke, "I'd like to be alone if you don't mind." Her voice was tired and meek. Jonathan knew he should say something to comfort her, this person he'd promised to love all his days, but he was ready to admit that the love they'd shared was gone. Stolen from them by the same man who came into their home and stole his wife and child. Jonathan dared to hope that Maestri might be able to turn up something of use. And, if fate had any sense of justice, he would find Jude and make sure he paid for what he had done to his family.

Jonathan rose from the side of the bed and left the room without a word. Once he closed the door behind him, he finished his scotch, the effects of which were beginning to buzz around inside of him once again. The television resumed its flurry of sound as Jonathan made his way downstairs. He wanted to go to Haley, but she was still upset with him. Jonathan remembered the angry words she spit into his answering machine. Something about never wanting to see him again. He heard the sound of a bath running upstairs. Good, maybe Nicki had finally decided to take a shower of her own volition. Maybe now that they knew for certain that their son was dead, she could start to move forward with her life. Jonathan pulled his cell phone out of his pocket and selected the name "Roth" from his contacts. Better to list everyone by their surname rather than run the risk of getting caught calling someone named Haley seven times in two days. The phone rang several times before connecting him to her voice mail. He disconnected the call. He'd already left her a few messages. He wasn't going to plead with her. There were plenty of other women around if she wasn't interested. Maybe she had gotten all she wanted out of him: down payments for both a condo and a car. Not a bad payout for a six-month investment when you thought about it.

Jonathan poured another drink, not bothering to mentally mark the fingers in his tumbler, just filling it up with scotch. The bath was still running upstairs. Jonathan wondered if he should check on Nicki. She certainly hadn't been in her right state of mind these past few months and the news of their son's death must have hit pretty hard. She had threatened to kill herself on more than one occasion, but never followed through with any actual harm to herself. Jonathan's own mind was still reeling from the confusing assault of emotions. He didn't feel like making the trek back upstairs, but his curiosity pushed him into action. Jonathan trudged up the steps on their plush white carpet without a thought for the scotch sloshing over the rim of his glass with every movement. From the upper level, the television masked the sound of the bathtub running. Jonathan returned to the master suite, not bothering to knock this time. An alcove amid the blankets and pillows spoke of Nicki's absence. Jonathan realized she was already in the bath and paused for a moment. He felt like he was invading her privacy by entering the bathroom uninvited, but then he remembered that Nicki was his wife and this was his house. He could go wherever he damn well wanted.

He crossed the room without another thought and walked through the archway that divided the carpeted bedroom from the marble-floored bath area. A tub sat in the corner beneath two panes of glass that met uninterrupted to form a window. Nicki's white breasts pushed above the red surface of water. She looked surprised to see Jonathan, but she said nothing to him. She just turned her eyes away from him back to the windows and the night sky beyond the glass. Jonathan stood there quietly for a moment before turning to leave the room. When he reached the foyer, he put his scotch down and grabbed his car keys. Haley might not be taking his calls but he still had a key to her place. Rage battered against the inside of his chest. He needed to get out of his house and he didn't know where else to go.

Cherie

19

The sun pushed its way in through the curtains until the assault bore down on Cherie's eyes and she was forced to wake and face the day. She rolled onto her side and looked at the digital alarm clock she kept on her nightstand, but hadn't set in months. Half past noon. Cherie let out a small groan as she rose to a sitting position at the edge of her bed. Her head throbbed and the previous night returned to her in a random sequence of images. Drinks at the Dilly Dally with Erick. Being ejected after 2 a.m. when the bar shut down. Finally, the Uber ride home. Why had she taken an Uber? Oh, yeah, Erick snatched her keys and refused to return them. That was probably a wise decision on his part.

Cherie reached for her purse which lay strewn across the floor next to her bed, its contents dispersed to suggest it was cast off with hostile disregard. She bent down to retrieve the scattered items, but her head spun and her stomach threatened to upend itself all over the carpet. Deciding to leave the purse for the moment, Cherie made her way through the house to the kitchen. Thankfully, the shutters remained drawn against the outside light. She should just leave them that way all the time, she decided. It would save on the cooling costs for the warm months remaining. She retrieved the Bloody Mary mix from the refrigerator. The fridge didn't hold much by way of food. Some leftover take-out boxes, a smattering of condiments, and a drawer full of aging produce she'd procured last Sunday when she'd decided she was going to get her shit together, at last. Apparently, that hadn't taken hold.

Oh well, she thought, there's always tomorrow. Right now, she just needed to get rid of her damn headache. She skipped the celery, she was out anyway, and carried her cocktail back to her bedroom. Once there, she curled up in her bed with her drink in hand and grabbed the television remote. She had been out when the news aired, but she had her television set to record it in her absence. The sleek hair and pink-painted smile of Haley Roth turned her stomach for a second time that morning. She didn't know why she did this to herself. She never missed a single segment of the Channel 9 News at Six, not one, but they always left her unsettled as a myriad of emotions contended for dominance in her heart and mind: rage and regret, nostalgia and hate, and finally, despair.

She had thrown away her whole career. And on what? A case that couldn't be cracked? A story that the public would never be allowed to hear? How many others, reporters and police officers, butted their heads against this very same wall since the blacklist was put in place? How many other voices were silenced in the name of public good? Once again, her despair would shift back to rage and Cherie's mind would begin to race through the cycle all over again. The alcohol helped with that. It slowed the endless spin of emotions and helped her dismiss her troublesome thoughts in the apathetic haze of booze. Sometimes, however, she got a little carried away and her consumption exceeded her intended effects. *Like last night*, she thought as her eyes drifted away from the screen to the handbag on her floor. She took another drink from her Bloody Mary to strengthen her constitution and stood up. Her head wasn't spinning any longer, but her stomach still felt queasy. Still, she could manage.

Cherie began gathering the displaced items that had fallen out of her bag. No keys, but she did find a note from Erick telling her to call him when she got up and he would drive her back to her car. She crumbled up the note and threw it back on the floor. She would call him later, when she felt like going outside and not a moment before. Maybe she wouldn't even call him today. She might just stay inside a couple of days and let him wonder. He should have given her the keys back once she was in the rideshare. Unless, of course, he didn't wait for her ride to arrive. That asshole. Her drink was almost gone, but the news program still had ten more minutes. Neal Doran's surgically stretched skin was plastered on the screen. He was gearing up to release some tragic news. Cherie could tell by the consternation on his face; the way that unnaturally smooth brow would ripple and his eyes squinted with the suggestion of thought. That was one person Cherie did not miss. More than fifteen years delivering news by his side and Neal Doran couldn't pull her face out of a lineup. Her tits, sure, but not her face.

Cherie rolled her eyes as Neal's "saddened but strong" voice started and she bent over to look under her bed for any additional items that needed to be shoved back into her bag. Suddenly, she heard a name that startled her. Cherie pulled her head out from under the bed where she was reaching for a lipstick that had rolled away and grabbed the remote in a hurry. She hit the rewind button. The familiar face of Nicole Mason-Lambert popped onto the screen beside Neal as he announced the woman had taken her own life. He blathered on about the series of family tragedies that had occurred in the recent months, including a miscarriage and the misfortunes of Southwest Resources. A miscarriage? They weren't just ignoring Nicki's abduction or the kidnapping of her child, but knowingly providing false information to the public.

She wanted to call the producers of the news show, to yell at them and remind them of the principles they'd sworn to uphold as journalists, but she was only one drink into the day. She knew it would do her no good. They would just say she was naïve, if anyone even bothered to pick up. What's more, the station was now complicit in a conspiracy to misinform the public, to hide the truth. There's no way they'd be willing to go against the HSA now and admit to knowingly reporting false information. She was all on her own and no media outlet would touch her. Deciding it was time for a second drink, Cherie grabbed her glass and headed for the kitchen.

20

The doorbell roused Cherie from sleep. She realized she must have dozed off sometime in the afternoon. It was dark outside now, judging from curtains which Cherie now found non-imposing. She turned on her side to look at the clock. Half past seven. The doorbell rang a second time.

"Jesus Christ, I'm coming," Cherie mumbled to no one in particular and forced herself from seated to standing. Who the hell was at her door? She padded out to the living room of her house and opened the front door.

"Of course, it's you," she said as Erick offered her a broad and toothy smile. "Where are my fucking keys?"

In response, Erick dangled her key chain with its BMW logo and then pointed to her driveway.

"I delivered her right to your door," Erick added.

Cherie snatched the keys out of his hand and muttered a "great, thanks," as she started to shut the door, but Erick stopped her.

"What the hell? Can't I at least call a ride?" Now it was Erick's turn to appear irritated, his dark eyes fixed on her.

"Use your cell outside. I'm not feeling very sociable," Cherie answered and started to shut the door again. And, once again, Erick stopped her.

"Hell, I've seen you far less *sociable*," he said, drawing quotations in the air as he exaggerated the word. "Five minutes and I'll be out. Let me just wait for my lift inside."

Cherie relented and stepped aside to allow Erick entrance to her house.

"You certainly don't look like you've seen the inside of your shower today," he said, stepping forward. As he moved past her, he added, "Doesn't smell that way either."

"Erick, if you're just here to give me shit you can wait outside. I will not have my car used as emotional leverage so just fuck off."

"Jesus, you're in an awful mood. You were in a much better mood last night, one that I might have taken advantage of, were I not a better man," Erick said, flopping down into a blue armchair, one of a matching set that flanked her sofa. All three were of a modern design that appealed to her taste once upon a time. Now, she saw them as uncomfortable and crafted from an annoyingly cheerful color palette. All soft blues and bright yellows and white. Very contemporary. Erick, in his brown slacks and creamy shirt, looked askew in her living room.

"Aren't you supposed to be calling a cab or something?" she asked in a sneering tone. She didn't want to let Erick inside in the first place. There was no way he was going to draw this out any longer than it had to be.

"Oh yeah," he answered with a false surprise and whipped out his phone. He selected an app and verified the address. Within minutes he had confirmation that a ride was on its way. Cherie remained standing. She didn't want to make a show of welcoming Erick. She just wanted to be by herself today.

"I assume you heard about Nicki Lambert?"

"You mean, have I heard the lies propagated by the HSA through those marionettes over at Channel 9? Then, yes, I saw the story." Cherie kept her anger in check. If Erick had half a brain, which she usually suspected he did, he could reason out how she might feel about all this. For years, she'd failed to realize how strongly she felt committed to the principles of journalism until those principles were called into question. Audra had even accused her of manufactured rage driven by self-interest rather than a true pursuit of justice. Cherie spent days mired in depression wondering if she was right. But, these days, any time she tied one on, a flurry of indignant rage threatened to rampage through her over the wrongdoings she witnessed. Sometimes she found herself ranting to strangers, or Erick, about the blacklist and the death of the media. No one seemed to care and that only made the fire inside her flare up to greater heights.

"There's nothing that can be done about it. You can

either shake your fist on a soap box or you can accept it and move on," Erick said with some finality. Cherie turned a scrutinizing gaze at the intruder. Is that what he came over for? To impart some sort of life lesson? To try and shake her out of this rut she found herself in?

"Get out," Cherie said, her voice firm to match the icy glare in her eyes.

"Oh, come on, Cherie," he whined. "My ride should be here any minute."

"Then it won't be a big deal to wait on the curb. Get the fuck out." Something in her tone made Erick rise up out of the arm chair and shuffle toward the door without another word.

"You know, you can be a real bitch," Erick imparted before he stepped over the threshold that divided her house from the rest of the world.

"I don't care," she answered as she slammed the door in his face. And she didn't care. She was beyond caring. Cherie locked the door, but rather than returning to her bedroom to resume the nap Erick had interrupted, she made her way to the kitchen to fix herself a drink. It was well past the Bloody Mary hour so she skipped the accoutrements and went straight for the vodka. Rather than calming her nerves, the drink seemed to make her only more restless. Cherie returned to her room and took a shower, switching the water temperature from scalding to bone-chilling and back again. She dried off and ran a comb through her hair, but the anxiety continued to mount. The alcohol was muddling her head, but it wasn't doing anything to numb her emotions. Cherie decided she needed to get out of the house.

She pulled on a pair of jeans, the only ones she owned,

and a flannel button-up one of her indiscretions had left behind after their short-lived tryst. She didn't know his name or phone number, not that she had any intention of reaching out even if such information had been made available to her, so she had no choice but to keep his shirt. Cherie found her gym shoes tucked into the back of the closet. Her personal trainer had been the first expense she'd nixed when finances got stretched a little thin. She figured she could maintain her fitness regime on her own, but within a few weeks, gym time was a thing of the past. Thankfully, her appetite had all but withered away since her termination so she didn't struggle to keep her weight down. She did notice, however, that her arms were losing some of their definition. If she didn't get back on track soon, she knew she was at risk of developing a hefty coating of flab. The same padding her parents claimed, "helped them through the winter months." She would get back to the gym. Maybe even tomorrow, she decided as she finished tying her shoes: enough was enough.

By the time Cherie reached the door her resolve was already weakening. She grabbed her keys and walked out the front door before she could change her mind. The fresh air made her feel lightheaded for a moment. Cherie leaned back against the doorframe to steady herself. After a moment, she felt more grounded and was able to move forward. Driving was a bad idea. She was sober enough still to realize that. She didn't want to go to a bar anyway. She just needed a walk; a chance to clear her head. When was the last time she just went out for a walk? She remembered that restaurateur she briefly dated about ten years ago. He would insist on an evening stroll after a late dinner. At the time, Cherie enjoyed their meandering strolls through the downtown area after a nice meal together, but she gave up those walks when she gave up the man. Sure, both were "nice" but neither was truly capable of holding her attention for very long. She probably hadn't been on a walk since the restaurateur unless you included walking to or from her car, walking around the mall, or walking on a treadmill at the gym while her former trainer increased the incline every three minutes. Never walking for its own sake. But tonight Cherie felt compelled to leave her house and her car to fill her lungs with the warm air of the city. Even if it was just a short walk.

21

Cherie walked past the condos and bungalows of her downtown neighborhood. She walked until her feet became sore and then fell into a comfortable numbness. She wondered if she was having a nervous breakdown as an unaccustomed calm encircled her. Aimlessly, she moved down streets and past strangers she chose not to acknowledge with a smile or even a glance. She kept her eyes fixed on the buildings, noting the variance in architecture that she'd never realized Phoenix contained. From Art Deco to Romanesque, the city had it all. How could she have never noticed all this before? She'd been living in the desert for nearly two decades, but all she could remember was the sandstone suburban sprawl and none of the distinction that filled her vision on this night.

She caught sight of a grand basilica on the opposite

side of the street. The archways and stone staircase looked vaguely familiar. Cherie realized she must have driven past this structure nearly every day on her way to the station. She never noticed the startling height or its outspoken beauty. Suddenly, the image of Nicki Lambert came to her mind. Catholics believed suicide assured a place in Hell, but Cherie hoped they were wrong about all that. She decided to cross the street and light a candle for poor Nicki Lambert in hopes that she somehow found herself someplace better. Cherie didn't wait to reach the stoplight, but cut straight across the street and hoped there wasn't a police officer around to witness her jaywalking. She didn't need any sort of hassle tonight, not while her mind was slowly unfurling its tight workings and the haze of booze was beginning to lift.

She made her way up the steps and, before she entered, Cherie noticed a message board covered in flyers. Maybe she should think about going to a meeting. Her drinking was out of hand and it had been that way for some time. Cherie decided that this might be the moment to admit she had a problem. Maybe she needed some help getting over the collapse of her personal and professional life. She made her way to the cork board and looked at the notices pinned up. A support group for victims of domestic abuse. Another for cancer patients. Narcotics Anonymous, Overeaters Anonymous, and, yes, Alcoholics Anonymous. Cherie's eyes kept drifting and then suddenly the word "Jude" caught her eye.

Cherie took a closer look at the photocopied flyer. It was advertising some sort of support group. Jude, the patron saint of lost causes, was willing to help those facing the seemingly insurmountable. The group met at 9 p.m.

on Thursdays. That was tomorrow, Cherie realized. She looked back at the notice pinned up for AA. That group met on Saturday mornings and Tuesday evenings. Cherie really didn't see herself waking up early to gather in a group setting. Maybe she'd try this Jude group out first and hope they weren't too heavy-handed with the religious stuff at the meeting. And, if it was, she could pretend she was going to use the bathroom and sneak out. No real harm done. Besides, if this was her sign, then God certainly had a sense of humor about things, Cherie thought and not for the first time. Jude, the villain who'd launched her on this downward spiral, was also the name of the group Cherie couldn't believe she was actually considering attending.

A stroll had done her considerable good, she decided, but she had done enough walking. Her feet gave a woeful throb beneath her. Cherie pulled out her phone and ordered a car to pick her up while she walked over to the corner to grab gin and tonic from a liquor store. Tomorrow was Thursday, after all, that meant she had one more night of heavy drinking before she had to set herself on the straight and narrow once again.

22

She looked at the clock on her phone. Twenty to nine. Maybe this was the sign she had been looking for, her way out of the dark cavern she had dug herself into. *Maybe they'll have lemonade and those hard little cookies that come in the tin*, Cherie thought as her stomach grumbled in reminder that she had eaten very little food, actual food, today. She pulled out the flyer ripped off the wall and set off in search of the address.

Cherie found a simple storefront with the windows blacked out and no signage to announce its presence. She looked at the clock on her phone. Ten to nine. The door was propped open with a cinder block and she noticed the circle of folding chairs set up inside. This had to be the place, she thought, checking the address again. A few people filed in around her and then a woman who looked to be in her mid-forties came to the door. She started pushing aside the cinder block with her foot.

"Are you here for the meeting?" she asked Cherie in a friendly voice. "The Saint Jude Group?"

"Yes, I guess I am," Cherie answered, not entirely sure she wanted to be here. Too late now, she decided, and entered the room. She took a few deep breaths to calm herself down and hoped no one would recognize her. There were a few motivational posters on the wall and a temporary table topped with a cheap plastic table cloth. Sure enough, a blue tin of butter cookies lay open for visitors. Cherie was disappointed to discover that instead of lemonade they were offering tiny bottles of water neatly lined up on the table. Nevertheless, she grabbed a bottle of water and two cookies before looking for an open seat.

There were only seven people present, eight including herself, and a dozen chairs arranged in the circle. There was a clock on the wall that looked like it belonged in any grade school classroom: white face and black hands within a chrome frame. The woman who greeted her at the door was the last to take a seat. As soon as she did, she folded her hands primly in her lap and began addressing the group.

"I'm Glenda," she said.

"Like the good witch?" Cherie asked and, when no one laughed or even smiled, she quickly realized this was not the place to be making wisecracks.

"Yes, like the good witch," Glenda answered after a telling pause. She had a short brown bob that stopped at her chin and a slender figure beneath that horrendous Soccer Mom pairing of capri pants and a polo shirt. "I see we have some new faces here tonight. Would you mind introducing yourselves to the group?"

A man sitting across from Cherie looked nervous as Glenda's eyes moved to him. She offered him an encouraging nod.

"Uh, my name is Grayson," he said in a tentative voice.

"Hi Grayson," the group replied in unison. Cherie suppressed a shudder. She'd forgotten how much she disdained group therapy. Her own shrink had recommended it some years ago to help her cultivate a stronger sense of empathy for her fellow humans. Cherie attended twice before deciding it was easier to just get another shrink. Nevertheless, she was here. *It was time to play along*, she thought, as Glenda's hazel eyes shifted to her.

"Hi, my name is Darcy," Cherie said, resisting the urge to cross her arms across her chest as she uttered her little white lie.

"Hi Darcy," the group replied.

"And who would like to get us started this evening?" Glenda asked, her glossy orbs roaming over the faces in the room: some eager, others eager to avoid attention. "Jennifer?"

Jennifer was a tattooed woman with stringy hair wearing a lavender tank top that showed the aging straps of a maroon bra.

"I stayed clean this week even though Tony came by and tried to get me to get high with him," the woman began, her eyes already beginning to swell with water. The group applauded her commitment and then lulled back to a quiet so Jennifer continued, explaining that her issues with addiction stretched back to her preteen years. Cherie struggled to keep her focus on Jennifer as she droned on about abuse that shifted from her father to the string of boyfriends that followed once she ran away from home.

Cherie suppressed an eye roll as tears began streaming down the younger woman's face. She hoped the next story wouldn't prove so riddled with clichés. She was already regretting walking through those doors to take part in this group therapy session. The cookies had been consumed before Glenda even began. Now, she just had to sit here and listen to these people blather on about their miserable lives. Jennifer reached her conclusion and collapsed into a fit of tears while the group applauded her a second time.

"Jennifer, thank you so much for sharing. We know you can continue your sobriety into next week. We're all here rooting for you. And who is your buddy on this?" she asked. Another woman in the circle raised her hand. Glenda smiled and continued, "Wonderful, Evelyn, we appreciate you making yourself available to help Jennifer through the coming weeks."

The group started clapping for a third time and Cherie considered leaving, just getting up and walking out of the room in the middle of their applause. Why did they have to clap for every goddamn thing? Was that somehow helpful in the emotional-healing process? The forced accolades of others? Cherie resolved to stay in her seat a little while longer. After all, she wasn't eager to begin the long trek home.

"Charlie, why don't you go next?" Glenda asked, addressing an older man with thinning hair and tired eyes.

"Lost my job more than two years back now," Charlie began. "My hands became too arthritic for work. Six months later, my insurance lapsed. Osteoarthritis, gets worse every year. Now it's in my spine and my knees. Can't straighten out these hands for nothing either." Charlie lifted his aging hands to show the curled claws his fingers seemed to be locked into.

"They called it early retirement, but that's not what it was. Retirement doesn't come at fifty-six without a pension or Social Security checks. I applied for disability, but it's two years gone by and I'm in my second appeal. Lost the house back in December. That's when the wife left. Went to stay with her sister in Bisbee. Now I hear she's taken up with a guy who owns a bar, some dingy joint that caters to bikers and the weird artists that live down there."

"Is your wife who you're angry with, Charlie?" Glenda asked, her voice echoing compassion.

"No, I guess not," he answered after a pause for deliberation. "I mean, I don't know if I would've stayed if the tables were turned. She's only fifty-three. That's still too young to be saddled with an old man who can't even lift a soup spoon to his mouth. We were never very good at putting away money. When we lost the house, I couldn't expect her to go live on the street with me. She said I could go with her when she went to live with her sister, but I knew neither one of us wanted that. Better to cut my losses than drag her down with me."

"Then who are you angry at?"

"The company, I suppose. I worked there for almost thirty years and they cut me loose the minute my hands stopped working right. I mean, there was probably something else I could've done for them. Worked there long enough, right? Could've been a foreman or maybe picked up a delivery route. I can still drive a vehicle, for now, at least. That way, I might have been able to keep my insurance and make it to the age when my Social Security kicks in. They just didn't care."

Cherie looked to Glenda, expecting her to do some therapist shuffle and turn the tables so that Charlie admitted he was really angry at himself, or maybe his mother or some other shit like that. The group leader surprised her by nodding her head in agreement.

"You have a right to be angry. You gave your life to a company that treated you shamefully. Abandoned you after you gave them years of service. Thank you for sharing, Charlie. I assume you're doing well in your new place?"

"Yes," he said, his eyes shifting slightly with embarrassment. "It was very kind of you folks to help me out with that."

"We're all here to help each other. That's the spirit in which the group was formed. We all bring our unique circumstances together and, together, we can overcome what might seem insurmountable."

The group picked up their applause yet again. When the hush resumed, Glenda spoke, "Darcy, would you care to share your story?"

Cherie jumped when she realized Glenda's eyes were on her and then she remembered the name she had given to the group. She didn't really feel like sharing, but she didn't know how to get out of this.

"Would it be all right if I passed on the first night?" she ventured to ask.

Glenda studied her face for an uncomfortable moment before she answered with a smile, "Of course. There is no pressure here. We'll invite you to share your story the next time we gather. Gina, how about you?" Glenda directed the question to the woman on Cherie's right with bright hazel eyes and her black hair pulled back into a severe bun. Cherie let out a sigh of relief. She didn't need to come up with a story to share with these strangers. Not tonight, anyway, and the likelihood of her return was growing smaller by the minute.

Cherie sat quietly while the remaining people present shared their soul-crushing stories of defeat. They were all defeated; beaten by life and the way the cards they were dealt always seemed to be stacked against them. By the time they were finished, the clock announced it was a quarter after ten. Glenda reminded the group they would be meeting the following Thursday at the same time. And then everyone rose as if it was the natural progression of their unspoken ritual. Cherie held her seat a moment longer so she could request a ride on her phone then she relinquished her seat in favor of another overly dry butter cookie.

Glenda cornered her before she could reach the table where the others had gathered after group. She put her hands on Cherie's upper arms in a gesture she probably considered warm, but Cherie took as imposing.

"I hope we get to see you here next week. It can be very cathartic to share your story with people who don't know you," Glenda said with a cheerful smile. Cherie shrugged off her hands and thanked the woman for allowing her to sit in on the group meeting. She left the room, forsaking that last cookie, deciding instead to wait on the curb for her ride.

Part 3: September

Haley

1

Haley locked the front door of her condo behind her, making sure to switch off the lights before she left. There was no reason to leave the kitchen light on now that Daisy was gone. She sighed, knowing it would be dark inside when she returned. Jonathan wouldn't be here, not tonight. It had only been a couple months since they buried his wife in the ground beside the body of his son. He insisted it was important to "keep up appearances" because "the family couldn't handle another scandal right now," but Haley couldn't help feeling slighted by his lack of attention. Ever since he showed up at her condo in tears, telling her they found his son's corpse then swearing love to no one but her, he had been distant in a way he never was before. Of course, it was that following morning that Jonathan received a call from his mother informing him that Nicki had been found in a bloody bathtub, her wrists slashed and life ended.

Jonathan didn't cry. He only grumbled, "Nicki committed suicide," to the space around her and then began scrambling to gather up his discarded clothing. He padded into the bathroom to take a shower without even a glance at Haley, who sat up suddenly as if a jolt of electricity had just shot through her body. Even now, recalling Jonathan's indifference as he told her the news caused an involuntary shiver to run through her. Maybe she had made a mistake letting him back inside that night, but she couldn't ignore his pleas through her door. When he told her about his son, she unlocked the door and folded him in her arms. She wasn't heartless. She couldn't ignore him, pretend she wasn't home or callously disregard the hurt he was feeling, but now that she was drawn back in, she wondered what she might have done differently.

Since their reconciliation, Jonathan had passed a total of twelve nights in her home. And he was always gone before the sun with promises that it wouldn't be like this much longer. The attention would die down and life could go back to normal. He didn't say "better than before" because that would be cruel. He had loved Nicki in his own way, enough to marry her, even if that love quickly faded in the wake of tragedy. He still needed to grieve for her. Haley could understand that. But then afterward, with Nicki gone, she was the only woman left in Jonathan's life. At least, she hoped she was. Soon he would be able to sleep over every night without worrying what the divorce attorneys might make of such behavior. And, after a prudent waiting period, they could be wed without hassle.

Haley flushed with shame realizing that she was reveling in another woman's death. That was wrong. Poor Nicki Lambert had a rough go of it; Haley thought back to all those months ago when she found her bleeding on the side of the road. Little did she know what sort of lasting impression that moment would have on the whole of her life. She didn't want Nicki to die. Hell, she *saved* her life and she would have done it again, even after her involvement with Jonathan. It wasn't her fault Nicki *wanted* to die. The loss of her child proved too much for her to bear. Haley could almost respect her for deciding to check out rather than continue through years of torment and the personal downfall that would surely accompany them.

By the time Haley pulled into the station's parking lot, she decided to push all thoughts of Nicki from her head. The woman had made her own choices. And, once again, Jonathan was left to deal with the media turmoil of his family's misdeeds. A new sprig of pity unfurled in her heart. Haley let it take root. She was being too hard on Jonathan. Of course, he *wanted* to be with her every night. He just couldn't be, not right now anyway. *I just have to be patient and all will play out in due time*, Haley thought as she marched through the building toward her office, pausing at Audra's desk to greet her assistant.

Haley was tremendously grateful that her relationship with her personal assistant seemed to turn a corner with Daisy's disappearance. She noted the iced green tea latte sitting on the edge of Audra's desk.

"Is this for me?" Haley asked with a smile.

"Of course," Audra answered in a cheery voice. "You're the only one here, besides me, who prefers tea to coffee."

"Better for the skin," Haley knowingly imparted. Audra might only be a year or two younger, but she hadn't a clue when it came to self-presentation or preservation.

"And it's very British," Audra added, giving her head one curt nod.

"Well, matcha is actually Asian. And you know how those people just don't age," Haley corrected her.

"And that's my daily serving of racism before noon. Thanks, Haley," Audra said. She followed it with a broad smile and Haley assumed she was just teasing her. Audra liked to tease her, to draw attention to her little missteps with language. Of course, she hadn't *meant* anything racist by what she said. Audra was just pointing out how it might sound to *others*. That could be helpful, especially when you had to maintain a public image. She didn't want a Paula Dean moment playing out on television.

Her private office was her sanctuary at the station. Haley decorated the walls with mementos that stretched all the way back to high school team sports. She thought she had arranged her knickknacks tastefully so as not to overwhelm the viewer. She had only been in here twice when it was Cherie's office. The space had seemed cold and impersonal, but professional then. Now she felt the office had a comradely air that Haley hoped didn't seem childish to others.

The thought caused an image of Jonathan's mother to surface in her mind. Well, at least, the image her mind had fabricated for the woman she had yet to meet; a woman her son described as tasteful and reserved. Jonathan had only told her a couple of stories about his mother, Patricia, but the woman sounded daunting. Nicki's emotional collapse caused his mother endless embarrassment which she would continually bring up around Jonathan, not that he could have done anything to prevent his wife's deterioration. Patricia would not approve of a new wife who posed the threat of ongoing public humiliation. Haley reminded herself she had a solid middle-class upbringing, maybe even upper middle-class. She had vacationed in Europe. Well, only once when her parents offered to foot the bill for a school-sponsored trip before she started college. Nevertheless, she had been *abroad*. She had a degree and a job that should impress any future in-laws. Haley made her way into her office while her mind started to wonder just how long Jonathan would wait to introduce her to his family. Surely Christmas was too soon, wasn't it? Six more months might seem more appropriate.

She let out a sigh as she sat down at her desk. Even if they had to wait a few years, she would still be getting married in her twenties. That was all that really mattered. Her only sister would be turning thirty-two next year and not a single proposal on the horizon. Haley could tell their mother was disappointed every time she brought up the subject of her sister and her perpetual lack of suitable boyfriend. And she ate carbs regularly. Haley was definitely the favored child of their mother, but their father was more partial to his bookish older daughter who shared his love of canned cheese and craft beer. She seemed to have a never-ending string of boyfriends in screen-printed t-shirts and yet she expressed no interest in settling down with any one of them, much to their mother's dismay.

Jonathan was a prize by comparison to any of those commonplace idiots her sister had paraded around family dinners. Or, at least, he would be as soon as she could bring him home to meet her family. Haley pulled up her itinerary on her computer and saw that she had an editing session scheduled this afternoon. How boring. She couldn't believe her producer insisted she learn how to edit her own segments from start to finish. There were people here who did that for Cherie. Haley didn't know if the station was planning on cutting some corners down the road, but she hated having to sit in while Doug and Renée ran through the footage gathered by the field reporters who, by the way, all hated her for overstepping them by landing Cherie Rodger's spot next to Neal Doran on the 6 o'clock news.

At least Doug and Renée didn't care about her sudden upward mobility. They seemed to hate everyone that appeared on the news equally. They called them "The Faces," as in "The Faces are going to need more screen time so cut away from the accident here." On top of that, Renée smelled like cat litter and cheap candles while Doug, if encountered in a bar setting, would be immediately dismissed as a creeper. Not how she cared to spend the afternoon, but if the boss wanted her to prove she was up to snuff in all areas, she could hardly complain. Before heading over to the editing room, Haley jotted off a quick text message to Jonathan just to let him know that she was thinking about him.

And she was thinking about him. All through the editing session and during her long, lonely lunch break, her mind was occupied with Jonathan and the mixed emotions surrounding him. By the time Audra told her she was needed in make-up, Haley was very aware that she had not yet received a reply from him. She checked her phone again just to make sure she hadn't somehow missed the chimes that alerted her to his messages. Haley considered sending him another text, but decided against it. This wasn't the right time to seem needy. Jonathan would be relying on her to be strong. Another desperate woman was the last thing he needed.

But the anxiety had already wormed its way in. Why hadn't he replied? One word would have sufficed. Especially the word, "Busy," which is what he usually sent her when work kept him from acknowledging her for extended periods of time. Sometimes, he would just send a little "xo" or something equally adorable.

By the time Haley arrived at make-up, Neal Doran was

already leaving. He gave her a wink as he passed her. That was the second time someone had winked at her today. Haley was beginning to feel like the whole station, or maybe even the whole world, was in on some secret she didn't know about, but everyone was assuming she did. She pushed the thought aside as she entered the room. Jayci was dressed in hyacinth purple from head to toe, a shocking contrast from her artificially red curls. Was it the anniversary of Prince's death already? No, that came in May when Jayci would put on this same getup and blast his greatest hits from her cell phone's wireless speaker bar.

"Perfectly on time! Sometimes, the day goes just right, like clockwork," Jayci called out in a melodious, if overly loud, voice. She was obviously in a good mood. "Come on in, girl, sit down."

Haley gave her a half-hearted smile and took a seat between Jayci and the wall of mirrors and lights. She quickly got to work: outlining Haley's eyes, coating her lashes in mascara and then separating them one by one before adding a second coat, contouring and powdering, and, finally, painting her mouth a burnished red. When Jayci stepped back to evaluate her work, Haley looked into the mirror and saw her reflection. She always looked older once Jayci completed her makeup for the cameras, but tonight she seemed ancient. Her eyes looked tired and her cheeks no longer had that fleshly look of youth. Maybe it was just her bad mood that was making her stare at her own face with such an overly critical eye, or maybe she was just now realizing that, whether or not she had aged, she would age. Her body would deteriorate quickly and, with it, her looks would go. She would be like Cherie

Rodgers, pleading for her job in the parking lot of the station. If she didn't marry, that is. *Marry soon and marry well.* And, with that thought, her mind went back to Jonathan.

"What's wrong today, Ms. Lovely? Some pretty thing got you down again?"

"Maybe," Haley answered with a juvenile shrug of her shoulders. She felt like a child and now it was spilling over into her mannerisms. She tried to buck up but only succeeded in jutting out her chin to an unnatural position.

"Don't think I wouldn't rather praise the very tall blond boy who ate all of my potato chips at the Red Lizard. It's just that I won't see him when I open my eyes. And I will see the sun," Jayci recited with a faraway look in her eyes.

Haley just stared blankly at her in response as her mind tried to lock away the words for later dissemination.

"It's poetry. Jack Spicer. I say it to myself every time one leaves me hanging," Jayci added in the silence left by Haley. "MFA, creative writing. Would you believe how much more I get paid to do this shit? Way more than I ever made as an adjunct. A whole different life. Can you imagine me in a suit and tie? Professor Wilson? It's all more like a nightmare than a memory. That's enough now. Get out of here, Ms. Broadcast," Jayci said smiling before she gave a nod of her head to indicate it was time for Haley to vacate her chair.

2

Haley unlocked the door to her condo as another wave of loneliness washed over her. Her two closest friends from college had wed the year following graduation so they rarely found time to spend a night out on the town with the girls anymore. Furthermore, no one from the station had extended an invitation to her for drinks after work since she'd moved from intern to weather girl. And now she had a boyfriend that she rarely saw. Haley sighed in the full knowledge that she was a social creature spending far too much time on her own. Maybe it was time to start thinking about another cat. There was little chance of Daisy returning to her now. Either she had found a new home or she was on her first grand adventure in the world. Or she was dead. Haley doubted she would discover the truth.

She pushed open her front door and noted that a light was on in the living room. An overwhelming rush of relief spread throughout her chest and limbs. Jonathan was here. Maybe he felt bad about not texting her back earlier and decided to come by for a visit. And, maybe, he would be able to stay over the entire night, now that he didn't have to rush off for Nicki. That familiar tinge of guilt arose, but Haley ignored it. She decided to be in a good mood. After all, it had been almost a week since Jonathan's last visit. Haley dropped her keys and bag on the kitchen counter and hurried into the living room where Jonathan was seated with a beer going over some files spread out on her coffee table.

"Busy day?" she asked, announcing her arrival. She

felt a sudden chill, moving from the blustery heat outside into the climate-controlled condo.

"Just awful," Jonathan admitted, turning around to offer Haley a wry and weary smile. "How about you?"

"Better now," Haley answered, trying to lighten the mood. She turned on her camera-ready smile for Jonathan's sole benefit and plopped down on the couch next to him. "Bringing your work home with you?"

"I just had some last-minute things I wanted to go over. I wasn't sure what time you'd get here," Jonathan explained, collecting the papers into files and then gathering the files until the table was tidy once again. "But it can wait. I'm really here to see you."

Jonathan's smile spread as he opened his arms to invite her to move closer to him. Haley thought there was something odd about his expression. Not his smile which was warm and familiar, but his eyes. Something seemed different about them. Haley nuzzled against his chest, trying to ignore the irksome idea, to pass it off as the utter nonsense she knew it was, but she couldn't. She leaned in to kiss him and then pulled back, leaving her hand on the side of his face so she could look into his eyes a moment longer. She saw the same unnaturally bright blue and inky irises looking back. Same shape, same size, but something seemed different: altered or absent. Now she was just being ridiculous. She leaned in to kiss him again. *See?* she told herself. *Same Jonathan.* Haley dismissed her concerns as frivolous as she stood up and led him to her bedroom.

The shifting pressure of the mattress woke Haley from her dozing rest. She lay on her side, facing away from

Jonathan. The glowing hands on her analog clock that sat atop her night stand told her it was a few minutes shy of midnight.

"Leaving so soon?" she asked in a syrupy voice. Haley rolled onto her back so she could make out the shape of Jonathan painted blue and black with night.

"No, I'm staying. Just thought I'd look over those files. They need my answer by morning." Jonathan's voice was temporarily muffled as he pulled his t-shirt over his head.

"Anything I can help with?" she asked.

"No, you need your beauty rest or you might turn into Barbara Walters," Jonathan joked and then laughed at his own quip.

"If only it was that easy," Haley moaned and turned on her side once again. Jonathan was staying. He would be here in the morning, right beside her in bed. He was just going to finish up some work. As the head of a major corporation, long hours had to be expected every now and again. Haley hoped he would still have time for summer vacations and weekend mini-holidays. Work hard, play hard. That was the way it was supposed to happen, right? Still, when Jonathan spoke of his father, he often mentioned that they didn't have much time together when Jonathan was a child. Always working, he said. Haley started to worry that Jonathan was already working too hard. Here he was, in the post-coital bliss of new love, and he decided to leave her alone in bed so he can burn the midnight oil. Just like that, her good mood plummeted.

She lay awake for two hours hoping that Jonathan would come back to bed. Finally, she fell asleep. When her alarm clock shocked her into consciousness the following morning, she couldn't help but notice that Jonathan wasn't beside her. There wasn't even a note telling her he had to rush off early. She shuffled into the living room to see if he had perhaps fallen asleep in there, but no, there was no sign of Jonathan. She checked the front door. At least he'd remembered to lock it this time when he stole away in the middle of the night.

Haley went back to her bedroom to retrieve her phone. She wanted to send Jonathan a message, but she couldn't decide whether to sound irritated or understanding. She weighed her options, but at that moment, she wasn't sure of herself. Yesterday, she reported news to the public she knew to be false. It was one thing to skip past the gory details last time when she first interviewed Jonathan all those months ago and the investigation was just getting underway. They didn't know what they were dealing with back then and she wasn't asked to lie that time, just to glaze over the kidnapping and focus on the story at hand: the water crisis in Harrison. This time it was a lie. She told herself it was a small one, but that felt like another lie.

She sat down on the edge of her bed with her phone in hand. More than her education in journalism, she just felt that lying was wrong and now she had to smile as she told those lies to millions of people. What was her alternative? To follow Cherie Rodgers and act like a crazy person? To set fire to her career before it even took off? To quit and let another pretty face take her place? Haley knew there were dozens of others who gladly would. She looked down at her phone.

The same could be said for Jonathan. Did she want these things, this man and this career, because other people wanted them? Because she was told she should want them? Because they were lucrative and came attached to money and power? Or did she really want them? More than that, what was the alternative? Haley picked up her phone and sent a message to Jonathan wishing him a good day and expressing her hope that she would see him again in the evening. Another lie. Before the year was up, she wondered if she would even notice them anymore.

Audra

3

Audra had avoided visiting Renn for more than a month. She spent that time at home, half-hoping that Marv might show up and beg to explain his absence, half-wondering if she would try to stab him if he did. She knew she saw him on that platform. She knew his face better than she knew her own. And, what's more, he saw her. How could he leave her hanging like this without any sort of explanation? It was downright cruel after the years they'd spent together. Audra felt like Marv was the only family she'd ever really had and he'd abandoned her.

True, her father gave her this house, one of a multitude of properties he owned around the Valley, but it was really more of an apology than a gift. He'd decided not to stick around once her mother started slipping, but he also didn't think to take his children along with him. Instead, he left them in the care of an unstable zealot. At sixteen, Audra emancipated herself and moved into a shithole apartment she could afford on a coffee shop gig. Marv moved in shortly after she turned eighteen. Once her dad discovered where she was living, he signed over the tiny bungalow she now called home. After that, she only saw her mother once or twice a year. Her father only expected an annual appearance at his Christmas Eve family dinner where Marv and Audra sat awkwardly opposite his two young children, the product of his second, and far more successful, marriage. Marv had been Audra's only real family and he just vanished without a word.

At first, she didn't know if Marv was seeking her out in order to reconnect. Maybe he found out what Jude was doing with the kidnapped children and wanted out. Maybe he came looking for her and found her with Renn and changed his mind. Maybe he was in Phoenix with Jude for Vanessa Kaine and just wanted to look at her once before he left again. Or maybe she and Renn were on Jude's watch list because they refused to drop the case, but Marv confirmed they had nothing to go on. The only thing that wasn't a maybe was that there were too many possibilities for Audra to know for sure and Marv didn't leave her any answers.

Her sorrow turned to anger and then back to sorrow again. Audra retreated into her own space as her mind roiled. Finally, she decided she had to find Marv; to tell him what he did to her, to say to his face that she hated him now and was glad he was gone. While she had been down at the station, he must have uncovered something in his research that led him to Jude. Audra had spent months after his disappearance hoping to uncover a bread trail to him through his computer, but she came up with zilch. No, Marv definitely hadn't left her clues that would aid her unveiling his discovery. She realized she would have to find it on her own. She went back to the message boards they had found during that week back in February which already seemed so long ago. New names, new messages, but there had to be something more, something hidden. Finally, when her frustration got the better of her, she hopped on her Vespa, now a lemony yellow color, and headed toward the Melrose Curve.

She used her key to open the door, hoping that she would find Richard Renn alone. After the weeks that had passed, she wondered if she should knock first, but decided against it. She found Renn exactly where she'd left him: seated at his computer in an undershirt with a holstered gun at his side. He looked up at her briefly without saying a word before offering her a stiff smile. Audra expected a "Nice to see you," or maybe a "Where have you been?" but neither escaped his lips. She set about making a cup of tea in silence. Renn was a difficult man to understand. Was he happy to see her or disappointed? Did he even notice her absence in the first place? Once she poured the hot water over her tea bag and left the mug to steep, she walked over to Renn.

"Miss me?" she asked, feeling like she was violating some unspoken oath by asking Renn anything pertaining to his emotions, especially in relation to her.

"Certainly," he answered, looking away from the computer screen to fix his eyes on her. His gaze became acute as he stared, scrutinizing her features for signs of the internal workings of her mind. She had seen him do this before, analyzing her body language and expression, reminding her that he was a behavioral analyst for the FBI not that long ago. Sometimes, she wondered how he'd managed to land that spot. Renn was smart, sure. She would even go so far as to say exceptionally intelligent, but he seemed a little out of touch when it came to understanding people.

"You didn't even give me a ring to make sure I was okay," Audra pointed out, surprising even herself. She knew their relationship wasn't some grand love affair. What did it matter if he didn't call to check on her when she didn't come by if she'd decided to lay low for a while? She was angry at a different man. She didn't need to entrap this one with some twisted game of emotional roulette.

"I didn't ring, but I made sure you were okay," Renn said, continuing to face her.

"What does that mean?" Audra asked suspiciously.

"I just went by your place a few times to check on you," Renn answered. "I wanted to make certain you weren't coming by of your own volition."

Audra's unruly laugh burst out of her. She smiled at Renn and said, "Coming from anyone else, that would be supremely creepy, but from you, it's almost romantic." She leaned forward and kissed him on the temple. When she rose up again, she noticed that his eyes were still locked on her. Audra smiled a second time and leaned down again, this time to kiss him on the mouth.

They didn't bother with the bedroom, but screwed on the dingy carpet next to his computer desk surrounded by seven months of useless research. It was so much different with Renn, but then again, Marv was her only basis for comparison. The disparity surfaced in her mind as she lay naked, except for her shoes, beside Renn, trying to catch her breath. She didn't force Marv from her mind. She allowed the memories to linger. They were helping to solidify her rage, allowing her to strengthen her focus on the mission at hand.

When she felt ready to move, she stood up and made her way to the narrow shower in Renn's bathroom. Once inside, she wouldn't be able to raise her elbows high enough to work her shampoo up to a decent lather, but it served its function nonetheless. She hadn't thought to bring along pajamas. Usually, she just slept in the slip she had been wearing under her dress that day, but the hot summertime weather had forced her to abbreviate her litany of underclothes. Audra grabbed one of the undershirts Renn had lying around his unkempt bedroom. She looked at the spartan features of the room: the unmade mattress on the floor that was his bed, the two plastic laundry baskets, six button-up shirts beside three sports coats and an equal number of pants on wire hangers in his closet. Audra didn't even realize that you could still buy wire hangers in the 21st Century.

Renn was back to his computer desk by the time Audra emerged fresh from the shower and wearing one of his shirts. He, of course, said nothing of her clothing choices, but asked if she was hungry.

"Starving," she admitted even though she knew it was an exaggeration.

"Folks these days still like pizza?" he joked. They had shared dozens of order-in pizzas over the past months.

"As long as there's pineapple on it." Audra's favorite pizza came topped with extra cheese and pineapple. Initially, Renn had turned up his nose at the suggestion, but once he'd tasted it, he seemed to come around on the subject.

"One pineapple pizza, coming up," he said. Either Renn was happy at her sudden return or something else had put him in a good mood. Audra chose not to question it. He was such a lugubrious sort, similar to Marv in that way, but he could be charming at times too.

4

"Don't you have to get to the station?" Renn asked the following morning as he prepared to head down to the office he shared with Gerry. He was pouring his coffee into a portable mug while Audra dunked a teabag into her own cup beside him.

"I called out. I had a few things I wanted to look into. Maybe a fresh take on Jude that's worth exploring. You don't mind me sticking around, do you? Maybe running some leads on the computer?" she asked tentatively. Renn had given her a key, sure, and sometimes she got home in the evening before he did, but she never just stuck around his place during the day while he was working. Audra realized she might have been a little presumptuous in assuming Renn wouldn't mind while he stood silently thinking for a moment.

"Well, someone should be here to take care of all that cold pizza in the fridge," he said finally and offered another uneven smile. "If you need me to bring anything home, just text me. I shouldn't be gone all night."

"Thanks, Renn," she said, and offered him a quick peck before he darted out the door. He was meeting with a new client this morning. She could tell by his tie. In all their time together, she never once called him Richard, even though she knew that was his name. He'd introduced himself as "Renn" and the name just stuck. Audra waited until she heard his car start before turning on her laptop. She considered telling him about her plan, but decided against it. Renn might try to talk her out of it.

Ever since she saw Marv at the Lightrail stop, her mind

worked furiously to uncover just how he had gotten in touch with Jude's organization. She wondered if, in his frustration at encountering the same dead-ends she had run up against, Marv had opted for a brute force attack to gain access to the message board's file transfer protocol. In doing so, he might have tipped off Jude's organization through his coarse means of hacking into their administrative accounts. Usually, Marv was much too cautious to implement such a sloppy method of breaking through a password, but maybe this time he wanted to be found out, just as Audra did. She'd built her own brute force program a couple years ago with Marv as part of a project they'd undertaken at SagaCity, a DIY hackerspace that they were a part of until Marv had a falling out with another member of the group and trashed his CPU. After the "incident" Marv was promptly ostracized by the group and Audra right along with him.

She couldn't blame them. Marv had a temper that landed him into all sorts of trouble over the years. That's exactly why she thought he might have been so brash as to use the program to break through the administrative login for the message board. It might take a couple of days, but she knew the brute force program would work. Of course, the program functioned just like its name suggested. It would submit hundreds of password variations in a matter of seconds using the dictionary as its source material. Audra had constructed her own program to cross-reference with the Bible as well. She'd originally intended to use the program to troll church websites, but after their departure from the group, she'd dismissed the joke as childish and didn't put the program into use.

A brute force attack on a website would alert any halfway decent webmaster to the failed login attempts. If their tech guys knew what they were doing, they would be able to trace the source of the attack to her if she wasn't hiding her location. And, if Marv was a part of Jude's IT support, he would definitely know where the attack was coming from. She opened the program and started its execution, drawing in a long, deep breath as she watched the rotating series of characters flash by faster than her eyes processed the information.

"Is this how you did it?" she asked the absentee Marv. "Is this how you led them to you?"

Audra wondered how long it would take for them to come for her, if it was even going to work at all. She decided to get up and take another shower, leaving the computer to work its magic while she readied herself for whatever was coming next. She had brought along a black t-shirt and black capri pants, the only dark clothes she owned aside from a dress she had worn to her grandfather's funeral. She wasn't quite sure why she felt she needed to tone down the color scheme today, but she went with her gut. Maybe Jude's organization would take her more seriously if she wasn't wearing a motley of attention-seeking hues today. After she was dressed, she helped herself to the leftover pizza in Renn's bare fridge and sat down to wait.

By sunset, however, she was frustrated and out of pizza. Renn had sent her a text to say that the new client wanted him to start right away and not to expect him home until early morning, if he returned at all. She decided to go for a ride, maybe procure some additional food for dinner. Audra grabbed the yellow helmet she'd left sitting on the kitchen counter. She'd bought the helmet to match the new paint job on her scooter, formerly Marv's scooter. With her keys and her backpack, Audra left Renn's place, making sure to lock the door on her way out, and hopped on her Vespa. She had grown quite attached to her new ride.

Audra decided a meal out might help her clear her head. Besides, Renn wouldn't be home for hours yet. If anyone came looking for her in her absence, they would just have to wait for her to return. Audra drove to a small diner that was popular with the local hipster crowd, which she found annoying, but they served a watermelon salad that had been on her mind all day. After consistently eating nothing but pizza for twenty-four hours, her body craved food that hadn't been mutated so drastically from its original form. She ordered at an outdoor window and took a seat on the picnic benches that provided outside seating to the diner's patrons. Audra didn't mind sitting outside, not tonight, even in the sweltering summer air. The diner provided misters that staved off some of the heat and the dwindling sunset was a sight to behold. She had lived her entire life within the Sonoran Desert, but the spectacle in the sky during its transition from day to night and then back again in the morning always managed to stop her breath. You never knew what you would see: pastel watercolors, acid visions, or chemical fires.

Cherie

5

Cherie never expected to return to the support group after that first meeting, but the following Thursday she found herself perched on those same metal folding chairs while Glenda welcomed the newcomers. The newcomers no longer included Cherie, whom the group still called Darcy, so she was expected to share when Glenda called on her. Cherie explained that she had lost her job when she was asked to compromise her morals and refused. She said little more. Cherie preferred to listen to the stories the other people in the group would share. The childhood abuse, the alienation and subjugation encountered in adulthood, the sense that each struggle was ultimately futile. Every story shared similar themes, but the plot points varied. For an hour or two, depending on the number of participants that evening, Cherie's own troubles obscured her sight as she sat entranced by the suffering of those around her. She felt a part of the whole miserable existence of humans, past and present.

At moments, she secretly worried she'd be found out. That Glenda would detect the slightest hint of joy Cherie took from their collectively expressed sorrows. With each passing Thursday, she began to enjoy the group setting a little more until, eventually, her concerns that she would be asked to stop coming led her to avoid Glenda like the plague after each meeting. If their group leader was gathering chairs, Cherie was helping herself to stale butter cookies. If Glenda made her way over to the snack table for a bottle of water, Cherie beelined for the door. After the third week, Glenda managed to corner her when Jennifer, their resident junkie, stopped Cherie to ask her for a ride home. Cherie sputtered out some excuse as to why she couldn't drive Jennifer home, or anywhere for that matter, when Glenda came up and snagged her by the elbow.

"Jennifer, I can drive you to the Lightrail station after I close up here," Glenda offered as she steered Cherie away from the others. Once they were out of earshot, she continued speaking, but in softer tones, "Now, *Darcy*, I know who you really are. I just want you to know that I completely understand why you won't share your real name with the group. A famous person like yourself has the right to a little anonymity every now and again, but I wanted to tell you that the group is a safe space to tell your story. I know you've been hesitant to share for some time now, but I really encourage you to open up. Talking about your struggle is the first step in healing."

"Can we skip to the second step?" Cherie had asked, half joking. Glenda didn't answer, only smiled at her and offered Cherie a patronizing squeeze on her arm before walking away to rejoin the others. Cherie was relieved she hadn't been asked to stop attending the group, but she wasn't entirely comfortable with this Glenda woman recognizing her. Then again, she had to expect as much in the city of Phoenix where her face had been on the nightly news for nearly two decades. Maybe she should be more surprised that the *other* people in the group hadn't recognized her. Still, most of these people seemed like they crawled out from under a rock for the weekly support group. She didn't expect many of them kept up with current events. But, her face had been plastered on billboards until recent months. Surely someone else here recognized her if Glenda was able to draw the connection.

Rather than increasing her paranoia, the idea calmed her somewhat. She wasn't one of these faceless nobodies that showed up to group week after week. During the following session, Cherie began to share additional details from her tale of woe, the one wherein she, the intrepid reporter, was coldly sliced out of the media when she tried to break a story that the people in power didn't want others to hear. She never mentioned Jude or the kidnappings, but she did identify the HSA as the culprit who blacklisted her story and cost Cherie her career. Glenda was right. Revealing her story to the group had a way of relinquishing some of the tight hold it had on her. The tension in her shoulders let up ever so slightly and Cherie was tempted to cry with relief, but she managed to maintain her composure, a skill she acquired during her years delivering the news with the same placid expression, no matter what was going on in her personal life or how deeply the story affected her.

Tonight, all she wanted was to release a few piddly details of her own descent from glory before sinking into the sea of sorrows belonging to those around her. She wanted that familiar sensation of rising up out of the water purified despite the degradation all around her. But, as Glenda readied to close down the group with announcements and reminders for the coming week, Cherie's peace of mind was shattered by a late arrival. At first, she couldn't place him. The stranger looked very familiar but noticeably different, like someone she hadn't seen since high school. Then he spoke, "Hope I'm not interrupting."

His voice, Marv's voice, came out of this ordinary-looking man in khaki pants with sandy brown hair. Cherie's eyes flew up to meet his, the same wintery gaze she remembered. He was looking straight at her. Cherie felt a trickle of ice down her spine and she considered bolting from the room, but she didn't. She held her seat and waited.

"Don't worry, Chad, we're just about done here," Glenda chirped. *Chad?!* Cherie wondered just how far Marv had wandered from the goth version of himself she had briefly known seven months ago. "Don't forget, folks. Same time, same place next Thursday. Have a good night and a safe week."

There was some scattered applause as the group broke for the evening. Cherie considered hurrying out the door without a word of acknowledgement for the man who'd disappeared all those months back, leaving poor Audra distraught and Cherie's investigation at a standstill. She also considered smacking him across the face for the trouble he'd caused both of them. But, instead, she rose and stood by her seat, waiting for him to approach her. She didn't have to wait long. Marv made his way straight to her.

"Hey Cherie, long time," he said. His voice was heavy with some unexpressed emotion. Was it guilt? Or perhaps regret?

"Long time, Marv—I mean, Chad."

"Yeah, about that. I think we should go someplace and talk."

Cherie felt a swell of apprehension. Wandering off

with Marv to some unknown location hardly seemed like a wise idea. After all, the man had practically fallen off the face of the planet seven months ago without a word to her or even Audra, his girlfriend, to let them know he was alive.

Marv, as if sensing her hesitation, continued in the silent void left by Cherie, "You know you want to know the truth. What could be more important?"

He was right. Even if it meant her life, she needed to know: about Jude, about his organization and its secret workings. She wanted to know about the children they stole and the endgame they had in mind. Even if she was risking her life, she knew it was a risk she was willing to take.

6

Cherie expected a blindfold or maybe the narrow confines of an automobile trunk. What she didn't expect was for Marv to offer to lock up as Glenda grabbed her purse and keys and led Jennifer away with the promise of a ride back home. Once the last of the group's stragglers made their way out into the city night, Marv locked the front door and cleared away the remaining cookies and the tiny bottles of water. Cherie grew impatient.

"So, Marv, where you been these past months?" she prodded. "I must admit I'm a little surprised to find you back in Phoenix."

"Just got back in August. Work kept me away. You know how it is," he answered, maintaining a casual lilt in his voice.

"I really don't, actually. You left someone behind that was awfully heartbroken," she continued. She didn't want to say Audra's name, not to Marv, who had so carelessly tossed her aside. Cherie didn't consider herself to be a person of excessive sentiment, but Audra's abandonment had gotten to her a little. Of the few things she knew about her former assistant, Cherie knew she had a difficult family situation so she felt this man was her only ally in this world. Marv, at least, had the decency to look ashamed. He didn't say anything else so Cherie left him to wallow in his thoughts as he finished tidying up the room. Finally, he was ready to leave. Cherie started toward the front door.

"This way," Marv said, motioning to the backdoor of the room that, until that moment, Cherie had barely noted.

"Where does this lead?" she asked, tentatively.

"To the heart of it all," Marv said with a smile as he pushed the back door open. Cherie saw a darkened corridor on the other side of the doorframe. It certainly didn't look like the heart of anything. It looked dusty from disuse with boxes piled up along the narrow hallway. But, she'd already decided she was going to see this through to the end.

"Lead the way."

Marv led her along the hallway, past lifeless doors and cobwebs until they came to a closed door rimmed in a faintly glowing light that seeped through the frame. He knocked concisely three times on the door and then waited. The door opened to reveal a young man standing in a sparse rectangle of a room. A square table sat at the center and a small desk occupied one corner with a computer taking up the entirety of its surface area. Cherie's eyes scanned the space before coming to rest upon the stranger. He had short hair bleached blond and a burgundy shirt with the sleeves cut off at the shoulder. The cargo shorts and sockless sneakers completed the look Cherie would expect to find on any state school undergraduate were it not for the gun clenched in his right hand. Cherie's eyes froze on the gun and, before she knew it, it rose in her direction.

"Cherie Rodgers, I presume?" the young man asked. Cherie didn't answer. She remained frozen where she stood until the man with the gun flicked the weapon with his wrist to indicate he wanted her to move closer. Cherie hesitated again, but she remembered the long, dark corridor completely devoid of any sign of life. Marv was still behind her and nudged her forward. She couldn't outrun these two men and she was pretty certain no one was around to hear her scream. She had no choice but to play along and hope that they wanted something from her other than her life.

She nodded at long last and stepped over the threshold into the small, unadorned room. There weren't any windows to the outside world or additional doors besides the one she'd just used to enter. The blond pointed to a chair and Cherie sat down without question. He handed Marv two sets of handcuffs which Marv then used to attach Cherie's hands to the side of her chair.

"Is all of this really necessary? It's not like I'm going to run off with two of you keeping watch over me," she argued.

"We might need to step out for a minute. Or Jude might want to speak to you all alone. Can't really say," the bleach blond said.

"And what's your name?" Cherie felt brave enough to ask. The younger man exchanged looks with Marv which told Cherie he was ready to hand over a lie.

"Mikey," he answered.

"Is that his real name, *Chad*?" Cherie asked in a snide tone. Marv barely had twenty-five years to call his own and this "Mikey" looked to be even younger. Cherie was on the verge of bitter disappointment. Of all the theories she'd postulated in recent months, she never expected Jude's organization would be managed by young miscreants. She began to worry that this criminal conspiracy was no more than a big hoax. True, they might have kidnapped children, but "Mikey" and "Chad" didn't look like they could lead a pack of mice with promises of cheese. They certainly didn't seem capable of igniting a revolution.

"Just shut up, *Darcy*," the one called Mikey growled at her. "We all need a little secrecy once in a while."

"What's really going on here?" Cherie asked impatiently. She didn't think these men were going to kill her. If that was the goal, they could have already done it. They wanted her to know something. Now she just wanted them to get to the point. Her arms were hanging awkwardly at her side and her wrists smarted from the metal handcuffs binding them. Neither of the men seemed inclined to answer her questions, but she persisted, "Well, what do we do now?"

Marv was the first one to speak up, "Now, we wait."

Without another word, the two younger men left Cherie alone in the room and locked the door behind them.

"Lot a good locking that door with my hands cuffed to this chair!" she called out after them, but if they heard her, they gave no indication.

Renn

1

The stakeout wasn't going as planned. Renn had been hired by a woman to spy on her husband whom she believed was indulging in extramarital affairs when she was out of town and, as a travel writer, her job kept her out of the Phoenix area rather often. Gerry had handed off the case to Renn because he was busy working three separate jobs this week and didn't have the time to complete the assignment himself. He'd considered passing on the assignment as well and, now with Audra's sudden reappearance, he wished he did. After four hours waiting outside the guy's office, digging up what he could from his tablet, Renn decided to toss in the towel early and head back home. Either this man was legitimately working extra hours or he was having an affair with someone at the office. Renn needed to do some more digging. Maybe Audra would still be at the apartment right now and she'd be willing to help him root out some information.

Besides, the new client he'd met with today was currently occupying his thoughts. When he arrived at his office, Renn believed it was to meet with a man by the name of Mike Anderson, but as soon as that slick silk suit walked through his doors, he recognized Michael Maestri.

"Mike Anderson, I assume?" Renn asked.

"Yes, I apologize for my little cover story. I was worried you wouldn't meet with me if I gave my real name," Maestri answered while still standing. Renn was seated at his desk, deciding whether or not to extend his hand in invitation to one of the two seats positioned opposite him. He had to admit he was curious about what Maestri was going to ask him so, after a few awkward moments, Renn finally offered Maestri a seat.

"And what is it I can do for you?" he asked.

Maestri shifted uncomfortably as if deciding how to answer.

"I heard you left the Bureau. Working freelance now?"

"According to the sign on the door."

"I thought it was interesting that you decided to stay in Phoenix. Your decision wouldn't have anything to do with Jude, would it?" Maestri asked, his eyes narrowing.

"Mr. Maestri, are you here to discuss a case or to question me personally?" Renn was already irritated with his decision to invite Michael Maestri to take a seat. He already had a case this week and another hook on the line for tomorrow. Maestri uncrossed his legs and leaned forward slightly.

"Mr. Renn, my employer has asked me to look into the matter of Jude and his organization... personally. I must admit, I'm at a bit of a loss on how to proceed. I contacted Special Agent Whitlock and he referred me to you. Said you quit the FBI and might be continuing the investigation on your own time."

"Whitlock sent you?" Renn asked, a hue of doubt in his voice. He didn't know what might have led Maurice to hand his name to this sleazebag.

"In all honesty, I did tell him there was a considerable amount of money attached to this undertaking," Maestri explained, leaning back in his seat once again. He offered up a smug smile and then crossed his legs so a tasseled loafer dangled carelessly in front of him. Talk of money certainly made Maestri feel more at home. He perceived himself to be in possession of something Renn might want and the slight discomfort that inhibited him moments before fell away. Renn's initial annoyance at Maurice for pointing Maestri in his direction began to abate as he considered how this might work to his advantage. After all, he was going to continue his investigation one way or the other. If one of the wealthy people victimized by Jude wanted to foot the bill, that might not be such a bad idea.

He got Maestri to agree to three grand a week, plus expenses and bonuses based on his final results. That would save him the trouble of having to take on other P.I. jobs if he didn't want to for a while. He could just focus on Jude when he had a new lead. And, with expenses included, traveling to follow up on new information would be easier. Hell, he might even be able to hire Audra full time. Her job at the station had been wearing her down for a while. And, during their time apart, Renn had realized that he valued her both personally and professionally. With that thought, he remembered that she had called out of work to remain at his apartment today. She would probably be there right now. Time to call it a night.

He started the engine on his Corolla. He preferred driving his Charger, but that car was more conspicuous on stakeouts. A Toyota Corolla, the second most popular car in the country, could hide in plain sight. Renn left the parking lot and made the short drive to his apartment. Audra's scooter wasn't parked outside. She must have run through the pizza and ventured out for dinner. Or maybe she went home again. Renn missed her during the time she was absent. He always knew the day would come when Audra would slip away as unobtrusively as she'd arrived. While she was gone, he didn't want to call her, to encourage her return. No, Renn wanted her to do what was right for her, but during that intercession of their relationship, he was surprised by the dull ache that continually spoke of her absence and the relief he'd felt when she came back.

The lights were on in his apartment. That was to be expected, but he couldn't tell exactly what had been moved during the day. A mug sat on the counter with that telltale teabag that reminded him Audra had stayed home, in his apartment, all day. Files had been straightened. The counters cleaned and then recluttered by an empty pizza box and teabag wrappers. Renn smiled, unaware he was doing so. Usually, disorder irritated him to no end, but with Audra, he found it endearing. She was so eager to be in the world that she left her mark upon it everywhere, between the litter and the jarring colors she picked out for everything she owned. She lived fully whereas Renn had always maintained a cold reserve. Instead of rankling him, he found these qualities strange and bewitching. Maybe he should reconsider offering her a job. If or when their relationship went south, that situation might prove more trouble than it was worth. Especially now that his feelings had somehow managed to tangle up around Audra in a way he didn't expect. Renn didn't want to get in over his head.

His thoughts turned around in his brain, but the creak of a hinge stopped the chaos in his mind immediately. It wasn't the front door that creaked. It was the bedroom door. Renn reached for the gun at his side.

8

"Stop right there, Renn."

He didn't wait to see who the voice was coming from, but dropped down into a crouch behind the kitchen counter and pulled out his gun.

"Wait a second. We don't want this to turn into a shooting match," the voice said calmly.

"Then get the fuck out of my place," Renn answered, still crouched low but slowly shuffling to the edge of the counters.

"Just put the gun away and come with us. We already have the girl," a second voice chimed in.

Renn closed his eyes for a brief second, weighing his options. If he put his gun down and went wherever it was these guys were planning on taking him, he'd be totally at their mercy. If he didn't, he might never see Audra again. At least, probably not alive. In all fairness, she had a pretty clear idea of the danger she was running into when she continued her search for Jude after Marv disappeared, but he didn't like the idea that she was tied up in some warehouse hoping he might swoop in and rescue her. Well, rescue might not be an option, but Renn decided that if she was going down, he'd go with her. It seemed like the noble thing to do. And maybe, just maybe, they'd be able to find a way out of this mess unscathed, even though Renn didn't believe that outcome was very likely.

He slid his gun against the linoleum floor and stood up. He hoped they didn't plan on killing him then and there. His eyes bore into the two men standing in opposition. One of the men was approaching fifty with graying hair and tanned, leathery skin. The other was younger, probably in his twenties, with sandy hair and sullen eyes. It was the eyes that gave him pause for a moment. Renn stared a moment too long and the younger man growled, "What?" in his direction.

"You look familiar to me," Renn said. "Do we know each other?"

"Just keep your hands where we can see them," the man replied, ignoring Renn's question. The man slipped the gun he was holding into the pocket of his hooded sweatshirt, a navy one that zipped up the front. "We're going to go out to the beige sedan outside. Just follow my partner and we won't have any trouble."

"Your name wouldn't happen to be Marv, now would it?" Renn asked, remembering the pictures of Marv that Audra had brought along for their initial meeting. Renn never forgot a face, even though this one was no longer surrounded by lank black hair.

"Shut up and move," the younger man grumbled, obviously irritated. Whether it was the assignment or Renn himself that rankled him, the detective couldn't say. If Marv, or Jude for that matter, had been keeping an eye on him, he was probably aware of the afterhours his former girlfriend had passed in Renn's abode.

They walked him out to the car, the elder of the two leading the way with Marv drawing up the rear. The older man opened the back-passenger door and indicated that Renn should take a seat. Marv moved around the car and climbed in beside him. The gun, Renn noted, had been removed from Marv's pocket and was now clutched in his hand, pointing in his direction.

"Careful now, son," Renn said in a steady tone. "You don't want that thing to accidentally go off."

Marv shot him a menacing look and replied, "What makes you think it would be accidental?"

"If you were just here to kill me, you would have done it already," Renn answered.

"Whatever. Just shut up and enjoy the ride," Marv said and then muttered something underneath his breath that Renn couldn't make out. The older of the pair climbed into the driver's seat and started the engine.

"Aren't you going to blindfold me?" Renn asked. "Isn't that the way this usually goes?"

Marv expelled a brief chuckle before answering. "We're not too worried about you telling anyone where we're taking you."

That was that. Wherever he was going, chances were it would likely be the end. He reminded himself he needed to hold on to hope. If not for his own future, then for Audra's. Whatever happened, he just hoped there was a way through this for her.

Cherie

9

Her wrists ached and she needed to urinate. She'd been tied to this chair for what felt like hours now, left by herself while they waited on this Jude person to return. Cherie decided to call out for help. Maybe someone passing by could hear her or maybe someone in the building would remember that she was chained up and let her use the bathroom.

Cherie unleashed a "Help!" as loud as she could muster. The one called Mikey burst into the room. She noticed he still held onto the silver gun with a long silencer attached to the end. Somehow the silencer made the sight of him all the more frightening. He could murder her in the middle of downtown, hide her body in the desert, and no one would even know she was dead. At least, not right away.

"Keep it down or I'll make you keep it down," Mikey threatened. It was difficult to feel intimidated by someone called "Mikey" but Cherie's eyes moved to the silencer again and her fear resurfaced.

"I have to pee," she said in a meek voice, trying to remind Mikey she knew who was in charge.

"So pee," he countered. "After tomorrow, we're done with this place anyway."

Mikey didn't wait to see her grimace before marching out the door. Before he slammed it shut on her once again, he brandished his weapon in the air as a threat. This guy was an idiot. Cherie wondered where they'd dug him up, but she couldn't deny the panic that silencer elicited.

How long would it take people to realize she was missing? A few days? A week? Maybe even longer, she realized with a heavy heart. She wouldn't be noticed when she didn't show up for work now that she was unemployed. At most, she called her parents once a month or so, and less since she'd lost her job. Erick was the only person who saw her with any regularity these days, unless you counted bartenders, but he hadn't been calling since she kicked him to the curb to wait for his ride. No one would know and no one would care. The news stations, if they even drew a correlation, wouldn't be able to report that Cherie Rodgers, once a popular reporter in one of the country's largest metropolitan areas, was murdered by Jude and his organization unless her corpse turned up. Even then, her name might even end up on that blacklist she hated with all her being. The HSA would be happy to hear she was taken off the map. No more pestering calls to inquire after the investigation, no more Cherie Rodgers threatening to go rogue with the story. Death would finally silence her.

Then again, Cherie reasoned, they wouldn't keep her tied up here for hours if they only meant to be done with her. Maybe they wanted to know what she knew, which was next to nothing. And maybe, she hoped, they would ask her to join them. She could only imagine what that might do to reinvigorate her career. She could infiltrate Jude's organization from the inside, learn their plans and secrets, and then reveal the truth about these so-called revolutionaries. Maybe that's why they chose her, so she could tell their story, spread their manifesto. Cherie adjusted her weight in the metal chair and a sharp pain in her wrist reminded her of the handcuffs. How much longer did they expect her to wait?

Maybe this was a test, her first test, to see how much discomfort she could endure. If they thought she would breakdown so easily, they had another thing coming. She had gone after difficult stories and harder interviews. She went on stakeouts for the Buckeye Butcher and she'd made the drive from Cave Creek to San Jose on the back of a Harley for a story about white supremacist bikers. She could sit handcuffed to a chair. But, as the minutes continued to tick by at an arduous pace, Cherie started to reconsider her commitment to this little game Jude seemed to be playing. That ride to San Jose on a motorcycle had left her ass bruised and her shoulders sunburned, but at least they had stopped for piss breaks.

Audra

10

She watched as the beige sedan pulled away from the duplex with Renn inside. She couldn't be certain without getting a closer look, but she was pretty sure that Marv was the guy in a dark blue sweatshirt with the hood pulled up over his head walking behind Renn. How on earth did *Marv* convince Renn to go along with him? It was hard to imagine Marv, even with a partner, getting the jump on Renn. They must have lied to him and said they already had her somewhere. She stayed out of sight, hoping they wouldn't notice the scooter which she left parked in a lot across the street. When she saw the van out front, she felt it was safer to approach the apartment on foot just in case someone was keeping an eye out for that lemon-yellow Vespa. She was ten feet from the crosswalk when she saw Renn being led out the door with another man in tow. She tried, as casually as she could, to move behind a parked Oldsmobile and watched through its windows as Renn quietly, and without struggle, took a seat in the sedan. The taller of the two men, the one in the sweatshirt, walked with a familiar gait, one she recognized as Marv's.

She waited until the car pulled away, heading north on the street, before rushing back to grab her scooter. She couldn't follow closely, but she knew the terrain well enough to keep an eye on the vehicle as it crossed the short stretch of downtown. Audra zipped down a few residential streets, ignoring the posted speed limits, trying to get a jump on the sedan. Once she saw the vehicle slip behind a building, Audra maneuvered her Vespa back into a nearby alleyway and waited a few minutes to make sure the car was staying put before she set off on foot. There must be a garage or opening large enough to admit a full-size vehicle. Maybe a warehouse in the back or something.

Audra wasn't sure what she should do. She knew Renn was in real danger, mortal danger, and considered calling the police. Then her mind flashed to Marv. Maybe the police didn't need to get involved. After all, they might only want to talk to Renn, to ask him about the brute force attack against their message board. Of course, he wouldn't know anything. It was Audra's program that had been attempting to hack into their administrative accounts. She was the one they were supposed to come for. This was all her fault. She used her smartphone to pull up an aerial image of the location. From the outside, the structure across the street looked like a single-story strip of empty stores, their windows black and awnings devoid of signs like those advertising pawn shops and yerberias further up the road. From above, she could see the connected mass that ran nearly a quarter of a mile from one side to the other. She found a place nearby to stash her ride and made her way on foot.

Audra slipped down the alley so she could come up on the building's west side. From there, she could access the back of the structure. Whether or not she could actually gain entrance was another question entirely. And, once she gained entrance, what guarantees did she have that she could get out again? *This doesn't seem like a smart plan*, Audra thought as she made her way along the street back toward the building where Renn was being held. She stopped at a bus stop and took a seat on the bench. What was she going to do when she burst in there? She might be able to handle Marv and his partner, but what if there were more? What good could she do Renn if they both landed in the clutches of Jude? She weighed her options.

Then Audra pulled out her cell phone. She quickly jotted off an email to Maurice Whitlock, Renn's former partner at the FBI, telling him that Richard Renn was being held at the given address in downtown Phoenix. She set a delayed delivery. If she didn't cancel the message in fifteen minutes, the email would be sent. She'd pulled the email address from Renn's list of contacts a few weeks back, before she knew for certain that Marv was still alive. At that time, she had begun to consider the possibility that Marv might actually be dead, murdered by Jude after he'd stumbled across some incriminating piece of evidence. She wondered if the same might happen to Renn and, if that happened, who she would turn to for help. His old partner surfaced in her mind. He was connected to the ongoing investigation into Jude and he knew of his partner's continuing efforts to uncover the truth about that organization. He would understand without Audra needing to divulge her involvement.

Now, it would seem, that precaution might pay off. She only hoped Special Agent Whitlock had an alert on his phone when a new email arrived. Otherwise, her backup plan wouldn't work at all. Audra shoved her phone into her pocket and left the bus stop. She continued north toward the building. Fifteen minutes. That didn't give her much time. She hoped she wouldn't waste too much of it trying to find her way into the building. Three minutes later, under the cover of night, Audra was making her way around the hidden north side of the structure. Thankfully, it didn't look like anyone was left outside to stand guard. A dumpster was pushed against the building. She didn't dare try the doors. What if someone was standing on the other side when she tested the handle? No, she needed to find a more discreet way in and around the building. Without another thought, Audra scurried onto the dumpster and, balancing herself on its narrow rim, she jumped to the edge of the roof.

Audra used her arms to pull herself on top of the building, praying no one was watching as she yanked her legs up behind her. She looked around and found two large air conditioning units affixed to the roof. Audra remembered when burglars had gained entrance to one of her dad's rental properties through the A/C and now she was hoping to do something similar. If she couldn't find a vent or other access point, she would have to push one of the big units aside. If she was even capable of such a feat, the noise would definitely alert people down below to her presence. She kept her fingers crossed as she began to explore the roof in the darkness.

Cherie

11

At long last, the door opened and Cherie was surprised to watch Glenda walk in with her short brown bob and daisy-patterned capri pants. She certainly didn't look like the head of a criminal organization until, that is, you got to her eyes. Hard, defiant orbs glared at Cherie. The warm and cheerful smile that Glenda wore on her face every week in group was gone. In its place was a sullen and menacing smirk.

"Cherie Rodgers, I would have liked to see you in group for a few more months before bringing you here, but it looks like our timeline has been moved up considerably," Glenda began. She took a seat across the table from Cherie and brought her elbows to the surface. Cherie remembered her hands were still attached to the chair in uncomfortable handcuffs.

"Glenda, any chance you could take these cuffs off before we settle into our conversation?" Cherie asked, sweet as sugar. "I promise not to cause any trouble."

"No, I don't think so," the other woman answered, a cruel twist in her voice. "Why don't we talk first and then we can see about those handcuffs?"

"I guess I don't have much of a choice in the matter," Cherie answered begrudgingly.

"Let's start with how you found us?" Glenda asked, leaning forward against her elbows as she spoke.

"What do you mean?" Cherie asked, confused. "I just

stumbled across the flyer for the group."

"You mean you just picked up our flyer through happenstance and made the connection? Did you come here expecting to infiltrate our group?"

"Listen, lady, I didn't even know this Jude had anything to do with that Jude until Marv showed up at the meeting tonight."

"You must mean Chad. We all take different names once we sign on. Whoever Chad was before, he isn't that person now," Glenda affirmed.

"You can't possibly mean you *chose* the name Glenda for yourself?" Cherie quipped.

"Coming from a woman who *chose* the name Cherie? From what I understand your real name is Charlene-Dean. Made a jump from white-trash to stripper when you changed your own name," Glenda retorted, aggravation surfacing in her tone. Cherie wondered how this woman could mastermind an organization as elaborate as the one that had been eluding both the FBI and the HSA for so long. This Glenda woman was too easily riled to orchestrate those kidnappings.

"I'm guessing you're not Jude," Cherie put forward her theory.

"There's where you're wrong. I am Jude, just as Chad is Jude, and a thousand other people are Jude. We're all Jude. We're all just parts of one organism."

"I want to be a part of it too," Cherie said, sticking out her jaw ever so slightly to demonstrate her resolve.

"You think it's that easy? You think you can just say you want to sign up and that's it? You have to be willing to give up everything. Everything you think you are and everything you hoped to become. All of that, gone. You haven't even considered the implications of what you're saying. You just want to make sure you walk out of this building alive." Glenda's face wore a stony expression. Her full lips pressed firmly against one another to form a thin line and the sharp jut of her chin tilted upward so she had to angle her eyes down to glare at Cherie.

"Everything has already been stripped away from me. There's nothing to hold onto." Cherie meant what she said. Her career, her future, she had been robbed of both because of that damn blacklist. All she had was in that room sitting across from Glenda. Her body, her mind, and her willingness to devote both to a cause. Cherie just needed to convince this woman that she was willing to commit herself fully.

"I don't think I trust you. Even as you're telling me that you're willing to give up who you are, you continue to think of the future you will have once you are able to return to your old life. The book you will write about the organization and its mission. Maybe you'll even be the one to document this momentous shift in human history. You don't understand that in order to move into this new world, you have to be willing to give up the old one. Not just your identity and everyone you've ever known or cared about, but even your life. You haven't hit bottom and you never will because you were born to excess and you don't know anything else. I can see its stain on you. You will never be able to let go of everything. It is too intertwined with how you see yourself."

"You're wrong! I have hit bottom. I'm right fucking there. I want to be a part of this, to be a part of something greater than myself, I'll give up everything right here and now."

"I'm sorry. I was wrong."

"Please, I'll do anything, anything you ask."

"Even lay down your life?"

"Yes," Cherie answered earnestly although she hoped it wouldn't come to that. She was willing to go to great lengths to prove herself to Jude's organization if it meant its inner workings might finally be revealed to her.

"Good," Glenda answered with a smile. A noise in the hallway startled the two women. Glenda rose from her seat, but Cherie was obliged to remain where she was. Glenda disappeared out the door only to return a moment later. "We're going to have to continue this in a few minutes. Sit tight."

Cherie rolled her eyes, calling out before the door closed, "Wait! I have to pee!"

No one acknowledged her. Cherie was left alone once again with her thoughts and her overly full bladder. Ten minutes later, her pants were damp and cold, but her bladder felt light and empty. They wanted to see her humiliated, fine, so be it. She just had to keep playing along and she would be in.

Renn

12

"Where's Audra?" Renn had kept his mouth shut for the entire drive. He'd kept his mouth shut as they pulled into what appeared to be an abandoned shopping strip and forced him out of the car at gunpoint. He'd kept quiet as they led him through the structure's dingy corridor, but when they told him to take a seat in an empty room, he decided to speak up.

"Sit down and we can talk about Audra."

Renn didn't like the idea, but what could he do? He took a seat and allowed Marv to handcuff him to the chair while his partner kept a handgun trained on him the entire time.

"Where's Audra?" he repeated.

"Hopefully, she's halfway to Mexico by now. It was a nasty little trick she pulled on you. Setting up that brute-force program to run from your apartment. Did you know she was doing it?"

Renn didn't answer. Marv took his silence as confirmation of his ignorance.

"Now that's a low blow. She should have at least *told* you she was going to try and infiltrate our network from your IP address, don't you think?"

Renn didn't know what to think. All he knew was that they didn't have Audra. Marv said he hoped she was on her way to Mexico. That meant she wasn't here. How could he be so stupid as to go quietly along with these two without asking for proof that Audra was in danger? Rookie mistake and, if he was being honest with himself, it was only because he allowed his feelings for Audra to cloud his judgement when he feared she was in jeopardy.

Marv stared at him with a self-satisfied grin. Renn had played right into his hands. Marv leaned in close so he was only a few slight inches away. Renn considered butting him right in the face. Maybe a busted-up nose would wipe away that smug look, but he remembered that the last time he popped someone in the face, it brought on a lot more hassle than it was worth. He needed to bide his time, to see what they expected of him. As far as he knew, Jude wasn't one for collateral damage. He acted quickly and precisely, snatching and executing children but not leaving a wake of bodies on the path to his goal.

Marv's gruff partner by the door grumbled a little, breaking the mutual focus that had risen between Renn and Marv.

"Hey, Chad," the man began. "We gotta check the other one. She wants to talk to this guy."

Chad? She? Questions started darting through his head as Marv stood up and made his way to the door.

"I'll be back soon," Marv promised. The minacious look on his face told Renn he should worry about his promise to return, but he had bigger problems at the moment. The door closed and he was left alone. His eyes moved over the room in careful scrutiny. Nothing of use. An empty table, another chair. A glass window covered in dusty mini-blinds. It was a small room and the way the doors were positioned made him think it was some sort of back office, the kind where you might see a jeweler working at his craft or an untrusting manager watching over his employees in the shop. Renn could try and bust out that window, but he suspected it would not lead to the outdoors. The dimensions were all wrong for a front facing window and he'd got a decent look at the building as they drove up to it. An empty shopping strip, the same kind that went up for sale around Phoenix all the time, just waiting for a developer to swoop in and make it new again. Glass fronted, so noise might be able to get out, but it was in a dismal neighborhood where people wouldn't usually be found walking except perhaps on the west side of the building which sat adjacent to a bus route. They parked on the east side of the building, pulled right in through an open delivery door into an empty warehouse at the back. Renn knew they hadn't walked far enough to put him in proximity of the street to the west.

Okay, so shouting wouldn't do him much good. It was a rough part of town and, moreover, Arizona still had a bit of that Wild West attitude. People would just shoot off into the air in anger or celebration here. He could be shot right in this building and the cops might not even be called about the noise. Renn bounced a couple of times in the chair, testing its strength. It was welded together to form a solid unit, like seats he remembered from elementary school. The chairs of today were usually so flimsy, he could decimate one against the floor or wall, but not this one. Nevertheless, he tried to pick himself up and toss his weight down against it in one final effort, but was more successful damaging his tailbone rather than the chair.

He considered the value of trying again. Even though he knew it was probably futile, he didn't want to give up quite yet. Renn readied himself for another battering of the chair when the door opened. A woman in her mid-thirties walked through the door, her chestnut hair cut to her chin and curled under in a bob ala Mary Tyler Moore. She looked like she was dressed for a mall, not an underground vigilante group, but her eyes suggested something sinister, maybe even maniacal. Yes, this woman wanted to kill him.

Audra

13

Audra found a crawl space that was accessible through a rusty grate held on by three screws. She had to use the small manicure set in her make-up bag to fashion a screwdriver, worrying the entire time about the timer ticking down on that email. She would prefer to do this without alerting the authorities, but she turned off her phone just in case they had a means of detecting her signal inside the building. Once the grate was open, she lowered her backpack through and wiggled in after it. She rose tentatively once in the crawl space, crouching to avoid hitting her head on the low roof. Audra tried shuffling along in a crouch, but eventually gave that up and opted for crawling along the narrow support beams that crisscrossed the crawl space.

She was near the west side of the building and she knew they had pulled the car in on the opposite side so Audra began making her way in that direction. A rat scurried across her path and Audra forced herself to hold back her scream. She was sneaking into the hideout of a criminal organization, one that kidnapped and killed children; she would not allow herself to be found out because she was scared of a rodent. Audra strengthened her resolve and continued forward. The crawlspace narrowed and then widened again as she continued toward the west side of the structure.

The ceiling beneath her showed considerable signs of

aging. Vents and lighting fixtures had fallen away or been removed. Never replaced, they provided small openings for Audra to peer through into the spaces beneath her. For the most part, the rooms were dark and Audra could make out nothing more than shadows and void. The dimly lit corridor was lined with refuse and boxes. She made certain to stay on the wooden beams because Audra knew that one false move could send her plummeting into the building below. She moved slowly even though she knew that the time she'd allotted for her rescue operation was ticking by steadily. Any minute now and her email would be on its way to Renn's former partner. He had to have an email alert on his phone, didn't he? Audra suddenly became very uneasy, worrying she might have gleaned a personal email address, one Maurice Whitlock didn't stay apprised of minute by minute. Too late to think about that now.

The sounds of voices rose up to her and Audra paused to listen. She couldn't make out the words, but one of the voices sounded like it belonged to Marv. Audra transferred her weight slowly, moving toward an open gap that she hoped would give her a discreet view of those below her. The voices became more audible, but, as Audra peered through the opening, her view of the men speaking was impeded.

"We're going back for the girl," an unknown figure said.

"Mikey can stay. I'm going with," Marv answered.

"No way, Chad. Glenda wants you here."

"I'm going."

"No way, no how."

There was a pause. Audra caught sight of a figure

moving through the dark space barely visible below. It looked like a man, but Audra couldn't be certain of even that much. It wasn't Marv. She knew that. He was tall and lanky, almost as tall as Renn. This man wasn't.

"We should've just waited for her to return. Then we wouldn't have to go back."

"You know the transport rules. One at a time. We would've had to kill that P.I. and Jude wants to know what he knows. He was part of the FBI investigation before the HSA picked up the case."

"We have someone there."

"Never hurts to double check."

Audra had to keep moving forward. Renn was in the building somewhere. She started to crawl, her ears ringing with every noise each subtle shift of her body created. Fear made her certain that the men below her would be alerted to her presence with every breath or movement. Thankfully, the voices stopped and she could hear the men making their way through the building back toward the west. She followed overhead, her hands pressed firmly against the wooden boards beneath her to help keep her steady while her knees ached increasingly with each passing inch. The passage narrowed once again before opening on to a much larger space. This must be the warehouse behind the building, the one where the car carrying Renn had disappeared.

She heard doors opening and closing, muffled voices, and the start of a car engine. Audra scanned the expanse around her. The crawlspace only reached four feet vertically and, in the dark, she had a difficult time establishing exactly how far it stretched around her. She sat crossed legged, stilled her breath, and listened. She could hear sounds in two different directions: one to the south and one further west. She decided to investigate the noise coming from the south first. Remaining on her hands and knees, she moved toward it.

A narrow shaft of light revealed another opening in the dilapidated ceiling, this one above an illuminated room. She checked the watch on her wrist, a Swatch watch that had been a gift from Marv for her twentieth birthday. The hands stood out in a glowing blue light. She had four minutes until that email went to Whitlock. Audra looked to the opening in the ceiling. There wasn't a board conveniently close to the gap that would permit her a view of what was beneath her. The plasterboard ceiling wouldn't hold her weight. She considered sliding a loose board in that direction, but worried about the noise such an action would generate. Audra leaned forward, putting her ear as close to the ceiling as she dared. Muted voices, a man's and a woman's, were nearly indecipherable. One of them might be Renn, but she couldn't tell for certain.

A distinctive voice cried out, casting a ripple of fear through Audra. She froze. That voice belonged to Cherie Rodgers. She'd heard it yell at her on more than one occasion back at the news station when Cherie was still gainfully employed. This time, the voice didn't sound angry, but exasperated. At least, Audra decided, she wasn't crying out from pain. Maybe Cherie was working with Marv for Jude's organization. Audra decided to continue moving in the direction of that voice.

Renn

14

"Agent Renn," the woman with the brown bob began as she took a seat across from him.

"Not anymore. Just plain old Richard Renn now," he answered.

"Of course, I'm Glenda. I just have a few questions. Won't take up too much of your time."

Renn wondered what the show of courtesy was all about. He considered reminding this woman that his wrists were handcuffed to his chair. He watched as her eyes drifted slightly to the side. She was trying to remember something, searching for a word or memory.

"At the time of your departure from the FBI, exactly how many kidnappings had been reported to your agency?"

"Twelve. The Lambert child was number twelve." Renn saw no point in lying to this woman. In his experience, Jude's organization was always a step ahead of them when it came to information. They probably had people inside law enforcement that kept them apprised of the internal workings on the investigation. This woman wasn't asking questions of her own accord. She was a cog, just as Marv was a cog. Renn just wondered how many pieces fit together to form the whole of Jude's organization. Renn ventured to put forward a question of his own, "Now, is this an interrogation or a conversation?"

"Just what exactly do you mean?" Glenda asked.

"Well, since I figure I'm as good as dead anyway, can I ask some questions? I'll die easier knowing why I was murdered."

"You think so?" Glenda offered him a sardonic smile. Renn noticed she was probably pretty. The woman had a heart-shaped face and a full mouth that might be inviting were it not twisted in a mocking grin. The bob and her pastel knit shirt made her look like she ought to be driving the kids home from soccer practice rather than leading an interrogation on behalf of a criminal organization. But, he had to admit, the latter did seem more interesting to him even though her eyes carried the glint of insanity.

"How can you be complicit in the murder of innocent children?" he asked.

"Men revile the things which they do not understand," she recited by way of answer.

"Then make me understand," Renn said.

"I'm afraid we don't have time for that tonight."

"I got all the time in the world."

"Once again, I'm afraid not. It's come to our attention that you continued your investigation after you left the Bureau. How many additional cases have come to your attention?"

"Six. Did you have anyone on the inside other than Cobar on the Lambert abduction?" Renn would answer her questions, but she would need to tell him a thing or two.

"Of course," she answered. "Each task force consists of a tech team, a team of rovers, and anywhere from three to ten internal agents."

"Rovers?"

"My turn," Glenda chirped with an artificial cheer.

"Where's the girl now?"

"What girl?"

"Come on now, Renn. I thought we were developing a friendly rapport with one another. Don't get smart with me now," Glenda said with a joking air, but Renn watched her eyes sharpen, honing in on his face with implied threat. "I know it was the girl that attempted to crack our system. We were ordered to bring her in. Just tell us where she is."

"I don't know and, if I did, I wouldn't tell you. Isn't that the line?" Renn tried to maintain the false joviality. There was no sense in turning things ugly. Not yet anyway.

"We tried tracking her cell phone, but she appears to have turned it off," the woman added. "No matter. Our team is looking for her now. She can't stay hidden long."

"Marv certainly stayed off the radar for quite some time. Audra could probably do even better. She's a smart one."

"Marv, as you insist on calling him, had our entire organization to assist him in staying hidden. I doubt the girl will prove so successful without our resources. Modern society is not conducive to secrecy." And, as if to prove no secret was safe, Glenda barreled into her next question, "Michael Maestri came to see you today. What did he want?"

Renn imagined her mentally checking off topics as she made her inquiries. Someone had told her what to ask. Jude operated an organization with many independent groups. He wondered just how autonomous each unit was? Could they effectively continue operations should the head be cut off? And, he wondered, just how far did Jude's organization reach?

"He wanted to hire me to look into your operation," Renn answered. Glenda laughed unexpectedly at his response.

"You certainly found us. Only thing is, I don't think you're going to be able to collect on that case."

"Right about that, it would seem. I didn't think you people were in the habit of leaving a trail of bodies behind. I mean, other than those kids."

"That was just the beginning, the first stage. There is so much more to come." Glenda's eyes grew distant for a moment as she added, "Therefore, repent; or else I am coming to you quickly, and I will make war against them with the sword of My mouth."

Renn recognized the words from the notes Jude left warning his future victims. Was this a group of religious zealots? Somehow, what Audra told him about Marv insinuated that the group was likely a revolutionary undertaking and not a religious cult.

Renn struggled for a moment to recall the words that waited for Jonathan Lambert and others of his ilk, each note scribbled by some child's hand.

"If you do not wake up, I will come like a thief, and you will not know at what hour I will come to you," Renn recited.

"Yes, the words of warning that so few heeded."

"Big on religion? Born again, maybe?" Renn asked.

"Not really. Just adopting a readily available language of prophecy."

Renn shifted uncomfortably. Glenda's eyes had assumed a feverish look. This woman was plagued by beliefs, but he wasn't sure just what they were. If only Renn could begin to understand those beliefs, to disseminate the ideas that led her to Jude and his organization, maybe he could learn more from her than she took from him. A knock surprised them both and a look of annoyance clouded her features before Glenda rose to open the door. She exchanged words with someone on the other side that Renn couldn't see from where he was seated. Without a word in his direction, Glenda vanished from sight.

Cherie

15

Glenda burst through the door with Marv in tow. They were involved in a heated exchange.

"We had two more days before we burned this location," she growled. "The new place won't be ready yet."

"The alert just came in. Police are on their way. Our guys on the inside said the call came from the FBI," Marv explained.

"You were followed," Glenda said abruptly, pausing to turn her enraged expression back at Marv. Cherie was momentarily grateful it wasn't directed at her.

"There's no way. Carl doubled back four separate times just to make sure," he argued.

"It doesn't matter now. We have to get out of here or we're all dead." Without another word, Glenda raised a gun that was clutched in her hand. Cherie hadn't noticed it was even there before, but there it was, silencer and all. Cherie started to panic.

"Wait, wait, wait, I can help you!" she asserted in a rush.

"And just what do you think you can do for us?" Glenda asked, tilting her head slightly to an angle away from the sightline of her weapon.

"Don't you see? I can tell the world about this. I can make sure everyone knows why you're doing all this. Surely, that has to be worth something?" Cherie began to pull again at her encumbered wrists to no avail. She could feel a trickle of blood running down her hands into the lines of her palm. Eventually, that blood would begin to drip to the floor beneath her. Maybe that would be the only mark she left on the world, that small speckle of blood on the cement floors of this disused building. The thought turned her stomach and, for a moment, she worried she might vomit. Try to be brave, she told herself. Don't go to pieces.

Glenda stood for a brief second in contemplation. Cherie almost dared to hope until, finally, Glenda offered a dismissive shrug and pulled the trigger. The bullet tore into her chest and pain shot through her entire body. She really did it. She really shot her. Cherie looked in confusion at the other faces in the room: Glenda's cold enjoyment and Marv's dazed distress. Without another word, Glenda slipped out of the room.

Marv remained standing next to Cherie as her limbs grew numb.

"I'm sorry, Cherie. No loose ends."

She wanted to say something to him. To yell at him or curse the day he was born. To say something, anything, to this duplicitous man who'd stood by watching as she was murdered. Cherie opened her mouth, but the sound emerged more like a gurgle. A waterfall of fear descended on her. She tried to still her thoughts, but it wasn't any use as she strained for every minuscule breath she could draw into her failing lungs. There was a sputtering sound that she worried was coming from her mouth.

Stay calm, she told herself. The police were on the way. Maybe an ambulance had also been called. Cherie tried to generate some faint glimmer of hope but her vision began to blur. She coughed and felt warm liquid leave her mouth. The world grew dark and calm and quiet.

Audra

16

Audra tried desperately to quiet her breath. She was on the verge of hyperventilating. She needed to be smart, to act quickly, and that meant staying calm. She watched through an opening in the ceiling as a woman with brown hair shot and killed Cherie Rodgers. Marv stayed right by her side through the whole event, not even a word of protest passing through his lips. How could he just watch her die like that? In Audra's mind the faces of all those missing children began flashing one by one. No matter their cause, these people were murderers, cold-blooded murderers. And Renn was in the next room, probably sitting in handcuffs just like Cherie, about to face his death.

It had to be her message that'd led to the police being alerted. That was the only reasonable explanation. This was her fault. She had to do something, but she didn't know what. She unzipped her backpack, unconcerned about the noise. She cast aside her extra dress and her makeup bag. There she found her emergency plan. All those months ago, when Marv disappeared, Audra believed he managed to locate Jude and his organization. She didn't for one moment think he was dead, but that didn't mean she refused to take precautions just in case her intuition misled her. After all, Renn was smart too, and he'd believed Marv was murdered and dumped in the desert. Audra decided to establish a little safety plan just in case the wrong person came for her. The Beretta Nano semiautomatic 9mm held six rounds in the clip, plus one in the chamber, and came in an adorable shade of pink called Rosa. She knew there were probably more important factors when selecting a handgun, but the pink polymer frame had sold her. Besides, a "Beretta" sounded serious and the gun merchant told her a 9mm was all you needed to put someone down, assuming you knew where to point.

Audra rose from her knees into a crouch and began scurrying to above the room where she had heard Renn's voice earlier. She moved a board quickly, listening to the exchange of voices from the hallway outside.

"Destroy the hard drives," the woman barked, presumably at Marv. "Meet me at the car in six minutes."

Audra slid a board over the stretch of ceiling to where she could reach the opening. She pushed her eye against the hole and saw Renn confined to a chair. He must be handcuffed just as Cherie was.

Audra noticed the heavy table positioned directly beneath her. She didn't have time to think. With the full force of her weight, she stomped on the narrow gap in the ceiling. The plaster began to give way. She stomped again.

Renn

17

A strange noise overhead startled him. His attention had been focused on the commotion on the other side of the door. Renn watched as a patch of ceiling fell to the tabletop in front of him. A puff of dust and probably asbestos rose up around it. A figure descended through the hole, lowered by her arms, until she fell the way of the ceiling chunk, landing with a thud on the table. Renn's eyes stretched to their full width as he took in the sight of Audra. The noise must have been noted beyond the door. Renn noticed that the voices in the hallway grew suddenly silent. Audra scrambled to her knees on the table as she pulled a small handgun out of the waistband of her pants just as the door flew open.

Glenda burst through the door, gun in hand, but Audra fired off a shot, hitting the woman in the shoulder. She fell back into the hallway, but the door remained open behind her.

"What in the hell are you doing here?" Renn sputtered out at Audra.

"I'm saving you," she answered as she slid off the table to her feet. "What does it look like I'm doing?"

"Looks like you're going to get yourself killed," he answered. The gun in Audra's hand was pink and black. Renn didn't know what surprised him more: the fact that Audra owned a firearm or that she'd managed to find one that matched her outfit. Renn looked to Glenda's form squirming in the hallway. He shouted at Audra, "She's going for the gun!"

Audra instantly stood up, her arm strong and extended with a practiced steadiness. Glenda was reaching for the gun with its silencer still affixed to its end. Audra pulled the trigger twice. Both bullets hit their mark with precision. Her body stopped moving and a pool of red began to grow around Glenda's chestnut bob. She leaned over Renn, trying to find some way to detach him from the chair.

"You need the keys," he said calmly. "How many shots do you have left?"

"Four," she answered, matching the placid tone of his voice.

"There's more of them coming," he warned.

"Just one."

Marv appeared in the doorway. He carried a gun similar to Glenda's right down to the silencer at the end. Audra stood up again, but she didn't raise her gun.

"Audra?" Marv asked with a baffled expression, already knowing the answer.

"Marv."

"You killed Glenda?" he asked, his gun still raised.

"She killed Cherie," Audra answered. Renn's mind flashed to Cherie Rodgers as he continued to watch the exchange between Audra and her former lover. He felt like he was intruding in a private conversation.

"Cherie was no good. You know that. You couldn't wash the corruption off her," Marv sounded indignant. The young ideologue. How could Audra ever have fallen for someone like Marv? Renn wondered. She seemed too smart for the likes of him. "You're not like them. You're good, like us. Uncorrupted. You can be a part of this, but we have to get out of here."

"Uncorrupted? You kill children."

"You don't understand yet. Come with me and let me help you understand."

"Oh, so now I can be a part of this? Why now? Why not seven months ago when you took off to join?" Audra's eyes burned as she glared at Marv.

"You had to get their attention on your own. There are rules. I couldn't do anything to tip you off or I was out. And out means dead." Marv lifted up his right hand, palm extended, as a peaceful gesture. He knew Audra well enough to know when her temper was rising. Renn noticed that he didn't lower his gun at the same time, but moved its barrel slightly away from her chest.

"Just get out of here, Marv," Audra said, her voice growing weary. "The cops are on the way."

Renn moved his eyes from Audra's quiet fury to Marv's own perturbed expression and knew before he spoke what his answer would be.

"I'm afraid I can't do that. You can come with me or you can die here with him. That's the way it has to be. I swore an oath. If I fail, I die," Marv said plainly.

"What about all those promises you made to me?" Audra asked. Marv didn't answer her but turned his gun so it was now pointed at Renn. Well, Renn decided, if Marv shot him it might give Audra enough time to fire one back at him before he could shoot her too. Renn only hoped that Audra could see that Marv would kill her if she left him no choice. "You would shoot me just like that?"

"Audra, the war against the rich is starting. You always knew it was coming. You knew it before I did. You always told me the world would turn to violence and it's happening. Right now, it's happening."

"I thought Jude only killed children. I didn't realize you people murdered anyone that got in your way." Audra was stalling. Renn realized she must have contacted the authorities. How long could she keep this up? When would the police get here? He pulled ineffectually at his wrists, trying not to draw attention to himself as he did so.

"The first woe is past; behold, two woes are still coming after these things," Marv recited.

"Then the sixth angel sounded his trumpet, and I heard a voice from the four horns of the golden altar before God, Revelations 9:13," Audra answered, surprising Renn once again. "Don't forget that I grew up around all that; just not my thing. And, really, I never thought you were the type."

"That's just how we deliver the message. The meaning is what's important. It's not about religion. It's about making people understand."

"So brainwashing and murdering children? You're really not selling me."

"The kids, that was only the first phase. The next part is coming. It's almost here."

"Oh yeah?" she asked sardonically, "What comes next? Raping and pillaging? Burning cities to the ground? Or does that come later?"

"Next is the culling," Marv replied in a grave tone.

"What the hell does that mean?"

"We go after the ones who are truly guilty of the crimes." His eyes grew more fervent as he spoke. Renn worried Audra might push him too far.

"Sounds like you should have started there."

Just then, the sound of sirens approaching in the distance distracted the pair and both turned their heads slightly toward the noise. Renn knew what came next. Audra drew up her gun as her head swiveled back to Marv. In that same moment, he shifted his weapon back from Renn to her. Marv hesitated for the briefest moment, no more than a flutter of the eye, but Audra didn't. She sent three bullets into his chest. Renn exhaled a long breath. He didn't blame Marv for hesitating even if it cost him his life. Renn didn't think he'd have it in him either. Audra didn't lower her weapon. By Renn's count, she only had one bullet left. He noticed a tremor move through her as Marv collapsed beside Glenda.

"Audra, get the keys to the handcuffs," he instructed. She didn't reply but did as he asked.

Audra stepped over Marv's lifeless form and rolled Glenda over to search her pockets. She came back into the room with the keys in her hands.

Audra seemed a little dazed. Her hands shook slightly as she fumbled with the keys. Once Renn had his hands free, he rubbed his wrists and offered to take her gun and its solitary bullet from her.

"Hurry, there might be others," he warned.

"The others left. They're looking for me," she answered, her eyes growing heavy with impending tears. Renn took her by the shoulders and fixed his grey eyes upon her watery gaze.

"Audra, he would have killed you. You did the right thing," he sought to reassure her. She was probably still in shock.

"I know. I just can't believe what a total and complete dick he was," she answered as two teardrops slipped from the corners of her eyes in perfect unison.

Audra

18

She stood over Marv crumpled across the open doorway. One hand looked to be languidly resting on the bloodstained pant leg of her first victim, the woman with the brown hair. Audra always contended that if she was forced to defend herself, she would do so without hesitation or remorse. Now that she had been called to act upon that belief, she found hesitation wasn't a problem, but remorse was another matter entirely. She stared at the fingers of his hand, almost expecting to see a twitch of hidden life. Slender fingers and long, the same that would brush away a tear or curl around her hand. Renn moved past her, taking her pink Beretta with him, and began checking the other doors. The two closest to her on the left were empty but when he moved to the door on the opposite side, Renn paused after pushing it open. He let out a long sigh.

Audra looked up from the corpses and settled her gaze on Renn.

"Is that where Cherie is?" she asked.

Renn didn't answer, just gravely nodded his head and moved into the room. Audra followed. Cherie's body was still seated in the chair, but she slumped backward as if she had drifted off to sleep in an uncomfortable position. The blood and matter clinging to the wall behind her told a different story. Audra felt a sharp inhalation filling her lungs and worried her stomach would upend itself. She slowed her breathing as her eyes focused on Renn. He was checking the computer, but she knew it wouldn't be any use. The woman told Marv to destroy the hard drives. They were probably soaking in a vat of acid somewhere in the building. Renn gave up as a loud commotion jostled the building. The police must be on the scene. Sure enough, within minutes the building was crawling with cops.

Audra felt herself being led away from the room. Someone offered her a blanket which she accepted despite the stifling September heat of the desert. She looked up from the coarse blanket and saw Renn near the building talking with a cheap suit. Police detective from the looks of it. Only then did Audra realize that she wasn't in the building, but outside of it. She was seated in the back of an ambulance, a blood pressure monitor attached to her arm. She must be in shock, she realized with a tinge of disappointment. At that moment, Renn looked up at her and smiled. He offered the cop a nod and started making his way toward her.

"You doing okay?" Renn asked with concern.

"Just a little shaken, I guess," she answered. Her senses were returning to her in full, but the emotional weight of her actions had yet to descend upon her. Instead, a strange lightness filled her head and limbs.

"Who taught you how to shoot like that?" Renn asked.

"My mom's family, they were doomsayers. Her brother taught me to shoot when he taught his own kids. Thought it would be a useful skill in the new world."

Renn looked startled. For the past six months, they had spent more time together than with anyone else, and yet, during that time, they had very few exchanges about their personal histories.

"I didn't even know you owned a gun."

"I didn't, not until after Marv disappeared. I knew he wasn't dead, but one can never be too careful." At the mention of Marv's name, she could feel sorrow at the edge of her being. How long until it swallowed her up? Maybe it would just continue lurking indefinitely, threatening to unleash its full force, but remaining in the shadows. She took a breath to clear her head. She'd done the right thing. Renn's voice brought her back to her senses and she raised her gaze to his.

"I should just hire you on the spot. We'd make a great P.I. team. Any other skills you've been keeping a secret from me?" he joked, trying to lighten the air around her. Audra considered his words. Private investigator didn't have such a bad ring to it. After all, journalism was out for her. The existence of the blacklist destroyed the ethical core of that profession. She couldn't see herself busting ass for some corporate gig, no matter the pay or the perks. She rebuked herself for thinking of such things while Marv was laying in the building in front of her, dead by her hand. Whatever, she decided; he would have shot her if she'd given him the chance. And, with that thought, the sorrow receded ever so slightly from her consciousness. She returned to Renn's question.

"I'm fluent in Spanish and Japanese and I studied Brazilian jiu-jitsu," Audra answered.

Renn's eyes flashed with surprise, revealing a wide rim of white around each grey iris. Suddenly, he laughed.

"Shit, I don't think I can afford you."

Part 4: December

Renn

1

"What have you got there?" Audra asked as she set her helmet down on Renn's desk. She had her own desk in her own office, but she still liked to march into his office when she finally rolled into work around noon.

"Whitlock sent over the files," Renn answered, briefly glancing up at Audra to offer her a smile. Her hair was a little longer, forming a sharp edge near her chin, but that wasn't what made her look older. Her brown eyes, a rich dark chocolate color that stood in contrast to her bleach blonde hair, had aged. Renn wondered if he should be sad to see the change take effect, but he decided against it. People grow up and Audra, after all, had been through a lot this year. On top of everything, she killed two people. Although it was in self-defense, he knew death had a way of changing people. That was to be expected. He returned his stare to the files before him.

"Well, then," Audra added as she turned to leave the room, "I guess I'll get started on my caseload. Why don't you let me buy you dinner and you can tell me all about what you find in those files later?"

Renn gave her a curt nod, his mind already sinking into the words on the pages before him. Audra was familiar with his gruff, absent-minded ways. She didn't seem to mind. And, one thing he'd learned about her in the recent months since he'd invited her to work with him, when she minded, she would say something. Audra didn't bottle up her aggression and then lash out unexpectedly. She gave you fair warning every time.

Three months and the investigation had made its first headway into uncovering the lengthy reach of Jude, an elaborate network built on people crushed beneath society's wheels. The organization established new connections in various cities through their support groups, seeking out the disenfranchised who had seen their lives destroyed, those most willing to give themselves entirely over to a cause if it meant some sort of justice might be served, some sort of better world promised. So far, they'd been able to uncover seven different sects running nearly autonomously, but Jude was still the missing piece. *If there even is a Jude*, Renn thought with a shake of his head. The woman he knew as Glenda was actually Ariel Dura, a surgical technician who'd lost both her husband and infant son when a faulty half-shaft on her SUV fractured without warning on a freeway, disconnecting the drive axle and causing a car accident. A recall was later issued by the manufacturer wherein they were accused of releasing the vehicle to the public in full knowledge that the half-shaft was problematic. She was believed to be the one with enough medical knowledge to facilitate the birth of the Lambert child without killing the infant or mother, even if that came later.

A young man who called himself "Mikey" but was later identified as Charles Montgomery, the son of a chemical company magnate, provided the most information once he and his partner were taken into police custody. At least this time, they were prepared for the arrest and searched the men top to bottom for cyanide capsules. Both were found to be holding the small, amber pills. Montgomery was restrained and, eventually, questioned at length by the HSA until he broke. Renn didn't want to imagine the interrogation means used to get the man to divulge the full extent of his knowledge, but whatever it was, the HSA proved effective.

His partner, on the other hand, opted to bash his own face into the interrogation table when left unsupervised until his frontal lobe hemorrhaged. The dead man was identified as Jackson Miller, a Wyoming factory worker who went missing in 2019, just a few weeks after his company released him as part of a massive layoff in an effort to reduce costs by moving manufacturing outside the United States. It seemed as if Jude was gathering up all the human odds and ends, all the alienated and dejected, and forming them into an army. Just to what end, Renn couldn't say, but it wasn't his job to guess anymore. He was ready to leave the questions to Whitlock and the HSA. He had other clients and other cases. And, as far as he was concerned, his work with Jude was over now. He just had one more phone call to make.

Michael Maestri was down at his office an hour after Renn placed the phone call. He burst straight into his office without knocking.

"Where's the fat, bald guy?" Maestri asked.

"You mean Gerry?" Renn replied. Gerry had originally shared the office space with Renn, but when he decided to retire in October, Renn saw it as the perfect opportunity to bring Audra in full-time. Audra left her job at the station after her ordeal had landed on the blacklist. "Gerry retired. I work with Ms. Maguire."

"She's a step in the right direction," he said appreciatively.

"Just sit down and shut up, Maestri. You seem too young to be so outdated." Renn could feel his irritation growing. Today, Maestri had added a burgundy scarf to his navy-blue pinstripe suit. "You hired me to find out more about Jude's organization and, more specifically, who was responsible for murdering Jonathan Lambert's son."

"Correct." Maestri settled into a seat opposite Renn and crossed his legs with a casual air. The man grated on Renn, with his tasseled loafers and vainglorious attitude. He was glad to be closing this chapter of his life once and for all. Renn pushed the file across the desk.

"You can keep that, but you're also welcome to have a look now. It seems a woman named Ariel Dura, who went by the name Glenda, headed the branch of Jude's organization that operated out of Phoenix. The HSA was able to connect her to a number of crimes, including the Lambert abduction."

"And where is this Ariel Dura? Has she been taken into custody?"

"She's dead. She died with two of her associates in September. I wanted to wait to give you the news until I knew enough information. The HSA is currently in the process of dismantling Jude's organization, city by city. Who can say how successful they will prove to be in their efforts. At least you know who the HSA believes to be responsible for the Lambert kidnapping."

Maestri nodded his head, weighing out Renn's words. Then he added, "And how much do you feel this information is worth?"

"You paid me weekly and covered my expenses. If we're done here, I believe a twenty-thousand-dollar bonus was promised if I delivered satisfactory information."

Maestri nodded his head again, but said nothing. Renn continued in his silence, "And if there is some sort of extra bonus for killing Dura, that should go to Audra Maguire. She pulled the trigger."

"You mean the cute broad I walked by?"

"Yeah, that woman has a real tough streak."

Michael

2

"Coffee or water?" Jonathan's assistant offered him while he was waiting.

"No thanks, Stephen," Michael answered. Jonathan was continuing the Lambert tradition of male assistants. Patricia thought a young, attractive woman might distract her son from his workplace responsibilities and lead to scandal. And, for Patricia, there were no other kinds of women.

"Mr. Lambert will see you now," Stephen announced with a warm smile. Michael noticed he did not stand up to open the door for him as was customary. Not like it mattered anymore. He had played his part and it was time for him to leave.

Jonathan kept his hair neatly trimmed and his face clean shaven these days. He also seemed to slow his drinking to the established norms for a modern-day businessman: no more than three before Happy Hour. Even Michael had to hand it to him, Jonathan appeared to have inherited his father's keen business sense. In a few short months, he'd managed to diversify the family holdings and already they were seeing sizable yields from those investments. Who knows what he could have done with a few years' time? But Michael knew he couldn't stick around and watch. It was time to cut ties. American capitalism had been good to him and he'd exploited it to his advantage, but the ship was going down and he had no intention of sinking with it.

"Maestri, what brings you around?" Jonathan asked, getting straight to the point. Usually when a meeting was arranged, Jonathan was the one who wanted to talk to Michael, not the other way around.

"I wanted to follow up on that information you requested. About the kidnapping." Michael said, as if Jonathan needed a reminder as to what information he was sent forth to find.

"Do you have something for me?" Jonathan asked, his eyes immediately coming to life with sudden interest.

"The member of Jude's organization who orchestrated Nicki's abduction is now dead," Michael stated plainly in hopes of the words maintaining their full effect.

"A member of Jude's organization, but not Jude himself?" Jonathan asked. Michael tried to hide his unease as he answered. Jonathan certainly had become a far more astute listener since he'd relinquished his day drinking. Michael didn't know whether to classify this as a positive or negative change.

"No, as far as the Homeland Security Administration is concerned, there is no Jude, just small groups across the country seeking some sort of vigilante justice. And, my sources at the HSA assure me that as soon as the group's coded message board was dismantled, all the active members scattered to the wind."

"So it's over?" Jonathan asked, his eyebrows arching upward with doubt.

"It's over." To confirm his assessment, he dropped a few glossy images on Jonathan's desk that he had purchased from the local PD. A man and a woman, both dead from apparent bullet wounds, lifeless on a stained, concrete floor. The image of Cherie Rodgers was mixed up with them.

"Was she one of them?" Jonathan asked and Michael felt the man's anger rising.

"No, they actually believe she was killed by the group because she was investigating them. She was found along with the other two," he explained. Jonathan's brow gathered in jagged disarray as he looked down at the image, but then he continued shuffling through the photos. There weren't many. Maybe a dozen. He ran through them twice.

Michael stared into Jonathan's face trying to read his response. Relief? Loss? Anger? Whatever Jonathan was feeling, he recovered himself well. Michael momentarily wondered if it was a learned behavior from Patricia or something he'd inherited in his genes along with his hair color and sharp nose. Finally, he gathered the photos together and placed them neatly in the top drawer of his desk. When his eyes rose to meet Michael's, they looked vacant.

"Anything else?" Jonathan asked. Michael didn't know if this was Jonathan's way of suggesting he was holding back or if he was earnestly inquiring for additional information. Maybe it was just Jonathan's way of dismissing him.

"I believe there is the small matter of payment."

"Oh?" Jonathan asked with a hint of surprise. "I thought I already approved the expenses for that private dick you hired. I didn't realize there would be more."

"Two million for proof of death. There's your proof of death," Michael said, pointing his finger toward the desk drawer where Jonathan had filed away the pictures.

"What?" Jonathan asked in exasperation. "Correct me if I'm wrong, but you didn't kill those people yourself. Where do you get off asking for two mill?"

"You didn't say I had to be the one to kill them. You said, proof of death. I got that for you. Now, I want what was promised to me," Michael gave a stiff nod of resolution and began removing the transfer documents he had arranged in the day between his meeting with Richard Renn and Jonathan.

"I said up to two million," Jonathan reminded him.

Michael wasn't going to quibble over money right now. He wanted out.

"Listen, Jonathan, your father was up to his neck in illicit dealings and I had my hand in every one of them. This isn't the time to renegotiate the terms of our agreement. I want the agreed upon amount or I'm taking this company apart when I walk out of here."

There. Michael laid it all out for him. He always knew he would need some sort of retirement plan once the old man stepped down and left his son in charge. That timeline changed when the water crisis hit Harrison and trouble came knocking on his door. They didn't just know about the misdeeds he'd managed to avoid prosecution over either; they knew everything. He was given a timeline and the option of walking away in exchange for his help. Of course, he didn't really know what he was agreeing to at the time, but at least he'd have the rest of his life to decide whether or not he'd made the right call. All he needed was an escape hatch. When Jonathan offered to hand the sum over to him in exchange for help tracking down his son's killer, he knew there was an opportunity hidden somewhere underneath his fear. Michael adjusted his tie while he waited for Jonathan to respond.

"And what sort of assurances do I have that you won't come crawling back here with more threats once the money runs out?" Jonathan asked, his blue eyes honed in on Michael's face.

"Sign these transfers and you won't ever have to see me again," Michael answered honestly. His flight was booked, his luggage packed; Michael just needed to see this one last piece fit into place before he was done with it all.

"That's a promise?"

"Guaranteed. I'll be out of the country before morning."

"Where do I sign?"

Jonathan

3

All in all, it had been a shit day. Jonathan derived none of the satisfaction he'd expected from seeing the people who'd murdered his son dead nor did he relish the joy of watching Michael Maestri walk out of his office for the last time. And a strange sense of guilt washed over him when he saw those pictures of Cherie, dead and tied to a chair in some abandoned building. She'd lost her job, her livelihood, and all because she was chasing down answers to the same questions he was asking. Jonathan poured himself a scotch and took a seat at his desk. It was almost closing time down at the office. He considered going to Haley's condo after work, but she had been pestering him about introducing her to his parents during the holidays. He couldn't stand the thought of dealing with that after the day he'd had. And yet, returning to his own home didn't sound appealing either.

Ever since Nicki's suicide in the upstairs bathroom, Jonathan hadn't once ventured up the staircase. Davina, their housekeeper, had seen fit to move his clothing into the downstairs guest suite where Jonathan had taken up residence after the abduction. Every time Jonathan saw the staircase, he remembered that night when he'd seen his wife in a bathtub, the water red from mixing with her blood. He'd left her to die. At the time, he'd felt numb; almost relieved to finally be done with Nicki and her drawn-out deterioration. In the months that followed, however, the image burned only brighter with time. He should just sell the house. His mother was right, as she usually was.

At the thought of Patricia, he wondered how she would respond to Maestri's sudden disappearance. Would the man try to say goodbye to either her or Wallace before he left the country, as he'd promised to do? Jonathan hoped he just vanished, never to return. And, what's more, he hoped his parents felt his absence. Maestri was never their son. He didn't care about them. Maybe they would see that now.

A knock on his door surprised him. It was almost five. He wasn't expecting anyone else today.

"Come in," he called out. Usually Stephen would ring him to announce a visitor, but maybe he had stepped away from his desk at this late hour in the day. The door opened and his assistant stepped inside, closing the door behind him.

"What is it, Stephen?"

Stephen was in his late twenties and had been hired as Jonathan's personal assistant when his father retired. Previously, he had worked as an assistant to the chief financial officer at a different company. He'd proved himself to be organized and diligent, but Jonathan doubted he would prove as resourceful as Michael Maestri. Maybe that wasn't such a bad thing, Jonathan reflected. Jonathan also recognized this man was a couple years older than he was. He wondered what it must be like to be working for someone younger than you; someone who, by the way, had inherited the company by birthright. What did it matter? Stephen certainly never seemed anything less than cheerful in his job posting.

Except, that is, today. His amiable smile was gone and his brow was contorted with heavy thoughts. At his side, he carried a leather satchel, the same one Jonathan had seen him arrive at work wearing every day. Jonathan began to worry. Did Maestri have some evil parting gift for him? Did something happen to his parents? Something was wrong.

"What is it?" Jonathan asked a second time, alarmed. Stephen's eyes flashed up to the surveillance camera in the corner of his office and then back to Jonathan.

"Therefore, if you do not wake up, I will come like a thief, and you will not know at what hour I will come to you," Stephen's voice sounded hollow, distant. The words reverberated through Jonathan.

"How do you know that?" Jonathan asked, rising abruptly from his chair. Those were the same words scrawled on the note that Jude had left on the boardroom table less than a year ago. Stephen removed a gun from his bag, a silencer attached to the end. Jonathan looked to the desk drawer where he had hidden a Walther PPK. He considered making a grab for the gun, but thought it wiser to wait and see. After all, Stephen knew the gun was there. He might just shoot him for trying.

"I am coming quickly; hold fast what you have, so that no one will take your crown," Stephen added, moving closer with his gun drawn.

"Just hold it right there," Jonathan sputtered. "What's this all about?"

Stephen's voice shifted again as he delivered another memorized line, "To him who overcomes, to him I will give some of the hidden manna, and I will give him a white stone, and a new name written on the stone which no one knows but he who receives it."

"Bread and stones are great and all, but I can change your life," Jonathan contended, his voice charged with new hope. "I can make you rich. I can give you a new life."

Stephen looked straight at the camera, away from Jonathan, and said, "The second stage is starting. Your crimes will not go unpunished. There's nothing you can do."

He fired off four shots, landing them all in his chest. Jonathan crumbled forward onto his desk while Stephen removed the silencer from his weapon and put both items back in his satchel.

"The new world is coming and we're going to bring it about. Your kind doesn't have a place there."

Stephen walked out of the office as calmly as he'd appeared, but for Jonathan, it was over.

Patricia

4

Patricia washed the makeup from her face. She usually waited until after dinner with Wallace, but not tonight. She felt tired, used up. Something was bothering her, but she was having trouble identifying it. Maybe it was just the string of lonely days stretched out in front of her. The loss of her lover was certain to weigh heavy, no matter how inconsequential she claimed Michael Maestri was to her. He called from the airport to say he was going on a trip and didn't know when, or if, he would be returning. His tenure with Southwest Resources had come to its close.

She wanted to call Jonathan right away to find out what happened. Did her son actually have the audacity to fire Michael? Surely, he must realize what an asset that man had been to Wallace and to the family's business dealings. Something told her Jonathan was keenly aware of Maestri's value and that was part of what always irritated him about the man. It was normal for a son to worry about being supplanted by his father's protégé, but Patricia could have told him not to worry about that. Maestri was useful, but he wasn't Wallace's heir. And, when it came to love, Patricia always told Jonathan that he should never bother fighting over scraps. Wallace loved himself so much he had little left to offer others. Besides, Jonathan was meant for better things. Bigger things.

Thinking of Jonathan reminded Patricia that she was not alone. She still had him. He would eventually remarry and start giving her grandchildren at what Patricia thought was a more appropriate age. She would also find another lover. She was young enough and she certainly aged well. Her mother always told her a woman could be smart and shrewd, expanding in knowledge and wisdom with each passing year, but she would always be valued by depleting external resources she could do little to maintain against the ravishes of time. Patricia worked hard toward maintaining her appearance and was proud of the results. Wallace, on the other hand, was deteriorating rapidly. Barely a decade separated them, but Patricia thought he looked ready for a retirement villa to await his death.

She patted her face dry with a towel set beside the sink and then tossed the towel into the woven laundry basket to her left. Looking at herself in the mirror as she brushed aside her hair, she noticed the silver strands mixed within the light brown and gold. She didn't mind them, but it might be time to start coloring her hair anyway. Much like Botox, it was better to start early to avoid any stark changes. There were few things she hated more than talk at the country club about her, and this year had been relentless. From Wallace's retirement and the scandal in Harrison to Nicki's "miscarriage" and suicide, it had been one disaster after another until she couldn't walk into a room without feeling a chill descend.

She kept attending her meetings and fundraisers. She kept her regular golf game on Thursday mornings and tennis on Tuesday with Mary, Stella, and Julie. Her schedule remained full but things still changed. Everyone was cordial, but beneath the social niceties, the warmth vanished. She tried to be dismissive at first, but as the months wore on, she felt depleted by the absence of connectivity. She would soon be like Wallace: a shadow self, similar in likeness, but devoid of substance as she went through the motions of the day. No, she decided, Jonathan would keep her tethered. Patricia always promised herself she would remain in check for her son. She just needed to find different charities to support and a different golf club. Let the members of the club see what happened when their businesses and pet projects didn't receive the Lambert money anymore. They would regret their behavior toward her.

Patricia straightened her back as her resolution solidified and then adjusted her blouse so its buttons aligned in a neat row beneath the diamond and pearl pendant she'd chosen to wear that day, the one she wore most often. At least she still wore actual clothes to dinner and hadn't resigned herself to pajamas yet, like her husband. Although she felt a three-martini headache coming on and might retire to her room for a day or two. Tonight, she wanted to have dinner with Wallace so she could let him know that Maestri had hopped a plane to Taipei. She wanted to see him hurt, dejected, when he realized that Michael had left without a word of goodbye. Patricia knew somewhere inside she wanted to see her own hurt reflected back at her on Wallace's face. She could leer at it, mock it, deem it pathetic and turn away from it. The pain might be more intense, at first, but she would move past it all the more quickly. She wouldn't dither over the conclusion of affairs. What would her mother say?

Patricia decided that her appearance was suitable for Wallace, in his robe, no doubt, and made her way toward the dining room. Her husband sat patiently waiting for her. Patricia remembered a rustic Italian soup was planned for their evening meal. She let out a long sigh. It was one thing to listen to him drone on about the news, but it was quite another to listen to him slurp his way through dinner. Just as she was about to take her seat, the doorbell rang.

She heard the maid's feet across the marble as she hurried to answer the door, but Patricia remained standing all the same. When she heard the voices, she started moving toward them.

Two men in cheap suits stood outside her door. They looked familiar.

"Mrs. Lambert?" one of them asked.

"Yes," she answered. Now, she remembered. She'd met them at Jonathan's office back in February. Right before Nicole was kidnapped.

"I'm Agent Garber and this is my partner, Agent Marcado. We're with the FBI."

"I remember."

"There's been an incident and we'd like you and your husband to come with us."

"Are we under arrest?"

"No, it's for your own safety," the agent named Garber answered.

"Then I'm afraid you'll have to provide us with more information before we're willing to leave. Or, better yet, contact our attorneys," Patricia replied.

"Can we come in for a moment?"

"No, you can tell me right now what's going on." She was done with law enforcement for the year. They had failed to protect Nicole when the grounds were crawling with police officers and even members of the Bureau. Now they wanted to whisk her away in the night to who knew where for who knew what.

Agent Garber looked to Marcado who gave a quick nod of his head.

"I'm afraid your son was shot today along with three other high-profile businessmen here in town, including Shah Patel of SP Electronics and Chris King and Alec Kaine of Kaine Health Solutions. All were shot in their offices and two died on the scene, including your son. So far, we've received 37 reports of similar actions in other cities."

Patricia couldn't breathe, she couldn't even see. She held onto the door in fear she would collapse. Jonathan was dead and, with him, all her hopes for the future. She tried to slowly draw air into her lungs, to stop the world from spinning around her. One hand moved to clutch the pendant that hung from her neck while the other gripped the door handle, keeping her steady. One of the agents moved toward her. She realized he was holding her elbow to assist her like some feeble creature. Patricia released herself from his grip and straightened her posture. The agent beside her cleared his throat and took a step back.

"We're not sure what these domestic terrorists have planned next so we're under orders to move people deemed in potential danger to a secure location until more information can be ascertained," he explained.

"Be that as it may, we have no intention of going any-where with you," Patricia said. "Please contact our attor-neys or return with a warrant if you expect us to cooperate."

She closed the door without another word.

Wallace called out to her from the dining room, "Patty, who was that?"

She ignored the question as she made her way toward

the stairs. If someone was coming for them, let them come.

Acknowledgements

I would like to thank my husband, Mark Anderson, for his unceasing support, for being my first and favorite editor, and for all the coffee. I would like to thank my mother, Zissel, for believing in my even more preposterous notions and my brother, Matthew, for "encouraging" me to share my works of fiction. I would also like to thank John and Amy Schorman, Mattx Bentley, and Aristotle Griego-McClanahan for sharing their technical knowledge. And, of course, I would like to thank Nick Courtright, Kyle McCord, and the good people of Atmosphere Press for helping bring this novel into being.

About Atmosphere Press

Atmosphere Press is an independent, full-service publisher for excellent books in all genres and for all audiences. Learn more about what we do at atmospherepress.com.

We encourage you to check out some of Atmosphere's latest releases, which are available at Amazon.com and via order from your local bookstore:

The Hidden Life, a novel by Robert Castle
Big Beasts, a novel by Patrick Scott
Alvarado, a novel by John W. Horton III
Nothing to Get Nostalgic About, a novel by Eddie Brophy
GROW: A Jack and Lake Creek Book, novel by Chris S McGee
Home is Not This Body, a novel by Karahn Washington
Whose Mary Kate, a novel by Jane Leclere Doyle
Stuck and Drunk in Shadyside, a novel by M. Byerly
These Things Happen, a novel by Chris Caldwell
Vanity: Murder in the Name of Sin, a novel by Rhiannon Garrard
Blood of the True Believer, a novel by Brandann R. Hill-Mann
The Dark Secrets of Barth and Williams College: A Comedy in Two Semesters, a novel by Glen Weissenberger
The Glorious Between, a novel by Doug Reid
An Expectation of Plenty, a novel by Thomas Bazar
Sink or Swim, Brooklyn, a novel by Ron Kemper

About the Author

Carly Schorman is a writer, blogger, and podcaster raised in a stretch of desert not intended for human habitation. She attended graduate school in San Francisco before returning to Phoenix where she currently resides with her husband. *The Saint of Lost Causes* is her first novel.

CPSIA information can be obtained
at www.ICGtesting.com
Printed in the USA
LVHW111102120121
676264LV00005B/52